He had to trust Doug Rawlings's judgment

No matter what the odds, no matter what the defenses, the sub skipper had to get in close enough to his target to loose his weapons and kill. With that mind-set, he was predisposed to look for counterattack options.

"What if he has an actual hot weapon on board?" Rawlings asked Brognola. "Along with the nuclear waste we know he had, maybe he has some kind of nuclear device, as well."

"Oh, my God!"

"That's one threat," the captain continued, "that we've never had a defense against—a nuke detonating in a harbor. If I was in Garcia's situation, that's what I'd do. And Miami is the perfect place."

Don Pendleton's Mack
Bolan®
Silent Running

A GOLD EAGLE BOOK FROM
WORLDWIDE®

TORONTO • NEW YORK • LONDON
AMSTERDAM • PARIS • SYDNEY • HAMBURG
STOCKHOLM • ATHENS • TOKYO • MILAN
MADRID • WARSAW • BUDAPEST • AUCKLAND

First edition March 2004

ISBN 0-373-61495-0

Special thanks and acknowledgment to
Michael Kasner for his contribution to this work.

SILENT RUNNING

Printed in U.S.A.

Revolutions are not made; they come.
                              —Wendell Phillips
                                1811–1884

When a people's revolution is helped along by
external forces, there's always an ulterior motive,
strings attached. When the "revolution" is a cover
for vengeance, the strings have to be cut and the
puppet master taken down.
                              —Mack Bolan

CHAPTER ONE

Cancun, Mexico

The famed "Strip" of the Mexican resort town of Cancun looked more or less like any other overly developed tourist trap anywhere in a tropical paradise. An eight-mile-long row of expensive hotels complete with tennis courts, well-tended gardens, towering royal palms, spacious pools and cabanas flanked one another along a perfect beach. Interspaced with the hotels were concrete, chrome-and-glass shopping malls, exclusive boutiques, world-class restaurants, glittering nightclubs and twenty-four-hour tequila bars. A brightly lit four-lane boulevard crowded with freshly washed cabs and colorful jitneys ferried the fun-seeking vacationers from one destination to the next.

The Hotel Maya wasn't the tallest building in the lineup, but it was easily the most impressive. From the outside, the hotel attempted to replicate the design of an ancient Mayan stepped pyramid as could be found at several of the neighboring Yucatan archaeological sites. If, that was, the Mayans had been able to build an eighteen-story pyramid in sand-colored concrete with bronze-tinted windows. Even a hardened pragmatist like Hal Brognola had to admit that it was impressive.

It was a warm, sultry evening, and the big Fed was standing on the balcony of his tenth-floor room of the Hotel Maya looking out over the Caribbean as a brightly lit cruise ship sailed out of the port. A raucous pool party fueled by Happy Hour drinks was in full swing around the pools in the courtyard below, and the live music was close to deafening. So far he hadn't spotted any young buxom women frolicking sans their bikini tops, but the sun had just gone down, so the night was young. A few barrels of cheap tequila later and the place would really start to rock.

This wasn't quite Brognola's usual environment. But he was in Cancun on business and had to admit that this faux pyramid beat the hell out of the normal venue for the biannual meeting of the Organization of Justice Departments of the Americas. Usually the international group met in far less spectacular surroundings noted mostly for their rubber chicken dinners and the Gideon bibles in every nightstand. He suspected that his friend Hector de Lorenzo, Mexico's attorney general, had a personal stake in the resort to have been able to reserve this swanky place for the week-long conference. With the attendees' tabs all being paid with the public dime, though, the hotel certainly wasn't going to suffer any loss of revenue with this crowd.

Plus, with everyone at the conference being either a police officer or justice department official, the staff wouldn't have to go far to call the cops if things got out of hand. Which he knew they would again this evening before much longer. There was nothing like turning a bunch of cops, lawyers and judges loose in a place like this courtesy of the public coffers. Most of the young women he'd spotted so far looked to be working girls instead of the usual mix of coeds and thrill-seeking, young urban professionals who came to try their luck in Cancun. Since there wasn't a dog among them, he figured they'd been flown in specifically to service the event. Again, he saw de Lorenzo's deft touch at work.

Brognola enjoyed hanging loose as much as any other overworked public servant and God only knew, he could sure use a few days off. But while this was a premier place for off-duty fun in the sun of any and every variety known to humankind, he hadn't come south to party. His mission at the conference was to try to get help with something that had been digging at the back of his mind. With the Western World focused so tightly on the "War Against Terrorism" no one was paying much attention to other potential hot spots in America's backyard. The Middle East crisis hadn't yet played itself out, and some doubted that it ever would. But it was still the number one topic on the national agenda and rightfully so; 9/11 wouldn't be soon forgotten.

Nonetheless, America had other, closer enemies who wished her harm and they couldn't be ignored. It was true that few of them presented as serious a threat as radical Islamic fundamentalists, but a nation, as well as a man, could die the death of a thousand cuts. His mission was to interest his colleagues in helping him look into something that seemed to be lurking just below the intelligence horizon. He'd had no joy with his quest so far; in fact, no one would even talk to him about his concerns. But this was just the second day of the scheduled week and now that the attendees had blown off a little pent-up steam, maybe he could get someone to listen to him.

He walked back to the well-stocked minibar in his kitchenette and was contemplating his choices when someone knocked on his door. He opened it to find Hector de Lorenzo and, even so early in the evening, the handsome, rakish, Mexican cop-turned-attorney general looked to be half in the bag and feeling no pain.

"Hal—" de Lorenzo hoisted his half-empty glass and rattled the ice cubes "—our dinner reservations are getting cold, *amigo*. And don't tell me that you want to eat alone in your room again tonight. I went to all the trouble to find us suitable dinner companions and, believe me, we don't want to disappoint them."

"Dammit, Hector." Brognola grinned as he shook his head. Hooking up with de Lorenzo was usually a one-way ticket to the Disoriented Express and this occasion was proving to be no different than usual. "You know how much I hate this social bullshit. I just want to have a quiet meal and go to bed by myself. I really don't need to have a bad head in the morning. I have work to do tomorrow."

"Hal, Hal." De Lorenzo shook his head in mock sorrow. "That's simply not done around here, and you know it. You have to show your country's flag, and wave it proudly, by sharing our libations."

The Mexican leaned closer and smiled. "Don't forget, we Latinos are a very social people and we're going to think that you don't appreciate our hospitality if you don't break bread with us."

As much as Brognola hated to admit it, he knew the Mexican A.G. was right. He needed to be seen as part of the extended regional justice family if he was going to get the cooperation he wanted when he needed it. "It's not the bread I'm worried about, Hector."

"Never to worry, *amigo*—" de Lorenzo beamed "—I'll see that you get served only the best tequila and not that rotgut you Yankees usually drink."

Brognola shuddered.

"I promise."

"Let me get my coat," Brognola grumbled.

"Good man," de Lorenzo said. "And I swear on my honor that you won't regret the evening."

Brognola had heard that line before, but maybe Barbara Price was right and he'd been working too hard and needed to relax a little.

DIEGO GARCIA GLANCED UP from the map of Mexico on the chart table over to the clock on the bulkhead of the spacious cabin of his pleasure boat. It was 2200 hours to the second.

"Team Six is at its launch point, Comrade," the radio operator reported from the communications console on the other side of the cabin.

Diego Garcia nodded. They were exactly on schedule, and he had expected nothing less of his men. The last two of his assault teams had a more difficult approach to make, and it would be at least another hour before they would be in position to launch. When his teams went into action, they would follow a series of carefully coordinated actions to ensure that his plan would succeed. Nothing less would be acceptable.

His command post this night was a sizable pleasure yacht cruising fifteen miles off the coast of the Yucatán Peninsula of Mexico in international waters. Anyone spotting the craft on radar or satellite would see only one more private boat sailing past the Cancun resort complex. Externally, nothing showed to make his boat stand out from the dozens just like it in the region. His communications antennas were all hidden, as was his defensive armament. He even had half a dozen women in bikinis up on deck to aid the disguise. Nothing had been left to chance.

A sharp stab of pain in the side of his head caused the Cuban to blink, but he ignored it. He had no time for anything as trivial as a brain tumor right now. In fact, for the next six months that the doctors had said he had left to live, he would have no time for it. In those few months he was going to be totally focused on creating a new New World Order in the Western Hemisphere that would be his last legacy to the world.

His plan wasn't just something he'd thrown together when he'd learned of his impending death. Not at all. It was a lifelong dream that had the full approval of the leader of Cuba himself. And while there would be no way to directly connect his operation with the Mother Country, Cuba would benefit greatly from it. She would finally become a real world power because of his effort, and his name would live forever in the minds of millions.

Diego Garcia, a ranking member of the DGI, Dirección General de Inteligencia, Cuba's intelligence service, headed up the supersecret organization code named the Matador. This section had been named for the brave men who stood alone in the sand facing brutal animals many times their size with only a slim sword in their hand to protect them. His motherland could never best the hated Yankees by brute force. There were far too many of them and they were too strong. But, as with the lone man in the arena, through bravery and a thin blade, even the largest raging bull could be brought to its knees.

Like the matador who faced the bull on the hot sand, Garcia didn't fear dying. When the tumor ate so much of his brain that he could no longer function, he would gladly put the muzzle of his pistol in his mouth and pull the trigger. His only fear was that he wouldn't live long enough to see the full extent of America's humiliation. The Yankees had ground his people under their heels for decades, and it was time for them to pay the bill for their arrogance. He envied the terrorists who had struck New York on 9/11, as the Yankees called it, but his operation would cost the Americans much more than just two buildings and a few thousand lives. They had caused the deaths of far more Cubans than that and one of them had been his dimly remembered father.

He remembered so clearly, though, his mother's face on the day his hero father had been buried. The Cuban leader himself had delivered the eulogy for him and the other Heros of the People who had fallen turning back the Yankee invasion at the Bay of Pigs. During the long speech, his mother had held herself proudly as befitted a widow of a martyr of the Revolution. She herself had been active in the Revolution and would go on to work for the DGI for the rest of her life.

On the morning after his father's state funeral, his mother had made him stand in front of a framed photo of Cuba's leader and recite a vow to dedicate his life to bringing death and destruction to the Capitalists who had killed his father. At the time he'd been too young to really understand what she was asking of him, but he had made the vow to please her. He had repeated it every morning since then and continued to do so to this day as the touchstone of his life.

That same morning, his mother had also started to teach him the things he would need to know to be able to carry out his vow. She had lived in Florida before the glorious Revolution and had started to teach him proper American English. As soon as he had the basics down, she went on to teach him how to blend in with the Yankees. Being from an almost pure Spanish bloodline, his features and coloring would allow him to pass unnoticed in the mixed American society.

After entering Cuba's secret service himself, he had specialized in the foreign branch of the DGI. With his mother's thorough training, he had been a

very successful undercover agent operating in
Florida, Texas and Louisiana. His successes were re-
warded with his appointment as the man in charge
of the top-secret Matador Section. The plan he was
implementing this night had already been in exis-
tence at that time, but he'd brought new ideas to it
and had expanded the program.

Within a very short period, the great United States
of America would be on her knees weeping, and he
would be a very satisfied man. Few men had ever had
the chance to be the driving force behind the destruction of a corrupt empire, and he would die happy.

Going to the head off the main cabin, Diego Garcia opened the medicine cabinet and took out the
bottle of pills that kept his growing tumor partially
in check. That the medication he needed to stay alive
had been developed in the nation he was trying to destroy was an irony that hadn't escaped him. Even he
had to admit that the Americans were very clever
when it came to the sciences and medicine, but they
were as heartless with their modern wonders as they
were with everything else. He had to have his medicine clandestinely purchased for him in Florida because the company that manufactured it wouldn't
allow it to be sold to the suffering people of his, and
other poor countries, at a price they could afford.

That was only one small thing that would be different in the new world he was giving birth to this night.

HAL BROGNOLA HAD to admit that de Lorenzo had been absolutely correct in insisting that he go to the dinner this evening. It would have been a tragic mistake for him not to have made the acquaintance of his dinner companion Elena Martinez. Being a staunch family man, he had no intention of taking this any further than enjoying dinner and a few drinks at the table. But it really would have been a shame to have missed this chance to even briefly enjoy the company of one of the most beautiful women he'd ever seen.

A man who was too old to properly appreciate feminine beauty was a completely useless article, and he was never going to get that old.

"Hal—" Hector de Lorenzo's grin threatened to split his face "—may I present Señorita Elena Martinez."

In his cop's mind, Señorita Martinez registered as five-six and a well-distributed one hundred and thirty pounds. The stats, though, didn't even begin to convey the effect of the complete package. The low-cut, tight-waisted dress she wore was a stunning advertisement offset by long hair combed down over her back.

"Elena," de Lorenzo said, turning to the woman, "my old friend Hal is one of the American President's most valuable advisers, so you should make him feel welcome to Mexico. I might need his help someday and I want him to remember me fondly."

The woman extended her hand and Brognola felt

like a fool, but he bent over it like a Spanish grandee in a forties Zorro movie. "I am honored," he said.

"As am I, señor," she replied with a smile.

"Let's eat," de Lorenzo said.

Dinner was being served in the largest of the hotel's open-air dining areas adjacent to the main pool. The scent of tropical flowers and salt water on the warm air and the flicker of torch lights created a romantic atmosphere. So did the intimate laughter of the young "dinner companions" each man had at his table. This was the most sexually charged event he'd attended in a long time where everyone still had their clothes on. With the pool close by, though, that could change at any moment.

The music from the live band wasn't as loud as it had been during Happy Hour, but it was still a force to be reckoned with. It did, though, make dinner conversations more intimate because he had to lean close to Martinez to hear her low, throaty voice. Which, of course, put him in olfactory range of the subtle mix of her expensive perfume and her natural pheromones. It was a very nice combination indeed and went well with her catlike eyes, silky long hair, low-cut dress, soft lighting, Caribbean rum and spicy food.

He was leaning close again, his face inches from her fragrant hair, answering one of her questions when a switch was thrown and the dining area was hit with harsh light from spotlights around the perimeter. By the time he could blink away the retina burn, a dozen black-clad men armed with AKs entered from the shadows and surrounded the diners.

"Aw shit!" Brognola muttered. He'd come to Mexico to chase a hunch, but it looked as though it had come chasing him instead. There was no way this was going to have a happy ending.

"Hal!" Martinez clutched his arm, her eyes wide.

"Just stay calm," he told her as he tried to figure the odds.

Since none of the diners had foreseen a need to pack lethal hardware while drinking and dining, there wasn't a gun in the crowd. The exception was the squad of waiters who had all produced handguns from somewhere, but it looked as though they were on the side of the intruders.

"Everyone stay where you are," one of the gunmen commanded in English and then Spanish.

When one of the diners jumped up, he was instantly shot. He fell dead across his table, scattering the dishes and drinks. This freaked his dinner partner, who also tried to run, only to share her companion's fate.

"Stay seated!"

If there was something that cops and prosecutors knew how to do it was to listen to men with guns in the hands. Another dozen gunmen started taking the diners and their companions from their tables and searching them before leading them away. When it came his turn, Brognola went along with the pat-down. This was no time for macho heroics. He did, though, try to steady Elena Martinez when the grinning thug took his time running his hands over her.

When they were both found to be clean, they were led away to the main conference room inside the hotel, where they found more armed men waiting for them. Whoever had put this operation together wasn't missing a trick. Once there, Martinez was led away to join the other women and Hal was sent over to join the men. The guards allowed no talking, so the men waited with their own thoughts and fears of what was coming next.

Brognola had no fears, though. He knew full well what was coming next. He just didn't know who was sponsoring this mass hostage taking and what they thought they were going to get out of it. Whatever it was, though, it wasn't going to be pretty.

CHAPTER TWO

Panama Canal

Dr. Richard Spellman wasn't a man who enjoyed wasting his time; he was much too busy for it. He wasn't one of those doctors who kept America's golf courses in business or one who took extended winter vacations in exotic resorts. For one, he wasn't a wealthy man, and two, he wasn't the kind of doctor who could take time off. He was an M.D. bench researcher in a university hospital; not too much downtime came with the job. While his salary was less than stellar by current medical standards, he didn't really care. He loved what he did. He loved it so much, in fact, that his wife had divorced him and taken up with a California plastic surgeon. Not only was she able to get her face-lifts and boob jobs done free now, but her new husband was willing to take her to exclusive, exotic locales and to parade her to show off his hand-iwork.

So, being on a cruise ship passing through the Panama Canal en route to the Caribbean was a first for Spellman and totally out of character. But it wasn't really a vacation, either. The sole reason he was on board the SS *Carib Princess* was that the Society of Genomic Research was holding its annual meeting on board, and he had been invited to present a paper on his work. Even so, if the association hadn't picked up his tab for the cruise and offered him an honorarium, he couldn't have afforded to attend.

He'd been prepared to really hate wasting the time both before and after he made his presentation, but he had to admit that he was actually starting to enjoy himself. He'd never been at sea before and found the experience strangely liberating. Also, after a couple of years eating his own cooking, he was thoroughly enjoying the ship's cuisine on his all-inclusive ticket.

Spellman stood at the rail watching the early evening jungle along the banks of the canal as the ship approached the eastern lock. In a little more than an hour, they would be in the Caribbean steaming for the island of Aruba. That would be another first for him; he'd never been to a tropical island. He turned when he heard footsteps approach.

"There you are, Richard," a woman in a light tropical dress said with a smile.

Dr. Mary Hamilton was the other reason he had started to enjoy the cruise. Since his divorce, his social life had been pretty much confined to exchanging mumbled greetings with the surly waitress in the restaurant where he had breakfast. When he'd found himself almost the only single guy in a boatload of doctors with their trophy wives and younger girlfriends in tow, he'd been a little overwhelmed. It made him realize how long it had been since he'd enjoyed the scent of a woman. On the second night out, though, he'd stumbled onto Mary.

She was a woman many men wouldn't notice. She wasn't a fashion plate, nor was she young enough to be a centerfold. She was, however, trim, confident and intelligent. That rare combination made her more than exotic to his eyes. Best of all, she was also a Ph.D. research director for a major pharmaceutical company. He worked in a smaller university setting, but their professional lives were similar and they could talk shop. Until meeting her, he hadn't realized how nice it was to be able to talk about his work with a woman who understood what he did for a living.

"You ready to go in to dinner?" she asked. "The eight o'clock bell just rang."

Being a man who hated to waste time, Spellman took her arm. "I'll tell you what," he said. "Rather than standing in line with the rest of the herd at the common trough, why don't we go down to that little French restaurant on the second deck and eat by ourselves. It seemed like a nice place, and the menu looked interesting."

He didn't add that this place he suggested was an intimate little bistro designed more for romantic encounters than for pedestrian dining. But if he was going to get to know this woman better, and he intended to, he wasn't going to waste any more time doing it.

"Great idea." Hamilton smiled. "I'm up for a few snails in garlic butter."

Spellman grimaced. He should have checked on her culinary preferences. But in for a penny, in for a pound. If he needed to, he'd introduce her to breath mints.

NGUYEN CAO NGUYEN stood on the deck of the blacked-out canal tug as it approached the stern of the *Carib Princess*. On deck with him were two dozen heavily armed Matador operatives in black combat suits. Another dozen men stood behind them ready to take command of the ship after the assault teams had secured it. Doing the takedown in the canal made it easier, and his allies at the eastern lock guaranteed that the ship's passage under new management would go without a hitch.

With the ship brightly lit, the Vietnamese had no trouble seeing the hatch open in the hull above the stern. A figure in a crewman's uniform rolled out a long rope ladder and lowered it over the side.

"Go!" he said in Spanish, and motioned to the waiting assault leader.

The black-clad commandos swarmed up the rope ladder, their silenced weapons slung over their backs, and disappeared inside the ship. To keep from being spotted, Nguyen had the tugboat captain back off a hundred yards while he waited. He didn't mind the wait because he'd been waiting for years to get his payback.

During the Vietnam war, Nguyen had been a young Vietcong agent planted in the USAID office in Saigon. In the aftermath of the Tet Offensive, he'd been exposed and sent to a South Vietnamese prison camp for six years. The North Vietnamese liberation of Saigon had freed him, but when he returned to what had been his home, he learned that his wife had moved in with an American foreign service officer in his absence.

The Yankee was already gone, having fled with the rest of his people in the last-minute evacuation, but Nguyen had hunted down his unfaithful wife and killed her and her bastard half-Yankee child. He could now see that it had been an impulsive act, but he'd been imprisoned for a long time. Had he taken the time to think about it, he would have still killed her, but might not have done it so publicly. His wife's family was high-ranking Vietcong officials, and he'd been forced to flee to Red China to escape their vengeance.

Even though China and the People's Republic of Vietnam shared the same twisted Oriental version of Marxism, they weren't quite on speaking terms. In the aftermath of North Vietnam's takeover of the South, the Chinese were concerned about continuing their expansionistic policies. The unsuccessful Vietnamese military incursions into the disputed Chinese border territory only confirmed their fears. Therefore, working on the enemy-of-my-enemy-is-my-friend theory, Nguyen was welcomed in China.

When his debriefing revealed his vast working knowledge of American military and political activities, the Chinese took him on as an agent in their intelligence service. After extensive training, he'd been infiltrated into a group of "boat people" refugees from Hong Kong being sent to the United States. Once in the U.S., he settled in Southern Florida and, on orders of his Beijing masters, linked up with the Cuban DGI agents active there.

The Chinese considered the Cubans to be rather unimportant in the grand scheme of world history, and bumbling, overly emotional amateurs to boot. But they were the sole Communist state in the Western Hemisphere and a good launchpad for China's plans for the region. And Beijing had been making plans for Latin America for decades. Since Chinese strategic thought was always couched in terms of decades instead of weeks, Beijing didn't mind letting someone else be their front man as long as it served their ultimate goals.

When Nguyen discovered the activities of the Matador Section and reported it to his Beijing handlers, he was ordered to try to get accepted into the secret organization and, given local Chinese assets, to offer the Cubans as an enticement. The Cubans fell for it, and Nguyen soon became Diego Garcia's second in command. As such, he was personally supervising the takeover of the *Carib Princess* as it was a critical element of Garcia's overall Matador plan.

If Garcia's operation was successful, it would advance China's long-range objectives without their having to expose any of their own operations. Best of all, if it failed, China wouldn't be caught up in the inevitable backlash. The Americans had been looking for an excuse to obliterate Cuba for many years now, and the Chinese didn't want Beijing to end up on the same nuclear cruise missile target list as Havana.

When Nguyen heard the code word over his radio, he motioned to his replacement crew that would sail the ship on to Cancun. As per his instructions, the assault team had executed the ship's captain and most of the bridge crew. The *Carib Princess*'s first officer, purser, engineering officer and the Black Gang had been kept alive, though. The Matador replacement crew was experienced with large vessels, but in case something came up, he wanted men on hand who knew the intimate details of operating this particular ship.

As soon as the substitute crewmen had climbed the ladder into the ship, Nguyen started up after them. His first act on board would be to notify Garcia that the ship was theirs.

RICHARD SPELLMAN grandly slathered butter on the last slice of thick-crust bread. "I swear this is the last bite," he said. "I'm going to have to call the ship's doctor and order a gurney to roll me back to my cabin."

Mary Hamilton smiled. "Coming here has to have been one of your better ideas, Richard. But wait on calling for the gurney, my cabin's right down the hallway."

"That's an even better idea," he said. "But on a ship, I think they call it a passageway."

"It still leads to my cabin."

Spellman signed his dinner check with his room number and stood. He was pulling Mary's chair back when he spotted a man in black heading down the passageway. He was carrying a submachine gun. A second later another gunman appeared. The ship had a small security force, but he'd not seen them wearing black combat suits nor packing automatic weapons. And the way these two men were moving told him that these guys weren't friendly.

"Come on," he told her quietly. "We've got to get out of here fast."

"What is it?" She frowned and turned toward the door.

He took her chin and turned her head back toward him. "Don't look," he said, "but something odd's going on. I just saw a couple of armed men in black SWAT suits in the hallway. Let's look for a back door out of this place until we can figure out what the hell's going on."

Hamilton was a decisive woman, but she was out of her element here and didn't mind him taking the lead.

The cook staff looked up from their chores when the two Americans walked into the kitchen. "Is there a back way out of here?" Spellman asked in English, nodding toward his companion. "Her husband is coming."

Keeping a straight face, Hamilton translated his question into flawless Spanish.

One of the cooks left his soup pot and showed them to a passageway behind the kitchen.

"I didn't know you spoke Spanish," Spellman said.

"You never asked."

"What else do you know that might come in handy right about now?"

She shook her head. "I can't think of anything."

"Keep thinking."

When the cook stopped in front of a door and said something in Spanish, Hamilton translated. "He says that if we need to hide from my husband, we can stay in here. There's a lock on the inside of the door."

"*Gracias*," Spellman said.

The cook grinned.

The storeroom behind the door was quite large and the door had been fitted with a pair of sliding bolts on the inside. A thick pile of blankets on the floor showed that this was a common trysting place for the staff seeking an afternoon delight.

"Just what we need." Mary chuckled.

"Complete with enough food and drink to last us for a couple of weeks." Spellman's eyes made a quick inventory of the shelves.

"Do you think someone's trying to hijack the ship?"

"I don't know, but we should be okay if we stay in here."

There was a porthole at the end of the compartment, but he couldn't see anything through it beyond the jungle lining the canal.

"How long do you think we'll have to stay here?"

"I'll be damned if I know," he replied. "But if we hear any shooting we'll be safe, at least until we reach a port somewhere."

She glanced down at the pile of blankets. "I'm sure we can stay busy till then."

Seeing the look in her eyes, so was he.

"This would've been better in my cabin." She smiled. "More comfortable."

He grinned. "I think we'll be able to manage okay here."

THE SPRAWLING PEMEX facility at Vera Cruz Llave was one of the Western Hemisphere's largest oil refinery complexes. Crude oil from dozens of Caribbean and South Atlantic offshore, deep-sea oil platforms was pumped in to be processed into everything from bunker fuel to Avgas. Because of the never-ending court battles being waged to terminate such industrial activities as refining in the United States, more and more American oil companies were sending their crude to Mexico for processing. This arrangement was a boon to the Mexican economy and got the environmentalists and their vulture lawyers off the backs of American "big oil."

Pemex wasn't unaware that their refineries were prime potential terrorist targets. Even with the successes of the ongoing war on terrorism in the Middle and Far East, Latin American terrorism was still a common fact of life. Here, though, it wasn't Islamic radicals causing trouble, but the home-grown whackos. There were still a few Marxists who still dreamed of dusty socialist glories to be won by the gun. But Native Indian separatists and would-be socialist land-grabbers were more likely to use terror tactics as were some of the drug cartels and out-of-office opposition parties.

As was common in all of Latin America, Mexico had more private security forces than it did police, and Pemex had the largest single security force establishment in the country. Sharp uniforms and modern weapons made the company cops look good, but the relatively low pay and almost complete lack of training made them little more than paper tigers. They would be no match for the forces Paco Domingo was moving into place against them.

Domingo was publicly known as the fiery leader of a militant oil field workers' union. To Diego Garcia, though, he was one of a number of deep-cover Cuban Matador agents who had been placed in Mexico years earlier. Some of these men had been undercover for more than ten years, but all of that waiting was over now. One of the main Matador targets this night was Mexico's petroleum industry, but other critical infrastructure systems would be taken over, as well. The electrical power generation facilities were high on that list as were the ports and the air traffic control system. And, of course, the presidential palace in Mexico City.

Come morning, Mexico would finally belong to the people. The rule of the powerful old families and corrupt business elites would be ended, and the people would be presided over by their "chosen" representatives—Paco Domingo and his deep-cover associates.

That thought sustained him when he drove up to the main gate of the Pemex complex. This was an impressive security hard point complete with razor wire, a remote-controlled traffic barrier, security cameras and half a dozen armed guards behind bulletproof glass. It looked formidable, but it was mostly show because the checkpoint was manned by idiots.

Domingo stopped his SUV in front of the barrier and honked. The security officer who came out of the booth recognized him and walked up to the open driver's-side window. "You've been banned from this place, Domingo. Move on before I have to shoot you."

"I have to talk to the company officer in charge tonight," he replied. "I've learned information about a threat to your plant and I have to tell him about it."

The guard laughed. "That's a new one coming from a union bastard like you. You'd be happy to see this place burn down to the ground."

"You idiot," Domingo gritted. "My people need their jobs here so they can feed their families. They're not crazy enough to destroy their own jobs. This is a foreign threat to the plant, and it's serious."

"Okay." The guard reluctantly reached for his radio. "But if this is some kind of a trick, Domingo, you're going to pay for it." He pointed to the video camera. "This is all on tape, you know."

"Just let me talk to the man in charge."

A few minutes later a BMW drove up, the barrier was opened and a man in a suit and tie walked through. "I'm Valdez," he said. "What's this about a threat here?"

"It's no threat," Domingo said as he pulled out a silenced pistol and shot the guard in the forehead. The company man got two rounds in the back as he turned and fled for his car.

Four black-clad gunmen stormed out of the darkness and rushed the guardhouse. A few shots later it was over. With the main gate secured, Domingo radioed for the rest of his assault force to move in. Twenty more armed, black-clad men emerged from outside the cone of light, slipped through the perimeter and fanned out, weapons ready.

The Pemex refinery was about to become the property of the people of Mexico.

A HALF AN HOUR later the leader of the strike team reported to Domingo. "The entire complex is in Union hands, boss."

"Good."

As with any successful revolutionary, Domingo never let the right hand know what the left was doing. His militant Union brothers might have been a little apprehensive had they known that he was working more in the name of the Cuban DGI than he was in theirs. It would turn out the same in the end, though, and that's what really counted.

"Comrade Engineers," he said, turning to the dozen or so grim-faced men standing around a van sporting caution markings, "it is time for you to do your part."

"Yes, Comrade." The explosives engineer smiled. When he and his men were done with their work, all it would take would be a single push on a button and the largest oil refinery in Mexico would go up in flames. And, until the rightful demands of the union workers were met, not a single drop of gas would leave the place.

Domingo reached into his SUV for the radio to make his report.

DIEGO GARCIA SMILED as he stepped off his boat onto the brightly lit yacht dock at the Cancun marina. The initial phase of the plan had gone like clockwork. The Cancun peninsula was completely secured, the *Carib Princess* was in his hands, as were as most of the targets in Mexico. He had expected nothing else from his Matador teams, but he knew that the Goddess of Fate could always unexpectedly deal herself into the game. She'd been smiling on him this time, though, which meant that the rest of the operation should continue according to plan.

When the sun rose over Latin America in a few hours, it would be on a new world in the making, a world of his making.

CHAPTER THREE

Cancun

The mood in the main conference room of the Hotel Maya could only be called grim. It was approaching dawn, and raw nerves had kept most of the conference hostages from sleeping. The heavily armed, black-clad guards had reacted swiftly with rifle butts to any attempts at conversation, so the men had been left to stew in their anger.

Hal Brognola was an old hand at the crunch game and knew how to keep his emotions firmly in check. He, too, was outraged at being taken hostage. But he knew that wasting his energy on things he had no control over was a useless exercise.

He'd catnapped throughout the night while still staying alert to exploit any opportunity that might have presented itself. Unfortunately, though, the silent guards hadn't blinked. With the dawn, additional armed gunmen walked into the room, which only increased the tension.

To some, the newcomers might have been a guard shift change, but Brognola had no trouble identifying that they were a command group. The head honcho was easy to spot. He was a light-skinned Hispanic who looked as if he had a Spanish grandee somewhere in his bloodline. He appeared to be in his mid-fifties and had a relaxed, military bearing. His eyes swept across the roomful of captives but revealed nothing. The way the other men treated him, told Brognola that the show was about to get on the road. He was glad to see the newcomers settle at one of the conference tables.

Not having been able to talk to his fellow captives, Hal couldn't even begin to guess what this was all about and he looked forward to going one-on-one with his captors. Being interrogated always worked both ways, and he should be able to pick up some information. There was no doubt that he and his fellow conferees had some perceived value as hostages. Were that not the case, they'd have simply been gunned down in reprisal for some real or imagined wrong done to someone, somewhere, sometime ago. The usual terrorist excuse for brutality.

They were considered valuable, so the only question was what they would be held ransom for.

He was a bit surprised when he wasn't the first man to be taken over to the head table. The American representatives bore the brunt of the kidnappers' displeasure so the others could see how tough they were on the biggest threat. His friend Hector de Lorenzo got first honors. Hal wasn't close enough to overhear what was being said, but Hector didn't hide the fact that he was royally pissed. The questioning was short, and de Lorenzo was led away.

When the A.G. of Panama was called out next, Brognola let himself relax. There was no point in getting amped up until his time came, but he automatically patted his empty coat pocket anyway.

He was catching another catnap on the floor when he was called for his turn in the barrel via a rifle butt in the middle of his back.

"Mister Harold Brognola," the honcho read in almost unaccented English from what looked like a rap sheet. "Let's see, you're usually called Hal by your good friend the President, right?"

"And you are?" Brognola answered the question with one of his own.

The honcho's eyes bore into him. "I would answer the question if I were you."

Brognola met his eyes and shrugged. "You know who I am. You have my passport."

The honcho nodded curtly, and the guard hover-ing over Brognola reversed his AK and slammed it into the pit of his stomach.

He'd seen it coming and tried to move with the blow, but it still took his wind. As soon as he could breathe again, he straightened.

The interrogator leaned forward. "Mr. Brognola, a man of your high position in government can't be stupid enough not to recognize the realities of what is taking place here today. You are my prisoner and regardless of who you might be in your American Justice Department, or who your friends in Washington are, whatever may be left of your life is solely in my hands now."

The honcho smiled. "You can play childish macho cowboy games with me if you want, but I can assure you that you will answer my questions sooner or later."

Brognola knew that to be a simple statement of fact. He had no amateurish illusions about the realities of going through an extended interrogation. But he wasn't about to play ball with this asshole until he absolutely had no other choice. If he was held long enough, or if they brought out the chemical interrogation gear, he'd have to talk. But he really didn't expect to be here that long.

As the honcho had said, he had friends.

"We'll see." Brognola didn't blink.

"Yes, we will," the man replied. "And by the way,

I am Diego Garcia. You are going to get to know me well before this is over."

A feminine scream split the air and the captives, not knowing who's woman was being mistreated, turned toward the sound. Brognola didn't, however.

"You've got some real winners working for you here, mister," he said, his eyes locked on Garcia's. "It looks like they have to beat up the women to get enough balls to talk to the—"

Focused on Garcia, Brognola didn't see the rifle butt coming this time, but he rode it out.

The Cuban turned to one of his gunmen. "Take Mr. Brognola to the jail."

"Sí, Jefe."

Garcia watched impassively as the Yankee was escorted out of the room. The report he had received from the Matador operative at the Latin American Desk of the U.S. State Department had been accurate. Hal Brognola was a force to be reckoned with, but he also had his weaknesses. What the American saw as his strength, the Cuban saw as something to be broken. His arrogance would also contribute to his downfall as would his protective instincts toward the women. Though the Yankee hadn't turned when the woman screamed, Garcia had seen the anger flash in his eyes.

Though the "interview" had been short, it had told Garcia much and confirmed that he had chosen his man well. Had he wanted, he could have arranged for the attorney general of the United States to have attended the conference and taken him hostage instead. But the American A.G. was always a political flunkey who had been given his job as a payoff for services he had rendered to the party of the incoming President. Brognola was a career Justice Department officer, and he had more than likely forgotten more about the workings of U.S. law-enforcement agencies than the A.G. would have time to learn before he left office. And his intimate knowledge was the goal.

If it wouldn't have tipped his hand, Garcia would have simply snatched Brognola and the Mexican de Lorenzo and let the rest go free. The other lawmen he'd gathered up were of little use to him except as expendable pawns as his plan played out over the next few weeks. And, to get what he needed from the Yankee, he fully intended to waste a couple of them. He would expend several of the women, as well, if that was needed to get what he wanted.

Except, of course for the delectable Señorita Martinez, Brognola's dinner companion. He was very careful about not sacrificing his top operatives.

THREE OF DIEGO Y GARCIA'S goons escorted Brognola to an SUV parked out in front of the hotel, handcuffed him and tossed him into the back seat. A short drive brought them downtown to a three-story building with an ornate, cast concrete, pseudo-Mayan facade. The sign carved into the facade, though, told it all—Municipal Jail.

Brognola was hustled in, uncuffed and shoved into an empty cell. Being in jail in Cancun wasn't like being locked up in the Mexican border towns traditionally seen in many movies. The resort town's facility had been built to house inebriated young American tourists and was more of a cheap but clean motel than a jail. Since the resort was one of the Caribbean's prime college break hangouts, they were aware that they had to treat their customers with kid gloves. If the cops traumatized a drunken frat boy, he and his brothers might not come back for spring break next year. So, for a jail, the accommodations in Cancun were first-class.

That was the good news.

The other side of that coin was that the jail had been built to modern security specifications. There would be no digging the flaking mortar from around a rusted iron bar and escaping from this place. The windows looked to be Lexan, the bars were stainless steel, the electronic lock on the door had been made in Dallas and the video camera watching him had originated in Pasadena.

At least, though, he had a comfortable place to lie down. That he was being housed alone in a four-man cell wasn't a good sign, but he had to play it as it lay. The best thing a man in his position could do was to eat and sleep every chance he could get because he didn't know when he'd get a chance to do either one again.

Brognola took off his coat, automatically checked his empty pocket one last time, placed it on one of the bunks, shook his thin blanket and stretched out for a nap.

He was asleep in minutes.

BROGNOLA WAS NOT surprised to be awakened only a few hours later. He hadn't been deceived by the shortness of his initial interview with Diego Garcia. The classic "false hope" gambit only worked with morons and drunks, and he was neither.

A short ride back to the Hotel Maya confirmed his suspicion that he was on for another round with the "Boss." The man was playing his hand by the book, chapter and verse. But since the big Fed had read the same book, he'd see if he couldn't stall the process. He was in no bloody great hurry, as McCarter would say, to get his ass stomped into the ground. In fact, to make this come out right, he needed to delay that part of the program for as long as he possibly could.

It was apparent that he'd been included in the bag, because Garcia thought that he was "friends" with the President. On paper he was listed as a Special Justice Department Adviser to the President, but that was just a long-standing cover for what he actually did. And it was imperative that he keep his real job from Garcia for as long as he could. As far as the man's thinking that he was one of the President's personal friends, he had no idea where that had come from. But since it was on the table, he'd use it to buy himself as much time as he could.

This time, Brognola was escorted into what looked in happier times to have been the hotel management's office suite. He was being taken to what looked to be the main office when the door opened and two goons walked out with Hector de Lorenzo between them. The Mexican's face was bloodied, but he only gave Brognola a quick glance. Hector was playing the game, but with Garcia's apparent intelligence sources, Brognola was certain that the bastard already knew of their long-standing friendship.

The office was large and tastefully decorated. A chunk of ancient Mayan carved stone was mounted on one wall, a minor Riviera painting on the other. Garcia was seated behind a huge, ornately carved, dark mahogany desk littered with enough electronic gear to run a fair-size war. Still working with an information deficit, Brognola knew whatever this operation was, it was no nickel-and-dime, hostage-taking incident.

"Mr. Brognola." Garcia greeted him and pointed to a chair. "Please have a seat. It is time that I let you know why you are here."

Brognola sat.

"Since it's been almost twenty-four hours since you were last in communication with your government, I thought I'd fill you in on what has recently happened in Mexico and, of course, your own country."

Brognola was interested but remained silent.

"You see," Garcia continued, "since you went down to dinner last night with the lovely Miss Martinez, the Western Hemisphere has changed for the better. The government of Mexico is now in the hands of its rightful owners—the people. As, by the way, are the nations of Panama, Guatemala and Ecuador. As a result of this, your nation will no longer be able to manipulate the destinies of those who live in what you North Americans like to refer to as Latin America. The Yankee hegemony has ended for all time."

"And how was this great feat accomplished?" Brognola asked.

"The will of the people is being brought to bear— and very successfully this time."

"Under the leadership of what Communist party this time?" Brognola made a guess. "China's?"

"Oh, no," Garcia quickly replied. "This is completely our own affair. Our socialist brothers in China have assisted us in several ways, true, but this is a spontaneous true expression of the people themselves."

"When pigs fly!" Brognola laughed. "Man, I can't

tell you how many times I've heard that crap about 'the will of the people.' All you Communists are the same, but it's never worked and it never will. The only thing that's going to happen to the people is that they're really going to get royally screwed now."

Garcia didn't rise to the bait. "Let me show you why it's going to work this time. As I said, this revolution has come directly from the people themselves, and it's long overdue. They have been repressed long enough and now they're finally taking back what's rightfully theirs."

He picked up a TV remote from the desk, clicked it and the set mounted on the wall flashed to a San Diego channel. A helicopter-mounted camera was showing a scene of some kind of massive riot with tens of thousands of people involved. It was so large that it filled the entire field of vision of the camera. It took several moments before Brognola recognized that he was looking at what had been the U.S.-Mexican border crossing point at Tijuana.

The barriers that had controlled the endless streams of traffic coming and going were gone. The buildings that housed the Immigration and Customs offices were being literally torn down by bare hands. The vehicles waiting in line to cross the border when the onslaught struck were being looted or overturned and set on fire.

A clearly panicked young TV reporter sounded

near tears as he did the voice-over. "We have just gotten word that the governor has called up the National Guard, but local authorities say that—" The transmission abruptly ended.

"Jesus!" Brognola said softly.

Garcia smiled. "Most of your country was stolen from my people and, as you can plainly see, we are taking it back now."

"We have an army, you know," Brognola said, "and we won't let something like this happen without responding."

"Most of your regular army is overseas fighting the so-called 'terrorists,'" Garcia stated accurately, "leaving your reserves and National Guards at home to protect you. And, do you really think that those soft, part-time, citizen soldiers are going to fire on unarmed women, old men and children and kill them? You Americans are cruel, but even I don't think they will do that."

Brognola was stunned. The United States military could bring almost unimaginable force to bear on any armed enemy. The stronger the enemy, the greater the force. But firing on unarmed civilians, particularly women and children, went against everything America stood for. America extended a helping hand to such people, not a bayonet.

Garcia leaned forward, his eyes glittering. "Take a good look, Brognola. You're watching the fall of the most corrupt government in human history, and it can't come a minute too soon for me."

The Cuban blinked and his hand flew to the side of his head. For a brief moment his eyes went unfocused, but it passed.

"And," he continued, "California isn't the only place where America is feeling the righteous rage of the people."

He clicked the remote again and a scene from what had to be the beachfront of a city in Florida appeared. A flotilla of boats, both large and small, were drawn up close to the shore and their decks were filled to overflowing. The smaller boats were heading in through the surf to beach themselves while people jumped from the larger ones to swim ashore.

A huge crowd had gathered along the beach and were successfully holding the police at bay to allow the boat people to reach land. Tear gas canisters were flying and the riot squads were out in force, but they were too few and were being pushed back. Every time one of the boats ran itself up onto the beach, hundreds more jumped down to join the crowds fighting the police.

As Brognola watched, one flank of the police line broke and the crowd surged forward. When one of the cops slipped and fell, he was trampled into the concrete. As soon as the mob reached the shops flanking the street, they started looting. As the camera panned, he saw smoke rising over a mall as another crowd blocked the fire trucks.

"That is right outside Miami Beach, Florida," Garcia said. "The boats are full of people from all over the Caribbean who have decided to immigrate to America so they can share the fruits of their ancestor's slave labor. The world is coming to America to take what is theirs."

"You're one sick bastard," Brognola stated.

The rifle butt to the back of his head sent him reeling into unconsciousness.

CHAPTER FOUR

SS Carib Princess

The requisitioned storeroom behind the cruise ship's French café had served well as an impromptu playroom, and Richard Spellman and Mary Hamilton didn't drift off to sleep until the early morning. Part of their sleeplessness, though, resulted from the occasional muffled gunshot heard in the night.

When sunlight streamed through the porthole on the two voluntary stowaways and woke Spellman, he glanced at his watch and saw that it was a little after nine. Getting up carefully so as not to wake Mary, he went to the porthole, but only saw open sea. Obviously the ship had passed through the canal into the Caribbean while they'd been in their self-imposed, but-not-completely-unwelcome exile.

"Richard?" Hamilton said.

"Right here." He turned back. "We're at sea, and my guess from the sun angle is that we're heading south. At least we won't starve, though. Hiding in a restaurant storeroom is definitely the way to stow away."

"How're we going to know when we're safe?" Hamilton asked.

"Damned if I know," Spellman admitted. "This sounded like a great idea last night and I'm convinced those were shots we heard, so I think we made the right move. The problem is that locked away like this, we don't have any idea what's going on out there. I've got a feeling, though, that I'm not going to be presenting my paper today."

The gunfire in the night had scared Hamilton as nothing else had ever done, but Richard'd had a calming effect on her and it was still working.

She smiled slyly. "I guess we'll just have to find something to keep ourselves occupied then."

RICHARD SPELLMAN was no sailor, but later that afternoon he recognized that the ship had reduced her speed and he chanced a peek around the edge of the porthole.

"Where do you think we are?" Hamilton asked.

"It looks like we're coming up to some resort mooring for cruise ships," he replied. "If I had to guess, I'd say that we're somewhere in Mexico. Maybe the Yucatán."

"What's going to happen to us?" the woman asked before she could stop herself. She hated playing the helpless woman with him, but she admitted to herself that she was scared. So far, Richard had been very calm, considering the circumstances, and in comforting her, had calmed her fears. Now that they had arrived at some kind of destination, though, the fear came flooding back.

"I don't have much experience at this kind of thing," he admitted, "but my guess is that we passengers have been taken hostage. For what, I have no idea. I don't know anything about Mexican politics.

"But—" he snuck another peek "—like it or not, I think that we're about to go to school for a cram course."

She shook her head. "How can you be so damned calm about this? I mean, I don't mind, but aren't you scared half to death? I know I am."

He turned back. "Sure I'm scared," he said. "Any rational human in this situation would be. But I'm saving it up for the right time to freak out. You know, a time and place where it might be useful."

She smiled in spite of herself and felt her fear ebb again. If she was going to die on this trip, at least she'd found someone she wouldn't mind dying with.

"You're a very funny man," she said. "And if we can get out of this mess, I think I'm going to want to see more of you. A lot more."

"That's a date." He grinned. "But first we have to figure out what in the hell we should be doing next. What do you think about trying to sneak off this damned thing as soon as it docks?"

She glanced around the storeroom. "There's got to be more room to run out there than there is in here."

"Good girl."

THE CRUISE SHIP was met at the Cancun moorage by Diego Garcia, a small fleet of buses and a couple dozen of his Matador gunmen. Nguyen Cao Nguyen, the first man down the gangplank, was met on the dock by the Cuban.

"Here they are, Comrade," the Vietnamese said, "packaged and delivered as you requested. Almost seven hundred and fifty of the international community's top medical men, their women and their children. And, as we expected, most of them are Yankees."

"Any casualties?" Garcia asked.

"None." Nguyen shook his head, referring to his own Matador team. The deaths among the ship's crew simply didn't count, and the passengers who had tried to resist were too few to mention, either. Since the bodies had been dumped over the side, he hadn't been able to reconcile the passenger manifest with the head count, though. But again, a few hostages more or less wouldn't really matter.

"Do you have the people I asked for selected?"

Nguyen nodded. "Of course, Comrade," he replied. A last-minute change to the master plan was to mix the political and medical hostages. He didn't understand the reasoning behind the decision, but it didn't really matter.

"Very good," Garcia said. "Bring them out now and tell your people to keep the ship ready to sail on a moment's notice."

This was another change to the carefully formulated plan he had helped put together, but again he had to go along with it. "Where?"

"Anywhere we might have to go," the Cuban said. "So have the fuel bunkers topped off immediately."

Nguyen took out a portable radio and spoke into it. "They're coming up on deck."

"As soon as they're transferred to the hotel," Garcia said, "I'll send some of the government hostages over to you. They'll be easier to guard here."

"I'm ready for them, Comrade."

Under the guns of the Matador guards, the selected passengers started to file down the gangplank and onto the waiting buses. The men were grim-faced, the women visibly frightened. These weren't people who were experienced with anything like this and their imaginations were obviously running away with them. There weren't that many children, but they had picked up on their parents' concern and looked dazed.

Garcia secretly smiled as the passengers were led away. Even though these doctors were educated, privileged men and women, like the rest of the Yankees, they were soft and would be no problem for him to hold captive for as long as he wanted.

THE TWO-SEAT, sea-gray camouflaged, Marine TAV-8B Harrier jet sat alone in a remote hangar at the U.S. Navy airbase at Corpus Christi, Texas. A squad of armed Marines secured the hangar from unauthorized visitors while the Navy ground crew gave the jump jet a final check-over. A figure in a flight suit broke away from the plane and walked to the locker room at the end of the hangar.

Marine Captain Fred "Mojo" Jenkins was the poster-perfect picture of a hot-rock Marine attack squadron aviator. Of medium height and in his early thirties, with a cocky, nonchalant bearing, he sported the typical buzz cut. He wore a half smile and looked at the world through steely eyes. His flight suit was covered with Tiger patches. Even so, he wasn't quite sure what to expect from his passenger on this classified flight. He'd never been involved with moving spooks before and had no idea what he'd gotten himself into. He'd made sure, though, to have his crew chief put an ample supply of burp kits in the rear cockpit.

There was no doubt in his military mind, though,

that he had to handle this guy, whoever he was, with kid gloves. The Commandant of the Corps himself had told him in no uncertain terms that the orders regarding this man had come down from the very top. That thought was foremost on his mind as he walked up to the man who, wearing an unmarked flight suit, was sitting alone in the locker room.

"I'm Captain Fred Jenkins, Sir." The pilot extended his hand. "Call sign Mojo."

"Glad to meet you, Captain." Mack Bolan stood and shook hands. "I'm Jeff Cooper."

Jenkins had seen enough spy thrillers to know there was no chance that was the man's real name. But this guy looked as though he could call himself the king of Egypt if he wanted and make it work for him. He was a big man, but not overpowering about it the way a SEAL or Recon Marine would have been. He wore his size well and projected a sense of total competence. There was nothing overtly threatening about him, but his blue eyes told you not to even think about fucking with him. All told, he looked as if he was the right guy to have at your side in a bar fight.

The pilot turned to the gunnery sergeant who'd overseen his passenger's suiting up. "Is Mr. Cooper briefed and ready to fly, Gunny?"

"Yes, Sir," the sergeant replied. "And I think he's done this once or twice before."

"Very good." Jenkins was curious, but knew better than to even think about asking questions. "If you're ready, Sir, we should launch. It'll be dark by the time we're over the target."

Bolan hoisted his black bag. "I need this stowed in your cargo pod."

"My crew chief can do that for you."

"Let's go."

JENKINS'S PASSENGER didn't display any of the telltale signs of being a Cherry flyer and there was no doubt that he'd flown in military jets before. When the F-14s of the CAP that had been ordered to cover his flight in showed up six feet off the Harrier's wingtips, Cooper hadn't even flinched. Even the link-up with the tanker for a quick, couple hundred gallon fill-up hadn't bothered him, and that was more than the pilot could say.

After the JP-4 top-off, Jenkins dropped down to wave-top level for the high-speed sprint to the coastline of the Yucatán Peninsula. The Harrier jump jet wasn't supersonic, but it didn't matter at that altitude. Once he crossed over the beach, the pilot flashed his "feet dry" code to the E-2C Hawkeye AWACS monitoring his mission and went on the terrain-following radar to continue keeping it low but out of the trees and native architecture. With his GPS nav system locked onto the LZ, he had no trouble locating the small clearing in the jungle a few minutes later.

Even so, rather than take a satellite photo's word on its suitability for a vertical landing, Jenkins clicked in the intercom to his back-seat passenger. "I've got the LZ in sight, Sir, but I'd like to make a flyover to check it out before I put us down."

"No problem."

When the pilot spotted no obstacles to landing, he cranked the Harrier around, viffed his nozzles down, went into a hover and sat his plane in the clearing.

"Thanks for the ride," Bolan said over the intercom as he unbuckled his seat harness and raised the canopy.

"Good luck, Sir."

Leaving his flight helmet and aviator survival vest behind, Bolan climbed down and shot Jenkins a thumbs-up. As per his preflight briefing, the pilot triggered the release to the cargo pod shackled under his right wing. Bolan's black bag fell to the ground and he quickly rolled it out of the way before shooting the pilot a second thumbs-up.

After answering with a crisp salute, Jenkins throttled up, hit his viffer control and the Harrier rose into the air. Balancing his lift, he fed in a little thrust and started forward. As soon as his air speed built to the point where the wings were generating enough aerodynamic lift to fly, he swiveled his nozzles all the way back and left town at top speed. Fortunately he didn't have far to go to reach international waters again and the protection of the F-14 CAP over the Western Caribbean.

He had no idea where his passenger was heading, but he wished him the best of luck.

BOLAN WAITED UNTIL THE SOUND of the Harrier echoed away in the surrounding jungle before breaking out his gear. Along with his usual personal weapons and equipment, he was packing heavily this time. With this being an open-ended mission, he had rations for three days, a pair of two-quart canteens, a larger than usual med kit, satcom radio gear and extra ammunition. He quickly got into his gear and loaded his weapons.

The pod had been sanitized of all U.S. military markings and could be safely left behind along with the equally sterile flight suit. By the time anyone found them, he'd have Hal Brognola back and they'd be long gone. At least, that was the mission profile, and until he knew something different, that's what he was going with.

He and Brognola had a history together that spanned almost his entire career, so when the President asked him via Barbara Price to try to extricate the big Fed from whatever was going on in Cancun, he hadn't hesitated.

Beyond their long friendship, Brognola was the leader of the nation's most secretive, clandestine operations organization known as the Sensitive Operations Group. When the nation needed a completely off-the-screen response to a threat or simply wanted to get some payback against evil-doers, Brognola's action teams were the President's first choice to take care of it.

Because of that, Brognola rarely traveled outside of the United States. And, on the rare times that he did, he was usually accorded Stony Man Farm blacksuit protection. This time, though, he'd figured that since he'd be in the company of the top cops from the entire hemisphere, personal bodyguards wouldn't be necessary.

That the President needed to get Brognola back as soon as possible went without saying. The information he carried in his head went beyond merely being damaging to national security. If the details of SOG were found out, it would be months, if not years, before the damage could be repaired. Bolan knew that Brognola was tough, but the risks of interrogation could never be underestimated, and it all hinged on him being able to stick to his established cover job. If Hal could force his kidnappers away from concentrating on breaking into that, Bolan should have enough time to get him out before it was discovered who he really was.

What should have been a simple hostage rescue operation was being complicated by a severe lack of intelligence. All communications with the region, even cell-phone traffic, had been cut and no one had any idea what was going on in the resort town. But if it had anything to do with what was happening in almost all of the rest of Mexico and the border states, the worst was feared.

The little information that had made it out of Mexico via satellite phones and TV hookups indicated that the nation was caught up in a bizarre revolution. The presidential palace in Mexico City had been taken over, along with most of the state governments. The armed forces were apparently also in the hands of the revolutionaries, as well as most of the major industries and services. That this was more than a traditional Mexican change in government "Pancho Villa style" could be seen in the reports of American business facilities being stormed and destroyed. Other foreign interests were being taken over, as well, but the main concentration seemed to be against U.S. property.

No one had any idea yet who or what was behind the sudden eruption of social unrest south of the border. It was as if the entire country had suddenly gone insane and the insanity was rapidly spreading northward into the United States. The famous border crossing at Tijuana had been stormed by tens of thousands of Mexicans and completely destroyed. The token Border Patrol and Customs police detachments had been overwhelmed and killed before reinforcements could be sent in.

The initial county and California Highway Patrol police units that sped to the scene had fared no better. Most of them, though, had managed to escape with their lives. When their guns hadn't been able to slow the hordes, they had wisely retreated back down the freeway hoping to put up roadblocks farther north.

Right before Bolan had taken off, he'd received a scrambled update reporting that the invaders had fanned out into the communities around the California border, hijacking vehicles and looting businesses. Police choppers were trying to keep track of them, but it simply wasn't doable. There were too many incidents to be tracked, much less stopped.

Adding to the problem was that other border crossings areas in Texas, Arizona and New Mexico were also being stormed and penetrated. Florida, Alabama and Louisiana were being invaded from the sea with the same success. If this wasn't brought under control immediately, the southern half of the United States was in danger of being overrun.

The President had called a state of national emergency and was federalizing all of the National Guard and Reserve units in the southern half of the country and sending them to secure the border. But it would be some time before any semblance of order could be restored to the thousands of miles of border and coastline. Even when that was accomplished, rounding up and deporting all the invaders would take even longer, maybe years. With more than eight million illegals living in the States already, finding and removing this new influx of invaders wasn't going to be easy.

Against that backdrop of pending national collapse, Bolan's job seemed simple. Go to Cancun, find Hal Brognola and bring him back.

THE HARRIER'S LZ had been plotted far enough away from the inhabited areas around Cancun so the jet couldn't be heard, thus Bolan faced a two-hour hike to reach his objective. An H&K 5.56 mm assault rifle ready in his hands, he checked his GPS, snapped his night-vision goggles in place and set out into the unknown of a world suddenly gone mad.

Bolan kept to the jungle for the first hour before coming across a dirt road that ran in the direction he was going. There was no traffic at this hour, so he used it to make better time. With his night-vision goggles in place, he had little fear of stumbling into an enemy patrol in the dark.

The dirt road intersected with the Yucatán Highway right outside the little village of Cancun. A few hundred yards farther on, he hit the first of the shacks on the outskirts of the village and stopped.

Twenty-odd years ago Cancun had been just another sleepy Mexican fishing village on the coast of the Yucatán and not even a very big one at that. Then the area had been "discovered" by modern financial conquistadors bent on conquering their share of the burgeoning Caribbean tourist trade.

Since Cancun had barely even been a village, the developers hadn't tried to do an Acapulco look-alike and build on the site's existing Old World Mexican charm because there simply wasn't any. Instead, they had gone for the gusto, building from scratch, U.S.-resort style. And since they hadn't wanted to get into the hassle of buying out the villagers and relocating them, they'd built on the then-empty, eight-mile-long sand spit across the bay from the village. The old dirt road through the town had been turned into a four-lane causeway leading from the airport to the hotels on the peninsula.

With only that one bridge between the peninsula and the mainland, whoever held the bridge controlled access to the resort. No one knew yet why the mysterious invaders had captured the strip at Cancun and the thousands of tourists vacationing there. Bolan had to admit, though, that the physical terrain was perfect for what they had pulled off. He'd studied the NRO recon satellite photos before getting on the Harrier, but he needed to make a personal recon before he decided on his move.

CHAPTER FIVE

From a hundred yards out, there were few signs of life in the old village of Cancun, the odd low-wattage light or candle cast a soft glow, but those were about the only lights showing. There was no civilian foot traffic and no signs of any vehicles, even parked, anywhere. Whoever the resort invaders were, they'd obviously swept through and secured this place, as well. But, the Executioner hadn't seen any foot patrols yet, so they might have gotten overconfident, which was fine with him. He liked it when his opponents were overly impressed with their own brilliance.

Bolan kept to the shadows as he made his way through the village. Were it not for the few faint voices he heard from some of the darkened dwellings, he would have thought the place had been emptied out. What inhabitants remained were keeping a low profile. He was moving quickly when a woman's scream, sounding louder because of the unnatural silence, split the night. A man shouted and the woman wailed again.

Against his better judgment, Bolan couldn't ignore it and went to investigate.

Following the sound, he came to a small adobe house a block off the main road. The front door was hanging wide open and a candle or lantern was burning inside, but the light was too dark for him to make out anything through the small window. Stepping up to the open door, he saw what looked to be a man struggling with a woman on the narrow bed against the wall in the corner of the single room.

In the dim light, he didn't have a clear, unobstructed line of sight, so his right hand whipped the Cold Steel Tanto fighting knife from the sheath on his assault harness. He was through the open door and across the room in three steps. The would-be rapist looked up from his work just in time to catch the blade as it slashed across his jugular.

The thug gurgled his death as Bolan grabbed him with his free hand and pulled him away from the motionless woman. She was unconscious, but breathing and didn't appear to be badly hurt. He laid his fingers against the side of her neck and found a strong pulse, so he just covered her.

Dragging the corpse outside, he closed the door

behind him before taking the body to a hiding place behind what looked to be a tavern. If there were other wandering thugs loose tonight, he didn't want someone to stumble over it and raise the alarm. From there, he continued on his way.

HAL BROGNOLA was still keeping to his sleep-whenever-he-could regimen. The world might be going to hell in a hand basket, but there was absolutely nothing he could do about it. Yet. He'd been awakened for the first meal his captors had provided in the late afternoon, wolfed down the beans and soft tortillas, used the urinal, crawled into bed and gone right back to sleep.

It was after dark when he was awakened by voices coming down the hall outside his cell. His watch had been taken away during the search the first night, so he had no idea what time it was, but it didn't really matter. He sat up, swung his legs over the side of his bunk and got mentally prepared to greet his visitors.

Two black-clad Latino gunmen entered the cell followed by a swaggering Diego Garcia. "How do you like your accommodations, Mr. Brognola?" he asked. "It's not quite your usual fancy D.C. hotel room is it?"

Brognola patted his narrow bunk. "Not bad for a Mexican jail." He shrugged. "I've seen a lot worse. The food's not quite up to Cancun's usual standards, though. I expected to eat much better here."

"You're eating what the people of Cancun eat on a daily basis," Garcia said. "They might be able to find work in your hotels, but they can't afford to eat the food they prepare for you."

"I don't think you kidnapped me to lecture me about the local cuisine, Garcia. There's not much I can do to improve the diet of your 'people.'"

"Your government has had a chance to improve the lives of the people of Latin America for years," the Cuban shot back, "but they have done nothing except to work hard to make it worse. Now that the people have taken things into their own hands, they will improve their lives for themselves."

"By invading the United States?" Brognola laughed. "And stealing what we Americans have created by our own ingenuity and our hard work? That's very original. I've never heard that one before."

"The people are only taking back what was taken from them in the first place," Garcia stated. "California, Texas and Florida rightfully belong to the Mexican people you Yankees stole them from."

"Don't forget Arizona and New Mexico." Brognola couldn't help himself. "We won them, too, when we beat your sorry asses in the Mexican War."

Brognola didn't even try to duck when Garcia swung at him. This guy wasn't too tightly wrapped, but as long as he could get him fired up every now and then, he wouldn't start asking the questions

Brognola didn't want to answer. He took the blow without flinching.

"Your arrogance is going to cost you dearly, Brognola." The Cuban almost spit the words. "I know that I could get a good ransom from your Washington friends for you, but I think that I'll turn you over to a People's Revolutionary Court instead to be tried for your crimes again humanity. The punishment will be to face a firing squad."

"Oh, please!" Brognola said. "Put me on trial in a kangaroo court and charge me with what? Being an underpaid career government employee?" He shrugged. "If I worked for the State Department, you might be able to make a case for my having repeatedly committed Crimes Against Common Sense, but I'm just a midlevel federal cop."

"A cop, as you say," Garcia replied, "who has the ear of the President. But your President is missing much more than just one of his many overpaid advisers. As of today he has also lost his source of cheap labor and a dumping ground for his toxic waste."

Brognola frowned. He was no stranger to the incomprehensible ravings of would-be, socialist "saviors of the people," but this was a completely new one on him. "What in the hell are you talking about?"

"The president of Cuba has just announced his recognition of the newly formed People's Republic of

Mexico," Garcia said proudly. "The Mexicans will now follow on the glorious path of the Cuban peoples to attain their true freedom from Capitalistic exploitation."

Brognola wanted to laugh but he knew better. This guy was rapidly descending into true paranoia. "In case you missed it," he couldn't keep himself from saying, "we're in the twenty-first century now. Che was the heart of the Revolution, and he's been dead for years so, for God's sake, get over it. After spilling his guts to the CIA, he got stood up against a shit house wall and was shot like a diseased dog."

Hearing the name of his personal hero spoken of so disrespectfully, the Cuban went berserk. Brognola's head snapped back from two blows to the face. The first strike opened a cut over his left eye and the second felt as though it had chipped a tooth. He'd been through worse and didn't react.

Garcia suddenly stopped and stalked out of the cell. One of the goons reversed his AK and smiled as he made as if to jab Brognola in the gut with the butt before following his boss out and locking the door behind him.

Brognola hid a smile as he laid back down again. Once more he had managed to deflect the conversation to lesser topics. But how much longer he could keep getting hit in the head remained to be seen. So far, though, he was taking it without incurring any permanent damage. Barbara Price was always saying that he was a hardheaded bastard, and now he was getting a chance to test that statement.

QUICKLY MOVING through the reminder of Cancun village, Bolan intersected the main paved road and followed it to the bridge that crossed the lagoon. As the photos had shown, the causeway was being guarded from the opposite end. A pair of open-top SUVs with mounted machine guns and searchlights were parked at the far end, and a dozen gunmen loitered nearby. It would be no problem for him to simply take out the security force, but this wasn't the time to make a lot of noise and leave more bodies behind. Someone was bound to notice sooner rather than later.

His only other choice was to make a half mile swim across the bay, which wasn't the option he would have chosen. Nonetheless, he headed south down the village side of the lagoon, separating it from the resort area, looking for an alternative to a swim.

A half a mile downshore, he came across a beach shack with several personal watercraft pulled up on the sand in front of it. A couple more small watercraft were under the roof of a lean-to in a state of disrepair; this, apparently, was a repair facility.

A quick check showed that all of the machines had been disabled by having their spark plugs pulled, but that was okay with him. The sound of an unmuffled two-stroke engine in the still night would attract a lit-tle more attention than he wanted. The watercraft would still float, however, so he looked around the shack until he found an aluminum paddle. Back on the beach, he chose a dark-colored Jet Ski, dragged it down to the water's edge and into the surf.

Straddling the saddle, he bent over the handlebars and paddled out into the lagoon at an angle away from the bridge. With few lights showing, there wasn't much chance of his being spotted against the dark water, but he kept low and paddled strongly, but carefully, so as not to raise ripples. The tide was with him and the trip across the quarter mile of open water went quickly.

On reaching the other side, he pulled the watercraft well up onto the sand and tipped it over so it would look as if it had been abandoned. He took cover above the surf line to orient himself; his GPS nav unit contained a downloaded map of the major buildings in the area. The Hotel Maya, where Brognola had been staying, was at the far end of the strip. But before checking out the hotel, he wanted to recon for a feel of the kind of forces he would be facing here and their locations.

There was an additional risk of exposure by doing it this way, but he didn't want to go to the trouble of getting Brognola out only to discover that there was no way for them to escape. He wanted to locate his back door first. Even then, finding the man was probably going to be more difficult than it really should be.

There was a comfortable sub-Q personal locator beacon often worn by people like Brognola—or people who were going in harm's way—that made finding them a snap. A single overhead pass of a satellite or spy plane would activate the beeper, and it would remain powered up for five days. As Bolan well knew, though, Hal didn't like to wear the miniature beepers, saying that they itched him.

For the lack of the locator beacon to follow, if Brognola wasn't being held in the hotel, Bolan was faced with the possibility of having to search more than a hundred buildings to find him. And, to make it even more difficult, according to the data dump he'd received right before he'd taken off from Texas, the airline manifests showed that some eight thousand American tourists had been flown into Cancun recently. Of course, there were also the thousands of Mexicans who lived and worked in the area to serve the visitors.

Finding the proverbial needle might turn out to be easier than this job.

WITH ALL THE ACTIVITY at the pier Richard Spellman and Mary Hamilton decided to wait for dark before trying to make an escape. They had also changed into fresh, starched sets of cook's whites they had found in the storeroom. They weren't the most practical camouflage to wear while trying to make a night-time break, but he figured that if they were spotted, they could be taken for the hired help, not escaped Americans on the run.

"If you think you can handle it," he told his companion, "it might work better if you lead off. With your Spanish, you might be able to talk our way out of trouble. I can pretend to be a deaf mute or something. But if it looks bad, get behind me real fast."

Hamilton smiled nervously. For someone who was more comfortable in a lab than a battlefield, her new man was proving resourceful.

Grabbing one of the extra tablecloths, Spellman tied the ends together to make a crude bag and loaded it with several plastic bottles of mineral water. Hamilton added a box of whole-grain crackers, some cheeses and a big tin of smoked salmon.

"How about some of those jazzed-up coffee beans?" Spellman asked. "We may need to stay awake until we can find a place to hide."

"Good idea."

Spellman slipped the locks on the storeroom door, opened it a crack and peered out. The passageway was clear, and he motioned for Hamilton to follow as he eased out into the hall. The deck they were on was two down from the main one. He expected the main to be guarded, but when he had boarded, he'd noticed a cargo hatch in the side of the ship on one of the lower decks. In L.A. it had been used to load passenger luggage and supplies for the trip. If he remembered correctly, it should be two decks down from where they were.

The passageway outside the café was deserted, and the pair quickly headed for the stairwell leading to the lower decks. The ship's passenger areas were carpeted, so Spellman barely heard the approaching footsteps in time to grab his companion's arm and get them both out of sight. The stair steps were also carpeted, which let them move quickly and noiselessly. Two decks down, they came to a hatch labeled D Cargo.

"This should be it," he said as he undogged the steel door and opened it.

The compartment behind the door was the size of a small house but was divided up into smaller sub-areas holding different cargos. Several of the cubicles held the passenger luggage he'd seen being loaded in L.A., and others held ship supplies. He motioned her inside and dogged the hatch shut behind them.

The steel deck in the compartment wasn't carpeted, so they stepped lightly as they crossed to the hatch on the outer hull. The sign on the steel door read Loading Berth.

"This should be it," Spellman said.

The controls for the hatch were simple, but he

opened it slowly so as not to make any more noise than necessary. The lights on the pier had been turned off, but the few lights burning on the ship illuminated about a six-foot gap between the hull and the dock. He looked inside the hatchway for a gangplank to bridge the gap, but there was none.

"Can you jump that far?" he asked.

Hamilton peered down at the water. "Maybe if you go first and catch me?"

"First I have to see if anyone's watching us," he said softly. "Grab my belt while I take a look."

"Be careful," she whispered.

Spellman held on to the door frame with one arm and swung out as far into the void as he could to look up at the decks above him. It was difficult to see anything beyond the expanse of the glossy white hull, but he caught moving shadows at both the bow and the stern before swinging back inside.

"It looks like they've posted a guard at both ends of the boat," he said. "But I don't think that they're looking this way."

Putting his hands on Hamilton's shoulders, Spellman looked her full in the face. "I think we have a good chance of pulling this off," he said. "If we can get off the ship, I know we can find someone to help us. I'll go first and if I'm spotted, I'll take off running to draw them away from you."

"I'll follow you," she said.

Spellman backed up a few feet, took a deep breath, sprinted for the open hatchway and leaped. He cleared the gap with ease, but landed hard. Getting to his feet, he made sure that no one was watching from the ship's decks before motioning for Hamilton to join him. As he had done, she backed off to get a run at it and cleared the gap by a foot.

He caught her arm as she came by and kept her balanced on her feet. "Good jump," he said softly. "Now let's get the hell out of here."

"You're limping," she said as they started off.

"I was never good at track and field. I hit wrong when I jumped, but I'll be okay."

"You sure?"

He grinned. "Yeah, I'm a doctor, remember?"

Taking her hand, Spellman led her across the pier into the cover of darkness.

WHEN BOLAN ENTERED the built-up area of restaurants and shops it was like being on an elaborate, full-size movie set after all of the actors and crew had gone home for the night. No one was on the streets, and none of the establishments was open for business. Again, a few dim lights glowed behind curtained windows, but that was all. Most of the streetlights had been turned off, as well, but that suited him just fine. Shadows were a scout's best ally.

A couple hundred yards farther on, he saw that one of the plazas along the main boulevard was brightly lit. Taking that as his cue, he decided to find out what was so important that it needed to be lit up. Coming from the side, he noted a handful of black-clad gunmen lounging around the entrance of a sizable building facing the square. The machine gun mounted on top of the SUV parked beside them told Bolan that the contents of the building had to be of interest.

When he got close enough to see the bars on the windows, he realized that this had to be the town lock-up. He had no way of knowing if Brognola was actually being held prisoner in there. But it was a jail and it was being guarded by the intruders, so before he moved on, he would take a look.

Slinging his H&K, he drew his Beretta 93-R and threaded the sound suppressor onto its muzzle.

He was working his way around the plaza when the gunmen made it easy for him. The guy behind the machine gun stepped down and said something to the others who laughed as he walked into the jail. That left him with only three targets to take down, and they all had their weapons casually slung.

Their confidence was admirable and showed that they had the entire resort peninsula under their control and weren't expecting trouble.

It was time to start changing that.

Bolan stepped unnoticed into the lighted plaza in front of the jail, the Beretta machine pistol held low against his leg.

"*¡Hola!*" he called.

The three gunmen turned and hesitated for a moment. This stranger was dressed in black, too, but by the time it registered on them that he wasn't one of them, he had the 93-R up and was firing.

Bolan's first 3-round burst took the man farthest from him, stitching a tight triangle over his heart. Retargeting smoothly, he put down the second man with another trio of 9 mm slugs before the first gunner hit the pavement.

The last guard had his AK halfway into position when a final short burst took him down, as well.

The only sounds of the hit had been the tinkle of empty brass on the pavement, the clatter of the AK hitting the steps of the jail and the soft thud of the bodies. So, before the machine gunner came back out, Bolan took the steps himself. He paused at the door, but the voices he heard inside didn't sound alarmed.

Swinging his H&K around on its sling, he switched his 93-R to his left hand and gripped the assault rifle with his right.

Show time.

CHAPTER SIX

Slipping through the door of the Mexican jail, Bolan rushed the room firing as soon as he had clear lines of sight to his new targets. Three of the black-clad men in the room had their backs turned to him, so the guy behind the desk with the surprised look on his face was targeted.

The man still looked surprised when he took a 3-round burst in the chest from the Beretta and pitched backward in his chair.

The others were turning to face their unexpected guest when a sustained burst from the H&K swept across the room at chest level.

That served for two of them, but the third man was faster than his comrades and dropped out of the line of fire as he fumbled for his piece.

Bolan tracked him with the Beretta and touched

off another silenced trio that dropped the gunman flat. The soldier stepped past the bodies and hurried behind the desk. A quick search of the guy who'd been sitting there produced a key ring with a plastic lock card, as well as several large numbered keys. The biggest key unlocked the sliding, barred door leading into the holding area.

The doors on the cells had regular locks, as well as electronic. In fact, when the power was cut, the mechanical locks worked as a fail-safe.

Hal Brognola was in the second cell Bolan checked out. The security light inside was dim, but there was no mistaking that huddled, sleeping form. The soft snoring told him that he was alive.

Bolan keyed the lock and opened the door. "You ready to go home, Hal?"

Brognola opened one eye. "'Bout goddamned time you showed up here, Striker," he growled.

The big Fed didn't look too much the worse for wear for his short imprisonment. He was rumpled, bleeding from one eyebrow, had a few bruises and badly needed a shower followed by a shave. But, at first glance, he didn't look to have sustained any major physical damage.

Bolan grinned broadly. "I got hung up going through airport security. I had to strip down to my shorts, 'cause I kept setting off the metal detector. You okay?"

"I'm fine now." Brognola sat up and reached for his jacket. "How bad is it?"

Bolan didn't have to ask him what "it" was. For a man who lived and breathed taking care of the nation's troubles, he could only mean one thing. "Have you been able to get any information down here at all?" he asked.

"The asshole in charge showed me some video clips of a Mexican mob storming the border crossing at Tijuana and some kind of small boat assault on a beach somewhere in Florida, but that's about it."

"That's pretty typical of what happened the first two days," Bolan confirmed. "There were also border town assaults in Texas, Arizona and New Mexico and they turned nasty real quick. We've got hundreds of police and firefighter casualties and the looting and arson damage in places like El Paso and Phoenix is extensive."

"How's the Man handling this?" Brognola asked.

"He's got everyone in uniform he can get on it," Bolan reported, "and they're starting to contain the intrusions. The damage to the border towns and southern Florida is running in the millions, but it's not spreading as fast as it was. For one thing, the citizens are taking this as a foreign invasion and armed home defense is a real popular topic right now. Neighborhood militia units are being sworn in to back up the police forces.

"If you're ready to go," Bolan went on, "let's do it. It's going to take a couple of hours for us to work our way back out to the PZ."

"Hold on, Striker," Brognola growled. "We aren't going anywhere."

Bolan had pretty much expected this response from his old friend and comrade-in-arms. Brognola had never been one to run from a fight no matter the odds. However, he had specific orders from the President of the United States. Brognola's input was sorely needed in this current crisis, and his orders were to get him back to Stony Man Farm ASAP.

"Hal, the Man told me in no uncertain terms that he wants you back at the Farm immediately to help him with this."

"The President's a good man," Brognola said, grinning, "and I know that he only has my best interests at heart, but the hell with him. I've got work to do here. That bastard Garcia's going down big-time."

Bolan shook his head. "Hal, I've got a Marine Harrier on call, and the back seat of that bird is waiting to evacuate your ass."

"That plane can just keep waiting until I'm done here," Brognola said firmly. "And you can consider your mission here to have been accomplished. I'm out of enemy custody and in no danger of being interrogated, so the country's secrets are safe."

"In case you haven't noticed because you've been

locked up, Hal," Bolan replied, "we're kind of light on the ground here to be trying to rescue several hundred American hostages. The Man is putting together a Marine landing force right now to come down and take care of that chore."

"I don't care as much about the tourists," Brognola said honestly, "as I do about the men who were at the conference with me. They're the top cops in their respective countries, and I've got a feeling that they're needed back home right about now. If this thing's spread as far as you say it has, Mexico's not the only place around here that's in trouble."

Bolan had to admit that there was a certain logic to Brognola's line of thought. While his briefings had been focused on the events that were taking place in Mexico and the United States, he knew that several other Latin American nations had also been hit by unexpected uprisings. In particular, Mexico's neighbors of Panama and Guatemala were also having major problems.

"And," Brognola added after a significant pause, "when I'm done taking care of that, there's a woman I want to make sure is okay."

Bolan was a little surprised to hear his old friend say that. Even on vacation Brognola wasn't known to go too far off the reservation. "And who's that?"

"Elena Martinez. I was having dinner with her when this thing went down, and she was taken captive."

"What do you know about her?"

"She runs some kind of social services center for the government working with the Indians down here in the Yucatán," he said. "She was only snatched up because she was having dinner with me. Garcia's thugs aren't treating the women they took that night very well."

Now that Bolan knew what was behind Brognola's request, he wasn't surprised. Hal was never one who liked to see women mistreated.

"If we find her on the way out," he said, "we can sure add her to the extraction collection. She can sit on your lap in the Harrier."

"Not good enough." Brognola locked eyes with his old friend and battle comrade. "I'm going after her when I go for Garcia. And if it'll make the Man happy, I'll tender my resignation from government service effective immediately. I have a current National Security Act form on file and, since we're not at war yet, I'm still my own man. I'll just exercise my right as an American citizen to opt out of working for the government."

Bolan paused before speaking. "Are you sure about that, Hal?"

"Damned straight." Brognola nodded. "I've never been surer of anything in my life, Mack. I've been doing this shit for years now, and I've suddenly come down with an urgent need to take some personal mental health time at a tropical resort. Call it a midlife crisis if you want."

He grinned. "After all, I did meet a Latin beauty and if that's not a midlife crisis thing for a guy like me, I don't know what is."

Bolan knew where this was going, but tried one last time to pull off a save. "Are you sure you want me to call it in to the Man that way?"

"It'd probably cause both of us a hell of a lot less grief if you didn't," Brognola admitted. "But I'm going to do what I have to do, so I guess you have to do the same."

Bolan knew when he was beaten. There was no way that he was going to walk away and leave Brognola in Cancun on his own.

"I'd better break the radio then," he said. "I don't want to have to tell the President of the United States that his number-one boy is playing hooky like a teenager. It might not look good on my report card."

"If you don't break that damned thing, Striker, I will," Brognola threatened.

"I'll just take the battery out," Bolan replied. "We might need it later, but as long as it's powered up, they can locate us."

"Do it then and let's get going."

WHEN THEY STEPPED OUT into the corridor, a voice called softly from the cell across the way. "Hal, it's Hector. How about letting me out?"

"Give me the key," Brognola told Bolan.

Bolan unobtrusively covered the cell as the door opened and a well-dressed but somewhat battered Latino stepped out. He kept his hands in the open as he nodded to Bolan. "Forgive me for overhearing," he said. "But it sounds like you two aren't leaving."

"Not right as yet," Brognola replied. "There's a couple of things I want to take care of here first."

De Lorenzo paused for a second. He'd had a hunch for a long time that Brognola was more than just another career Justice Department official assigned to advise the sitting American President on law-enforcement issues. Exactly what he really did to earn his federal paycheck wasn't clear, but seeing that a commando had been sent to rescue him spoke volumes.

That Brognola had chosen to stick around when he had a way to get out safely said even more about him.

"Need some company?" de Lorenzo asked.

Brognola turned to Bolan. "He's a good man, Striker. I don't know how well he can shoot, but I know that he's steady and reliable."

The Mexican realized that while Brognola was a high-ranking officer, it made sense that the commando was more or less in charge of the rescue operation and would have the final say. "If it matters," he broke in, "I was the best shot on the National Police pistol team for three years running."

Bolan extended his hand. "Jeff Cooper," he said.

"Hector de Lorenzo, current A.G. for the Mexican government by way of the National Police."

Bolan assessed the man. "Aren't they missing you up in Mexico City right about now?"

"Could be," de Lorenzo replied. "But, to be honest, I don't have any idea what's going on up there recently. I've kind of been out of touch."

"We don't know exactly who's doing what," Bolan said, "but the word is that the presidential palace has been captured and the government has been deposed. All communication facilities have been taken over so the only news that's getting out is over cell phones, and even that is spotty."

"What a time to be away from the office," de Lorenzo said softly.

"I don't think you could've done any good if you'd been there," Bolan said. "The coup was apparently well planned. Even the armed forces have been taken over."

"What's the plan?" he asked.

"I'm going to try to find Señorita Martinez," Brognola growled, "and then I'm going after the bastard who's behind this."

"The one who calls himself Diego Garcia?" de Lorenzo asked.

"Yeah," Brognola replied. "You know anything about him?"

"Only that he's a Cuban as are most of the rest of those bastards."

"You're kidding!" Brognola exploded.

"Nope." De Lorenzo smiled grimly. "He speaks good Mexican Spanish, but his mother tongue is Cuban Spanish and he still has a bit of an accent. The last I saw of him, he was still at the hotel," de Lorenzo added. "And it looked like he was planning to stay, as he was setting up a command post."

"What in the hell does he think he's going to do with a couple thousand North American tourists?"

"Other than hold them hostage?" De Lorenzo shrugged. "I don't know. But with all of us from the conference in custody, he's crippled the justice systems and police forces of most of Latin America. If he's planing some kind of widespread revolution in the region, with us out of the way, he's got a damned good start on pulling it off."

"That was my first thought," Brognola said. "And I figured that I'd try to see if we could slow him down."

"If we're going to take on these people," Bolan broke in, "we need to help ourselves to a little more ordnance. And we need to do it quickly before someone notices the bodies outside."

"Since this is a police station," de Lorenzo said, "there should be an armory around here somewhere."

It was right around the corner from the holding cells, and another key on the ring opened the door.

The offerings were a little better than Bolan had expected. Brognola found himself a Remington 12-gauge pumpgun and a bag of at least a hundred rounds of double-O buckshot. He also spotted a 1911 .45 in a Western-style holster and belted it on. A couple boxes of ammunition went into his jacket pockets until he could find something better.

De Lorenzo took an M-16 from the rifle rack and found an assault vest with loaded 30-round magazines, which he put on over a borrowed olive drab police field jacket. A pistol belt with a holstered 9 mm Smith & Wesson and a sheathed Ka-bar fighting knife went around his waist.

Bolan was well heeled as it was, but he added half a dozen old World War II pineapple-style fragmentation grenades to his load. He had no idea what they were doing in a cop shop, but they might come in handy. He had a double basic load of 9 mm for the MP-5, but he helped himself to another two hundred rounds in boxes.

"How about the rest of these men?" De Lorenzo pointed back to the cells where half a dozen men were being held. "Most of them are from our group."

Bolan and Brognola exchanged glances. "They might present a problem for us if we let them loose, Hector," Brognola said carefully.

"You don't want their help?"

"I'm afraid that they'll just get in our way," Bolan

explained. "We'll have a better chance of doing what we're going to do if we do it alone. We don't want the opposition to get alarmed."

"They're Latino men," de Lorenzo stated, pointing out the obvious, "and they're really going to be pissed if they can't get into the fight, too."

The last thing Bolan needed was a bunch of angry senior police and justice officials stumbling around alerting the opposition to what was going down.

"The only reason that you're coming with us," Bolan said, "is that Hal recommended you. I'll free them, but if they want to get themselves killed, they'll have to do it somewhere far away from us. If this thing's going to work, we've only got a small window to do what we're going to do. We don't have time to be baby-sitting people who shouldn't be in the line of fire in the first place."

De Lorenzo had been a cop long enough to know where the commando was coming from and had to admit that he was right. Senior government bureaucrats weren't exactly his first choice for men to make up a strike force, either. He had no idea what the three of them alone would be able to accomplish, but he, too, was Latino and he had to do something.

"Give me a moment," de Lorenzo said, "and I'll try to explain it to them so they'll understand."

"Make it quick."

The Mexican hesitated. "And if I can get their sacred word to go to the south end of the island and hide, can I turn them loose?"

Brognola nodded and Bolan handed over the key. "Tell them to give us a good head start."

The two Americans heard raised voices, and de Lorenzo wasn't smiling when he came back. "I'm going to take a lot of grief for that when this is all over."

"If they come out of this alive," Bolan said, "they'll get over it."

"If any of us do," de Lorenzo added.

BOLAN CLEARED the plaza in front of the jail before he let Brognola and the Mexican come out. "Let's get these bodies inside," he told them.

After concealing the corpses, Bolan disabled the SUV and the machine gun as a matter of covering their rear.

"You said you last saw this Garcia guy in a hotel?" Bolan asked de Lorenzo.

The Mexican nodded. "Yes, the Hotel Maya. It's where we were holding the conference."

"How far is it to that hotel?" Bolan asked.

"About three miles," de Lorenzo replied.

"Let's get moving."

On the other side of the jail plaza, a few more streetlights had been left on, giving the deserted resort a surreal look. Cancun was a 24/7 kind of town, and thousands of young men and women should have been crowding the streets looking for a good time in paradise. Many of them would simply find Tequila-fueled oblivion along that route, but that was part of Cancun's fabled charm. But not only were the streets and bars devoid of carousing tourists, the Mexican nationals who lived and worked in the town were gone, as well.

"Do you think that he ran off all the locals?" Brognola asked, turning to de Lorenzo.

"I doubt it. I don't think he has enough men here to make a sweep like that. They're probably just holed up in their houses and shops waiting for this to blow over. It's in the blood of the Mexican people to keep out of the way of revolutions."

"Smart."

"They've had a lot of practice."

The sound of an approaching vehicle sent the trio into cover around the side of a building as an open-top SUV drove past with three men in the back guarded by two gunmen. The three prisoners looked to be tied up.

"It's heading for the jail," Brognola observed. "We're about to be made."

"This way," de Lorenzo said as he led them down an alley off the main street.

The three men faded into the darkness.

CHAPTER SEVEN

Richard Spellman and Mary Hamilton kept to the shadows as they quickly made their way across the open area around the pier where the *Carib Princess* had been tied up. Spellman had no idea where they might be able to find safety from whoever had taken over the ship, but he knew they had to get as far away from it as they could. A few blocks from the pier, they entered the dense downtown area of Cancun, packed with bars, eateries, tourist shops and strip malls.

They were surprised to find the area dark and completely deserted, all the shops closed. "Everyone's gone," Hamilton said. "What do you think's happened?"

"I don't know—" Spellman looked around slowly "—but it doesn't look good, and it may have something to do with the hijackers. I think we'd better keep out of sight until we can figure this thing out."

He took her arm and started down one of the side streets. He had absolutely no idea where he was going, but vaguely hoped to find some signs of life and someone who might take them in for the night.

BOLAN, HAL BROGNOLA and de Lorenzo kept to the side streets as they made their way north to the Maya Hotel. So far, the only signs of the terrorists they had encountered had been the occasional SUV patrol. Pausing to clear an intersection, they spotted two figures a block away moving furtively in the dark.

"Those don't look like Garcia's men," de Lorenzo commented. "Not wearing white clothes like that. They might be local hotel workers."

"Let's see if we can catch up with them," Bolan said. "They might be able to fill us in on what's been going down around here."

"When we get close enough," de Lorenzo said, "I'll call out so they don't think we're with the bad guys."

The trio was a hundred yards away and closing fast when a half dozen black-clad gunmen burst from the shadows in front of the fleeing pair, their weapons at the ready, and surrounded them.

A woman's scream cut the night. "Richard!"

"They're Americans!" Brognola said.

Bolan and Brognola moved into action with de

Lorenzo right behind them. "Take the right flank and wait for my shot," Bolan told the Mexican.

De Lorenzo held his borrowed M-16 at port arms as he ran. He had no idea how the rifle was sighted in, but at that range, an inch or two off of battle sight zero wouldn't really matter. As he'd told the commando, he'd been on the National Police pistol team, but he'd also been through the assault tactics course with the M-16 and had fallen in love with the shooter.

They had covered half the distance when the guy who looked to be in charge of the squad of thugs stepped forward. He had some kind of club in his hand and drew it back to strike one of the people in white. Bolan paused and snapped off a shot from his Desert Eagle. The roar of the big .44 slug echoed as it took out the back of the thug's head.

Like the other gunmen, the two Americans in white froze.

Bolan shouted, "Get down!" When they dropped, clearing the field of fire, the killing began in earnest.

Brognola was still a little far away for accuracy with his pumpgun, but since firepower conquered all, he ripped off a couple of blasts of double-O buck anyway. De Lorenzo halted to get a better firing platform and snapped out controlled 3-round bursts.

The gunmen had been stunned by the unexpected intrusion, but they reacted fairly well. Their main problem was that they weren't experienced night fighters and the targets were running. Also, the AK was notoriously difficult to control in bursts of sustained autofire.

One guy did know what he was doing, and a well-controlled short burst of tracers sliced through the air inches in front of de Lorenzo's head. The Mexican dropped into a crouch and put a well-aimed 3-round burst into him.

Bolan had accounted for two more with the Desert Eagle when the last two thugs finally realized their mistake and made a break for the shadows. The Executioner acquired the lead runner in his sights and put a .44 bullet in the middle of his back, slamming him facefirst into the dirt.

Brognola got the last one with a double pump from the Remington.

When the firing stopped, the two Americans got to their feet and looked around in shock. When one of them turned out to be a woman, Brognola cradled the smoking Remington in his arms as he walked up.

"It's okay now," he said. "You're safe."

"Thank you, thank you," Mary Hamilton sobbed as she hugged him. "They were going to kill us and you saved us."

"I can't say that you're completely safe now, though," Brognola said as he gently disengaged himself. "We think the entire peninsula is under the control of some kind of terrorist organization."

"Who are you two and what are you doing here?" Bolan asked.

"I'm sorry," the man replied. "I'm Dick Spellman and she's Mary Hamilton. We were on the *Carib Princess* for a medical society meeting, and the ship was hijacked as we were leaving the Panama Canal. Mary and I were eating in one of the little cafés below deck and I spotted gunmen with automatic weapons in the passageway as we were leaving. Not knowing what was going down, I found a place for us to hide and…"

Spellman quickly recounted their hiding in the storage room behind the café.

"That was real quick thinking." Brognola praised him. "Good work."

"So you never had a chance to really find out who those men were or how many of them were involved?" Bolan asked.

"No," Spellman replied, "I'm sorry. It happened too fast and all I could think of was getting out of sight."

"Do you know how many people were on the cruise?" Bolan kept pumping for information.

"At least 750 according to the handout we got when we came on board."

"And they're all doctors?"

"Mostly medical researchers and their families, and they're from all over the world."

Bolan and Brognola exchanged glances. Next to having an equal number of widows and orphans, a boatload of doctors and their families was about the best bunch of hostages a terrorist could ask for.

"But I don't understand," Hamilton said. "Why was the ship taken over?"

"Well," Brognola explained, "it's real simple. It was taken over so the terrorists could hold you all hostage to protect themselves from a retaliatory attack. We don't know what their ultimate plan is, but it has to be big. The Mexican government has been taken over, and we've also had problems at our southern borders, so this is larger than just the capture of the tourists here at Cancun and your ship."

Spellman didn't think to ask these three mystery men who they were or what they were doing; he just saw them as their only hope of salvation. "Can you help us get out of here?" he asked.

"The President has a rescue force on the way." Brognola told the lie smoothly. "They should be hitting the beach in a little over twenty-four hours."

"The Marines?" Spellman brightened.

"Yes. If you can find a place to hide until they get here you'll be safe."

Since he was familiar with the area, de Lorenzo stepped forward. "We don't know how much of the area the terrorists are controlling," he said. "But if you head south along the beach you should run into other people who are also hiding, and they will take you in. Just be on the lookout for gunmen in black. They're the terrorists."

Spellman had been hoping that these men would be able to do more for them, but obviously they were on some kind of mission against the terrorists. "We'll be careful," he said. "And thanks a lot."

"Good luck."

IN HIS COMMAND POST in the Hotel Maya, Diego Garcia went over the printouts of the latest reports from his Matador groups in Mexico. It was amazing how easy it had been to bring the country to its knees with just a few hundred men in the right places. Even the takeover of the presidential palace and the National Assembly had been child's play and had required very little killing.

Gaining control of the Mexican military forces had been a bit more of a problem, but select officers in positions of high authority had been deep-cover Matador agents. The army's chief of staff had met with an unfortunate accident, but his successor was part of the Matador team. The air force and navy had come under his control just as easily, and only a couple of so-called counterterrorist battalions deployed against guerrillas along Mexico's southern border weren't under Matador control.

With the military's aviation assets either grounded or controlled by his operatives, however, those few units wouldn't present much of a threat at this point. Once the army had been properly purged, he'd use them to neutralize the few holdout units.

The Yankees had finally reacted to the invasions of their southern borders, but the damage had already been done. The estimates were that between eighty and a hundred thousand people had flooded into the border states and it would take months, if not years, to run them all down. Not all of them had been Matador operatives by any means. But all it took was for a couple of his men to aim the mobs against high-value targets and turn them loose to do the damage he wanted accomplished. The Yankee news reports of widespread looting and arson told him that the plan was working as he had intended. With the Yankees tied up in their own backyards, they wouldn't be interfering in Mexico's internal affairs.

"Comrade Colonel," one of the Cuban's subordinates said as he hurried into his office. Diego Garcia wasn't a colonel, but he liked the sound of the military title. "Someone killed the guards at the jail and freed the prisoners."

Garcia didn't believe what he was hearing. The town's police force had been disarmed and locked up along with all the private security guards employed by the various hotels. The only people in town with weapons were his men. "How did this happen?"

The man shrugged. "No one knows, Chief. We were delivering another group of prisoners and found the bodies of our men had been dragged inside. It looks like they were caught by surprise."

"How many dead?" The Cuban had planned this

operation down to the last round of ammunition and operative. He had enough men to completely cordon off the peninsula and to guard his thousands of hostages. He also had a fair-size reserve force. But he wanted to keep his reserves free in case a situation came up that required reinforcement.

"All of them are dead, Comrade, all eight."

"And the prisoners?" He was holding only a few men in the jail, but they were important hostages.

"All of them escaped, Colonel," the man said. "And it also looks like they took some of the police weapons to arm themselves."

"Does it look like they had outside help?"

The man shrugged. "There is no way to tell, Comrade Colonel. None of our men fired their weapons, so it looks like they were taken by surprise."

"Pull one of the squads from the eastern end of the bridge and tell them to replace the jail guards," the Matador leader commanded. "And tell the comrade at the bridge to make sure that the explosive charges are ready to be set off."

"Sí, Comrade Colonel."

"And track those people down," Garcia ordered. "All of them. There's no way for them to escape and I want them back. Tell the comrades not to worry, though, if they have to kill a few of them. Except," he quickly added, "I need that Yankee alive at all costs. And, if they can, the Mexican de Lorenzo, as well."

"Sí, Comrade."

As soon as the Matador officer left to carry out his orders, Elena Martinez came out from the back room of the office. She had changed out of her party dress and was wearing Matador black.

"I didn't think Brognola had it in him to do something like that," she said. "He seemed just like all the rest of those Yankee political flunkies."

"There's something about him that doesn't fit with what I was told," Garcia said. "Unlike the others, he wasn't at all concerned about being taken hostage. He taunted me like he was a man who had no fear of the future. You know, I think he escaped so he could try to kill me and disrupt the plan."

Martinex was all too aware of Garcia's growing paranoia. He was a brilliant planner and his thirst to bring grief to the Yankees drove him relentlessly. Of late, though, he seemed to have slipped into very self-centered thinking. She had reported her concerns to the Cuban leader, who had ordered her to keep an even closer eye on him.

She didn't know how much closer she could get to him than sharing his bed, but much was riding on the success of this Matador operation. Garcia was the architect and driving force behind the project, but if it looked as though he was losing contact with reality, her orders were to eliminate him. If that became necessary, Nguyen Cao Nguyen would step in to take the plan to its conclusion, and she would step up to the second-in-command position.

It would be poor payment for Garcia's years of faithful service to the Revolution if he had to be removed. But the Cuban people deserved only the best and if a man, any man, was not up to the job, he was expendable.

"Let me go out to look for him," she suggested. "I should be able to bring him back."

"Tonight? You'll get shot by our own patrols."

"Not if I wear the same dress I was wearing when I was 'captured.' You can tell our men to be on the lookout for me and if the Yankee sees me, he'll think that I managed to escape, too."

"It's a big town."

"But if he's coming here like you think, he'll be somewhere between here and the jail."

"I'd rather you stayed here and guarded me," he replied. "I have to oversee the plan and if I am killed, it will surely fail."

"I will not let him get close to you," she promised soothingly. "But to do that, Diego, I have to have complete freedom of movement, you know that."

The rational part of Garcia's disintegrating mind did realize the truth of what she said. Elena was one of Cuba's most effective operatives, and her personal kill list was impressive even by Mossad standards. As a favor for the PLO, she had even taken out one of Israel's superspies in Spain. A soft Yankee bureaucrat like Brognola wouldn't stand a chance against her.

"Good idea," the Cuban finally agreed. "But see

that Juan knows that you are leaving the headquarters so he can increase the security on me."

"Certainly."

Elena quickly changed back into the red fiesta dress she had worn at the dinner. She'd positioned the thigh holster for her silenced Makarov pistol on her left leg and her stiletto sheath down the back of her neck. She would have preferred to pack her Czech Skorpion machine pistol, but that wouldn't fit her cover of a woman needing rescuing.

She had no doubts that if Hal Brognola was coming back to the hotel, he would be coming for her; he was that kind of old-fashioned man. It had taken her a little longer than usual to get a read on him at the dinner and had been surprised when she did. She'd been prepared to have him start pawing her over the shrimp cocktail, the usual response she got from men his age, particularly Americans. Surprisingly, though, he had turned out to be the prefect gentlemen companion, comfortable with himself, urbane, witty and well-mannered.

It had been a long time since she'd been around a man like him, and it was almost a shame that she was going to have to kill him.

She left the hotel through one of the side doors and slipped into the warm night. Once in the dark, she mussed her hair and carefully tore the bodice of her dress to expose half of one breast. If she was going to claim that she'd been manhandled, she had to look the part. Men were such fools.

She hurried toward the jail, keeping in the shadows as she knew Brognola would be doing. She hadn't pegged him as having had much military experience, but even a rookie cop knew enough not to walk down the middle of a deserted street in enemy territory.

JUAN GOMEZ DIDN'T trust that Martinez bitch as far as he could throw her. She and her big tits had the chief eating out of the palm of her hand. And, for all his brilliance and dedication to the Revolution, Diego Garcia was an absolute fool when it came to women. The fact that Gomez swung the other way predisposed him to not trust any woman, but that particular woman was pure poison and he hated it that a man he admired couldn't see her for what she was.

He went back into his makeshift command center, spotted Jésus Delmonte, one of his top field operatives, and called him over.

"The chief wants me to let the patrols know that the bitch Elena is loose on the streets," he said quietly. "She's supposedly going after the Yankee bastard who got away from the jail."

"Why is she doing that?" Delmonte asked. "We have our men out looking for him already."

"Damned if I know, but I don't like it," Gomez growled. "I want you to follow her, find out what she's up to, who she meets and if possible what she says. I don't trust the bitch, and if it looks like she's playing the traitor, kill her."

"But—"

"You will do as I say," Gomez snapped. "And if it comes down to that, so be it. I'll tell Diego that the Yankee killed her."

Delmonte's heart really wasn't in this, but he knew better than to even try to cross Gomez. Those who thought that homosexuals were soft had never seen him kill a man with his bare hands. Rather than end up dead himself, the operative grabbed his weapon and his radio and headed out.

"Keep me updated," Gomez called after him.

"Yes, Comrade."

Outside the hotel, Martinez had already disappeared and none of the guards had seen which way she had gone. Delmonte figured, though, that she had probably headed south in the direction of the jail, and he started running that way. She was moving quickly, but two blocks on he caught sight of her when she passed close to one of the streetlights that was still burning. In that red dress, she stood out enough that he should be able to keep her in sight.

Slowing so she wouldn't hear his running footsteps, he closed to within half a block of her right as she turned off of the main street and plunged into the crowded buildings of the side streets.

Elena Martinez watched from the shadows as Hal Brognola and the two men with him moved north down a side street. As she had suspected, he had to be gallantly heading back to the hotel to "rescue her." It was a magnanimous gesture given the circumstances, but she wasn't the kind of woman who needed any man's help. She was surprised to see the other two men with him and didn't like the odds. She figured, though, that she should be able to cut Brognola out of the pack, take care of the other two and return the American to Garcia.

She mussed her hair some more and started breathing heavily. As soon as she was panting, she dashed out of the shadows, looking back over her shoulder as if she were running from someone.

From half a block away Jésus Delmonte saw Elena Martinez break into a run and, without thinking, took off after her, pulling his pistol as he ran. If she was meeting someone, he had to find out who it was.

CHAPTER EIGHT

Bolan heard running feet approaching and spun to see a woman in a red party dress break out of the shadows. He was covering her with his H&K when Brognola IDed her.

"Hold your fire," he said. "It's Elena, the woman at the dinner I told you about."

"Elena!" he called as he stepped into the open. "It's Hal! Over here!"

Hearing the shout, the woman turned and raced for their protection.

Now that she was closer, Bolan could see that her dress was torn, her hair was disheveled and she kept glancing over her shoulder as she ran as if she were being pursued. Sliding his aiming point past her shoulder, he went to his night optics and saw a man running after her. He had a pistol in his hand, but it wasn't aimed at the woman. When he stopped and brought it up, Bolan fired.

The woman screamed at the shot and ran to Brognola. "Oh, God, Hal!" she panted as she clung to him. "He was trying to kill me."

Martinez didn't know who the man's victim was, but he had to be one of Gomez's men sent to check up on what she was doing. The Matador security chief was the one man in the organization she had never been able to work with at all. The fact that he enjoyed rough sex with teenage youths probably had a lot to do with it.

She could also see that she wasn't going to make much headway against the two men who had hooked up with Brognola. She had met de Lorenzo before the dinner and knew that he wasn't a fool. The other man with him had the look of a Special Forces operator, probably from their famed Delta Force, and he wasn't going to go along with her program, either. She didn't like what she saw in his eyes.

This created a problem for her. She could let herself be "rescued" and continue on with them in the hope of finding a better opportunity, or she could go out in a blaze of glory right here and now. She didn't have a death wish, but she had never failed on a mission and wasn't about to now. Brognola was a big man in Washington, and his loss could only help the plan.

"Please—" she swayed as if weak in the knees "—I need to sit down."

Brognola put his arm around her. "There's a bench over there."

Martinez allowed herself to be led to the decorative wooden bench in front of a small garden plaza. The trees above them threw deep shadows and, if she played it right, she should be able to quickly take out Brognola and escape through the garden.

She pretended to stumble and went down to one knee. When Brognola bent to help her to her feet, her hand came out from behind her neck, the thin blade of her razor-sharp stiletto poised.

Bolan caught the flash of steel out of the corner of his eyes and had his 93-R in his hand without even thinking about it. The 9 mm round went into her right shoulder, the blow knocking the knife away as it spun her, sending her to the ground.

"*¡Tu Madre!*" she spit as her left hand went down toward her thighs and came up filled with steel. Bolan fired again and this time the round took her between the eyes.

Brognola stood in shock.

"That's some dinner date, Hal," Bolan said as he walked over and picked up the stiletto from the ground. It was a professional assassin's tool, not a woman's date-rape hideout piece.

"It's a good thing that Garcia broke up your little party the other night before she talked you into taking her back to your room. If you had, you'd be wearing this thing between your shoulder blades."

De Lorenzo was also in a state of shock at the near assassination of his friend. "I swear on my mother," he said. "I did not know anything about this, Hal. She was recommended to me by the state governor as being a woman of high standing and character and he told me she was a looker, not an assassin."

"It's not your fault, Hector," Brognola said. "I've always been a sucker for a pretty pair."

"And for a setup," Bolan added. "This wasn't an accident. Someone wanted you out of the picture. Now that your damsel in distress's no longer in play, you want to go home?"

Brognola didn't even hesitate. "Not on your life, Striker. I'm really pissed now. I don't like being set up and I want Garcia's ass."

"You know—" de Lorenzo bent over the corpse of the Cuban who had been following Martinez "—if we're going after Garcia, we need to know how he's got that hotel defended. This guy's about my size so what about my borrowing his uniform and making a recon of the place?"

"Won't your Mexican Spanish give you away?" Brognola asked. "You said that all of his top men sounded like they were Cubans."

De Lorenzo smiled wolfishly. "There's a side note to my résumé you might have missed, Hal. I served at the Mexican consulate in Havana for a couple of years after it opened in the early nineties. I can speak Spanish with a good Cuban accent."

Bolan smiled. The only thing the Mexican could have been doing in Cuba was spying, so he would have needed to speak the local dialect fluently. Mexico had diplomatic relations with Castro's Cuba, but the DGI wasn't above making the spies of even friendly nations disappear if they could catch up with them.

"You sure you're up to this?"

"As you gringos like to say," de Lorenzo said with a grin, "been there, done that."

"You've got the lingo, partner, I guess you're elected then."

Since the Cuban hadn't been carrying a rifle, the Mexican left his M-16 with Brognola. He did, though, switch his Ka-bar fighting knife to his waist belt under his borrowed black combat jacket. The Cuban's field belt with the holstered Makarov pistol went over the jacket.

"Let's see if we can get down there before dawn breaks."

THE MORNING SKY didn't dawn clear over the Caribbean, and it didn't dawn as much as the sky ever so slowly grew lighter. It also wasn't the usual overcast, gray coastal day that occurred occasionally even in paradise. The sky had a strange, solid, yellowish cast. The air was dead-still, and the flocks of seabirds that normally cruised above the surf line had all but disappeared.

Bolan, Brognola and de Lorenzo had moved to within sight of the Hotel Maya. Dressed in the black uniform of the dead Cuban officer, the Mexican was ready to make his probe of the hotel.

"We have a hurricane coming," the Mexican announced as he cast his eyes skyward. "It's a little late in the season for a storm like that, but it looks like we've got a big one moving in."

"How's that going to affect this place?" Brognola looked concerned.

"Cancun's built to take the storms," de Lorenzo replied. "The developers knew full well what the weather's like around here, and the major buildings should ride it out okay. About the worst thing that will happen is that the waves will swamp the seaside restaurants and the rain will wash out the dirt roads on the mainland, flood the fields and trash a few farmers' huts."

"And give us good cover," Bolan added. "If we wait till the storm hits, the opposition'll be ducking for cover in the hotels, and they're not going to be out looking for us to be mounting an assault."

"And where are we going to find cover from it?" Brognola didn't like what he was hearing at all. He was a man who usually rode out storms, natural or manmade, in the snug surroundings of an operations center and watched the relay on real-time satellite imagery. Hiding out in the open while Mother Nature did her best to eradicate him wasn't his modus operandi.

"We'll just stay low and hang on to a tree if we need to," Bolan replied.

Brognola turned to de Lorenzo. "Just how hard are those winds going to be blowing, anyway?"

The Mexican shrugged. "Well, with a real good storm, we can get up to two hundred kilometers, that's about one hundred and twenty of your miles an hour or so. When the coconuts ripped off the palm trees are flying parallel to the ground, that's about two hundred klicks. But when they start going up into the air like rockets, it's more like—"

"I don't want to know," Brognola said.

"Don't worry, Hal," de Lorenzo said, grinning. "I'll let you know when you need to grab on to a tree. And," he added, casting his eyes skyward again, "I think I'd better get going while we still have time."

"Good luck," Brognola said.

De Lorenzo gave a mock salute.

HECTOR DE LORENZO walked up to the Hotel Maya as if he owned the place.

Diego Garcia had placed a pair of gun jeeps in

front of the entrance and a gaggle of AK-armed thugs were lounging around smoking and drinking beer out of bottles.

De Lorenzo got a couple of hard looks from the guards, but ignored them as there was almost no chance that the gunmen could know who he was. He continued on with the studied arrogance of the Latin officer class and entered the foyer. Inside, he was just one of many functionaries scurrying around trying to look busy.

He nonchalantly turned left at the decorative fountain by the reception desk and headed for the bank of elevators. The door was closing on his car when a gunman reached out to stop them.

"Comrade," the man said, nodding as he got in the elevator.

De Lorenzo nodded back without speaking as even a Cuban revolutionary officer would. He punched the button for the rooftop restaurant on the eighteenth floor and was surprised when the gunmen did not select a floor for himself.

At his floor, the man held back while de Lorenzo stepped out ahead of him. Still playing the officer, de Lorenzo continued to ignore the man and walked onto the observation deck outside the restaurant. The deck extended around all four sides of the pyramid and would gave him a good viewing point to look down on Garcia's defensive positions and guard posts below.

He was checking out the beach side approaches when he heard the guard walk up to him. He turned slowly as the gunman halted a pace away from him, his AK held at port arms.

"Comrade?" the man said.

"What is it?"

"The colonel gave orders that no one but the sentry is to be allowed on the observation deck," the man said. "I will have to report to my watch leader that you were here."

"My friend," de Lorenzo said with a smile, stepping forward and placing his right hand on the gunman's shoulder. "I like to see a man who does his duty. For the Revolution to be successful, we all have to do our duties no matter what they are. I commend you on your zeal to follow orders."

The gunman swelled with pride. This man wasn't a stuffed shirt like most of them were. Maybe he should forget that he had seen him in the forbidden area. After all, he was one of the Matador officers.

De Lorenzo's right hand clamped down on the muzzle of the man's AK as his left flashed out from behind his belt. The point of the fighting knife went in under the man's rib cage and slid up into his heart.

The dutiful sentry gasped, shuddered and died with a puzzled look in his eyes.

De Lorenzo lowered the body to the ground and wiped the blade of his knife on the corpse's shirt. Who said that growing up in a rough part of Mexico City didn't have its advantages? His uncle had been one of Mexico's most famous knife fighters and had taught him how to survive with a blade. Now, to get rid of the evidence.

The restaurant had one of those stainless-steel carts the waiters used to serve fresh carved prime rib at the diner's table. It was at least six feet long and had a round, hinged metal cover over the top. A perfect place to hide a body.

Being careful not to get any of the man's blood on his uniform, de Lorenzo dragged the body over to the cart and opened the cover. As he had expected, the inside serving area had been emptied and cleaned after the previous night's meals. The hapless guard was stuffed into it, his knees drawn up to his chest to make room. Since he didn't want anyone to find the guard's AK and ask awkward questions, he put the weapon in with him. Even a deluded Marxist deserved to go out with his gun at his side.

After rolling the cart back into place in the kitchen, he went to the sink and washed a small bloodstain from his left sleeve with cold water. After patting it dry, he went back to scoping out the hotel's defenses. He wasn't sure what the three of them alone would be able to do once they got inside. The commando seemed to be capable of infiltrating by himself, but if their goal was to kill Diego Garcia, he and Brognola would be useful as a diversionary force to make it easier for him to get in. This half-assed "revolution" had to be stopped in its tracks, and killing the Cuban was probably the fastest way to put an end to it. This kind of organization was always run with top-heavy leadership, so to take out Diego Garcia should disrupt whatever their plans were. If the majority of the Cubans were as stupid as that sentry had been, de Lorenzo thought it shouldn't be too much of a chore.

After storing the enemy's dispositions in his mind, he took the stairs back down. Every couple of floors, he left the stairwell and went to the small observation point at the end of the hallway to see if he could spot more details of the security positions.

Rather than go back out the main entrance, he rode the elevator to the first basement level. Finding it empty, he explored the passageways until he found a door leading onto the grounds. Keeping clear of the Cuban positions he had spotted from above, he made his way back to where the two Americans were waiting.

"HE'S GOT A LOT of people there," de Lorenzo reported when he rejoined Bolan and Brognola. "But the Maya's not going to be that difficult to infiltrate.

I mean, it's a hotel and there are several ways to get into the main building that he doesn't have well covered."

He eyed Bolan's silenced H&K subgun. "With your silenced hardware, you should be able to get in and make the hit. I think that if Hal and I provide some fireworks from out front it might make it easier for you to zip in and out."

"Where will I find him?"

De Lorenzo knelt in the dirt and began to sketch a map of the lobby. "He's taken over the manager's office suite, and it's not hard to get to if you come in from the back. There's a basement tunnel here…"

Bolan watched the Mexican sketch a plan of the ground floor of the hotel and asked a few questions before mapping it in his mind.

"Actually," the Executioner stated, "that's not a bad plan if we wait for the storm to add to the confusion. With you two drawing their fire, I should be able to get in and out of there with a minimum of hassle."

"Then what we do?" de Lorenzo asked.

"Then we'll start taking out the rest of those bastards."

COLONEL PABLO MENDEZ was one of the few field-grade officers in the Mexican army who had more combat time than he did time spent sitting behind a desk. He'd had his buckle in the dust from almost his first assignment years ago as a newly commissioned lieutenant and had kept it there. On top of that, most of his "desk time" had been spent at Fort Bragg and Fort Benning in the United States Army schools learning how to be an even better combat officer. He was both U.S. parachute and Ranger qualified and had done extensive counterguerrilla work at the JFK Special Warfare Center at Fort Bragg.

He'd put his military expertise to work mostly in the southern part of his country although he'd been loaned out to several other Latin American nations to help them curb their own insurgency movements. There were still several ragtag bands of leftover Marxist guerrillas loose in the region's jungles, but mostly the enemy now were the private armies of the cartel drug lords. And, in many aspects, they were even more difficult opponents than the old-style idealistic guerrillas. For one, they were better armed and were more brutal. But, Marxists or drug lords, he had gone head-to-head with them and bested them all.

Whatever was sweeping over Mexico now, though, might turn out to be his toughest fight yet.

He had been in the southern Yucatán when the word came down from army headquarters in Mexico City that he was to immediately cease all operations, return his troops to their home base and stand down. The officer passing on the message couldn't give him a reason for the orders, and Mendez instantly smelled a rat. One of the dirty little secrets about the workings of the Mexican National Police and military forces was that they weren't free of political meddling, and the orders sounded political.

Right after that message, he started receiving radio and cell phone intel from some of his fellow officers saying that the army leadership had been overthrown by some kind of radical group. One by one, though, they went off the air and he feared the worst. His being in the field instead of back at his headquarters was purely a fluke. Two companies of his Ranger-trained Panther counterterrorist battalion were deployed on a training exercise in the Yucatán, and he had flown in to take a look at their operation.

Not long after the radio calls ceased and a few of the locals reached his lines to report that a group of terrorists had apparently taken over Cancun and were holding the tourists hostage, had it all come together. Someone was taking over the government of his country. He couldn't turn his back on an outrage to Mexico such as that, and he clearly saw his course of action.

There might not be anything that he could do about whatever was going on in Mexico City, but he and his men could sure as hell take on a terrorist group in nearby Cancun, and he would.

For that kind of operation, though, he needed to react quickly. But when he'd called back to his home base, he'd learned that his choppers had been grounded on orders from army headquarters. He had the JetRanger he'd flown down in, but his jungle fighters had been operating on foot and from a small fleet of two-and-a-half-ton trucks. Trucks weren't as fast as choppers, but they were all the mobility he had and they would have to serve.

Using his tactical radio, Mendez quickly recalled his units, ordering them to pull back to the closest pickup points to wait for their truck transport.

As soon as the first truck was loaded, he dispatched it down the dirt road in the jungle toward the village of Cancun with orders for the soldiers to establish a perimeter east of the village and to wait for the rest of his troops. It would take a couple hours for the trucks to get all of his people in place. But when he did, he was going to kick some major terrorist ass, as his American friends would say.

As long as he was alive, his nation wasn't going to fall to any bunch of thugs. And freeing Cancun was a very good place to start saving Mexico. North American tourism was the lifeblood of Mexico's economy. Without a steady stream of tourist dollars coming in, the nation would collapse. Considering the blow the resorts had taken from the shutdown of air travel in the aftermath of 9/11, any further erosion of the American traveler's confidence in Mexico's safety would be an unmitigated disaster.

CHAPTER NINE

Diego Garcia looked up from the paperwork on the desk when his communications officer hurried into his commandeered operations center.

"Comrade Colonel," the man said, "we are intercepting tactical radio messages from a Mexican army unit working in the border region. It's from one of those Ranger units the damned Yankees trained at their School of the Americas. Their commander is refusing to obey his orders from Mexico City to return to their base."

"And…?"

"Somehow they heard about us and they say that they're moving in to retake Cancun."

Diego Garcia pushed his chair back and went to the map tacked up on the wall. "Do they have any helicopters?"

"We don't know yet."

"Find out!" The Cuban blinked his eyes at the stabbing pain that flashed through his skull. "I must know what I am facing here! A commander must have information before he can make his plans."

"As you command, Colonel." The man hurriedly left.

Garcia turned back and studied his map. The Cancun peninsula wasn't only the perfect place to hold hostages, it was also easy to defend. If the Mexican Rangers didn't have helicopters, they would be forced to try to come across the causeway to get at him, and the bridge was easily defended. Explosive charges had already been placed on the bridge supports and, as a last resort, it could be destroyed.

He had no doubt that his fighters could hold their positions in Cancun long enough for his other Matador units to solidify their grip on Mexico. The reports from his teams in Panama and neighboring Guatemala indicated that they were also making satisfactory progress. Once everything in those three countries had been secured as required, he could go on to the next phase of the operation and strike directly at the major weakness of the Yankee economy.

While that part of the plan was going well, he was very concerned that he hadn't heard back from Elena. He had been a fool to let her go out alone like that, but she had her ways of getting him to agree with whatever she wanted to do. Now that the Mexican army had discovered them, he needed her to help him organize their defense. He called for his security officer.

"You want me, Chief?" Juan Gomez asked as he walked into the room.

"Have you heard from Elena?" Garcia asked.

"No, Sir," Gomez met his boss's eyes squarely. "Not since she went out last night."

Gomez, having also not heard from Delmonte, figured that the two had somehow crossed paths and killed each other. He would miss Delmonte; he'd been a good man for jobs like that. But if the Martinez bitch was finally dead, it would be a good exchange. Now maybe he could keep Garcia's mind on the operation at hand.

"I will tell the patrols to keep a sharp eye out for her, *Jefe*," Gomez stated, playing the game.

"Please do, Comrade." Garcia's voice had strangely softened. "She is essential to our success."

Gomez sincerely doubted that, but held his tongue. Regardless of his boss's weakness for women, he was a brilliant revolutionary.

"Also," Garcia added, "we have intercepted radio messages from a small Mexican army unit that is moving toward us."

Gomez didn't like that at all. Their takeover of the army headquarters in Mexico City was supposed to have short-stopped that kind of interference. The Matador troops were good men and well trained, but they were lightly armed and not up to fighting regular army units in open battle. "Do we know who they are yet?"

"One of the units that guard the border with Guatemala. They call themselves the Panther battalion."

"That is not good," Gomez said. "Those units are said to be well trained."

"We will be safe here," Garcia replied. "They will not dare attack us in force. They know that we are holding hostages against that."

Gomez didn't share his leader's optimism about the value of the hostages as human shields. "Let me alert our men," he said. "We can't always count on the enemy doing what we want them to."

"Do that," the Cuban said. "And let me know the instant you hear from Elena."

"As you command."

ONCE HIS ORDERS had been issued, Mendez left his senior officer, Captain Stephen Ortega, behind to supervise the load-out, boarded his JetRanger and flew to the designated assembly area east of the village of Cancun. He had the pilot keep low on the approach so they wouldn't be spotted from the resort area.

As he flew over the jungle with the treetops tickling the chopper's skids, he couldn't help but notice the overcast, yellow-tinged sky and realize that a storm was moving in. It was rather late in the season for it, but a little bit of a blow wouldn't be too much of a problem. His men were accustomed to working in any kind of weather. In fact, depending on the situation, a storm delivering blinding rain might even work to his advantage. He'd keep a close eye on it as the situation developed.

When the pilot reached the cleared farmland to the east of the village, Mendez had him get down even closer to the ground. It had rained recently, so the ground was wet and the rotor blast didn't throw up a dust cloud. Once they set down, he decided to make a personal recon of the approaches to the bridge.

"I'm going into the village," he told the pilot as he unbuckled his seat harness.

"I'll go with you, Colonel." The pilot reached back behind his seat for his weapon.

"No, Jorge. I want you to stay here and monitor the radios for me. And if I'm not back in an hour, I want you to tell Captain Ortega to do what he thinks is best. But I want those bastards cleaned out of there as soon as possible."

The pilot saluted. "As you command, Colonel."

As Mendez entered the edge of the village, he was surprised to find it apparently deserted. Absolutely no one was in the streets, and the shutters were closed on all the windows.

Even though no one moved on the streets, Mendez stayed fully alert and proceeded cautiously. When he reached the lagoon side of the village and saw the two dozen black-clad troops guarding the far end of the causeway, he knew what he was up against. Finding a concealed position, he took out his field glasses for a closer look.

Through the binoculars, he saw that the gunmen were armed with AKs and RPGs, the standard armament of Marxist insurgents. The machine guns mounted on the open-top SUVs were also Russian made. He could make out what looked to be an 82 mm mortar set up on the other side of the bridge, but that was all he saw in the line of heavy weapons. Fortunately they didn't seem to have any of the 12.7 mm heavy machine guns the Marxists usually favored, and that was a good thing. Going up against the heavy guns would cost his men dearly.

After marking the enemy positions on his map, Mendez went back to the assembly area to work up a plan of attack while he awaited the arrival of his troops. His two infantry companies were jungle-infantry armed and totaled about 120 men. He had no idea of the size of the enemy force, but to control the real estate they had taken over, as well as all the tourists, they had to outnumber him badly. If he went by the tactical manual, he was in no position to be making a direct assault.

The book said that an attacker needed to outnumber the defender by three to one. But the Panther battalion didn't back off from the odds no matter what. They were accustomed to going up against greater numbers and using their superior fighting skills and tactics to determine the outcome of the battle. He was a realist when it came to combat, but he also knew his people.

Even so, the plan of attack was going to have to be well thought out so his troops would have the chance to use their superior training to the best advantage. With the bridge being the only conventional axis of advance, he decided to make a feint against it while he tried to move the bulk of his forces across the lagoon somewhere else.

Though the resort area was a peninsula, in that one end was connected to the mainland, the map indicated that a land neck at the north wasn't passable for normal traffic. In fact, it showed that the road winding through the broken terrain was more of a donkey trail than something even a four-wheel-drive truck could navigate. Men on foot could walk the trail, though he doubted few locals even bothered and many didn't even know of the track, which favored what he had in mind.

Even though his forces were small, Mendez broke

them down into even smaller units. They were jungle fighters and were trained to operate in small teams. If he put them out in small groups, he might be able to deceive the enemy into thinking that his forces were larger than they actually were. That kind of deception might not work against regular troops, but these terrorists were likely half-trained bandits as they always were.

He smiled grimly as he drew avenues of attack on the map with a grease pencil.

RATHER THAN WAIT for all of his troops to assemble, Mendez took the officer who arrived on the first truck aside and gave him his mission. Lieutenant Simon Villa was what his old American Ranger buddies would have called a "hard charger." A graduate of the Ranger school himself, Villa was on his way to becoming a legend in counterterrorist jungle warfare. He wore a pair of holstered 9 mm pistols on his field belt, and his men called him Pancho. He was famous for taking on the most daring tasks and somehow pulling them off.

"Yes, Colonel." Villa grinned as his operation was explained. "If you can truck us up to here—" his finger stabbed the hills on the map just north of the peninsula "—we should be able to get through there in a little more than an hour. Then, depending on how well the enemy is patrolling the neck, we should be able to either sneak through or blow our way through those bastards in short order."

"What I'd rather have you do," Mendez replied, "is to create a diversion up there for the rest of us. Make them think that you're the main attack, or at least a flanking attack. Once you're drawing their attention to the north, I'll mount another diversion against the bridge and then push the rest of our people across the lagoon to the south."

Villa rested his hands on the butts of his two Smith & Wesson semiauto pistols and grinned. "I think we can manage to do that, Colonel."

"You'd better be able to, because I don't have enough men to rescue your young ass if you get into trouble."

"That will not happen, Colonel."

The second truckload of men arrived just as Villa was moving out with his platoon. These men Mendez sent into the village to secure it and to be the main diversion force that would make the attack against the bridge head.

"Make sure to keep out of sight," he told the veteran sergeant in charge. "We have to coordinate your attack at exactly the right time, and I don't want them to spot you before that."

The sergeant turned his eyes skyward. "Make it after the rain starts, Colonel, and they'll never see us until we're right on top of them."

The troops from the third and fourth truckload would be his main attack.

"Go down the south shore," he told Captain Ortega when he arrived, "and see if you can find enough boats that you can use to cross the lagoon. When you find them, let me know and we'll kick off."

"Yes, Colonel."

NOW THAT THEY HAD a plan, Bolan, Brognola and de Lorenzo had to wait to see if the Mexican's prediction of an incoming hurricane would come true. If it did strike, it would provide perfect cover for what they had in mind. If it didn't, Bolan would still make his solo insertion, but he would wait until dark.

"Let's pull back," he said.

They were moving away from the hotel when several truckloads of gunman, rocketed down the main boulevard toward the south end of town.

"I wonder what that's all about?" Brognola asked.

"They're sure as hell excited about something," de Lorenzo said.

"Since we're waiting for the big blow to hit, why don't we head back down there to see what's going on?" Bolan suggested. "We might be able to pick up a few targets of opportunity."

The three went into the maze of smaller shops and bars on the lagoon side of the peninsula and headed south toward the causeway. At the main intersection south of the jail, they spotted a sandbagged position manned by a squad covering the road from the bridge. It was apparent that something had stirred the hornet's nest. The gunmen were alert behind their barricade as if they expected to see the enemy come charging across the bridge to assault their position at any moment.

"Those boys are nervous," Brognola observed. "Something big's going down."

"Whatever it is," Bolan replied, "I think we can give them something more to worry about to raise their stress level a little. You two keep my butt clear, and I'll see about doing a little ankle-biting."

Bolan's H&K wasn't particularly suited for sniper work, but he'd worked with worse and he did have a plus-two optical battle scope mounted on the weapon.

After Brognola and de Lorenzo were in place to cover his withdrawal, Bolan slowly worked his way forward and found a covered position 150 yards short of the barricade. With the enemy all dressed more or less the same, he couldn't tell who the group's leader was, so he chose a target at random and squeezed off a single shot.

A well-placed 5.56 mm round to the head produced spectacular results. The gunman's head appeared to explode in a cloud of red.

His comrades reacted instantly and started offloading ammunition at anything they could see. An RPG gunner popped up, a grenade ready in his launcher as he frantically looked for the sniper.

Rather than target the gunner, Bolan zeroed in on the rocket in the front of the launcher and fired again. The detonation of the warhead ripped through the gunmen, slashing them with red-hot frag.

Instead of remaining where he was and taking out the rest of the squad, Bolan withdrew before he was spotted. After rejoining Brognola and de Lorenzo, the three went to find another group of terrorists to harass.

"CHIEF," Juan Gomez called as he stormed into Diego Garcia's office, "I'm getting reports that someone's attacking our outposts in town."

Garcia ignored him and asked, "Do you have anything on Elena yet?"

Her body had been found an hour ago along with that of Delmonte, and Gomez had half a mind to drag the corpse back and lay it on Garcia's desk. The bitch was dead, and she was still causing him trouble. But he knew that the situation was too critical to have his superior distracted any more than he already was.

"Considering what's going on," he said, "I can only believe that she fell victim to whoever is shooting up our outposts. I'm sure that if she was alive, she would have returned by now."

Garcia rubbed his temple. "I never should have let her go out alone last night. She is a soldier of the people, but she is still a woman and she should have been escorted."

"Comrade Colonel—" Gomez could hold it back no longer "—we have a mission of great importance to accomplish here, and every one of us is expendable except you. If Comrade Martinez has fallen, you must follow the example of our glorious leader and march past her body without looking back and concentrate on the job at hand so the people will emerge victorious."

A look came over Garcia's face Gomez had never seen before.

"Do you dare question my judgment of what is important? Our leader himself chose me to lead this operation, so are you questioning him? Only he himself has the power to instruct me, and he is satisfied with what I have done so far. We will be victorious, and the Yankees will suffer as they have never suffered before. If they think that attack in New York was a great blow, when I am finished with them they will never stop weeping."

"I meant no disrespect, Comrade," Gomez said quickly.

Garcia leaned forward, his eyes glittering. "If you ever say such a thing like that to me again, I will have you taken out and shot like a dog, Gomez. Your life is valuable to me only as long as you are serving the cause and carrying out your orders faithfully. As our president himself said, the faithful must never waver in their devotion to the duties they are given by their leaders."

Gomez was a dedicated Cuban Communist, and his entire life had been spent in service to the Cuban people. No one had ever talked to him in that manner, and it was only his years of rigid obedience to those appointed over him that kept him from killing Garcia where he sat. The mission did come first, but when it was over, Garcia would pay for this. Gomez wasn't a man who ever forgot an insult.

"As you command, Comrade," he said as he stiffly turned and left the room.

LIEUTENANT SIMON VILLA had positioned his men on the flat land at the northern end of the peninsula in double quick time. Pushing his points well out in front of his main body, they had run almost all the way along the trail through the jungle at the neck of the peninsula. When they reached the bottom of the bluffs, he moved into a defensive position and called a ten-minute rest break.

While his nineteen men drank from their canteens and checked over their gear, Villa broke them down into five-man hunter-killer teams. That was their usual tactical grouping and it should work as well here as it did in the jungle.

At the end of the break, he dispatched one team to the Caribbean side of the peninsula, one to advance up the lagoon side and the other two to come right up the middle. Their mission was to kill any terrorists they saw without getting into a major firefight. If it got too heavy for them to deal with, they were to retreat to the hills.

After making a short report back to his colonel, Villa took command of the fifth team himself and headed off toward a golf course he could see in the distance. He didn't expect to find too many terrorists playing golf, but you never could tell what the bastards would be up to.

Terrorists of any and all stripes were the lieutenant's avowed enemies. One of his cousins had been caught up in a bank robbery being conducted by one of Mexico's so-called Marxist liberation front gangs and had been killed in the cross fire. At the funeral, he had vowed to his aunt that he would devote his life to getting revenge for the death, and he had done so.

When they got closer to the green, Villa was pleased to see an open-top SUV with three gunmen inside and a machine gun mounted in the back drive onto the course and park. The terrorists had good fields of fire out there in the open, but he had no intention of getting too close to them. Ranger school had taught him the value of making a long-range kill. He had several trained marksmen in his platoon, and his best was in his team this day.

"Can you take him out, Paco?" he asked his designated shooter.

The Mexican sniper grinned. "Do beans go with tortillas, Lieutenant?"

Villa laughed. "Let's do it."

CHAPTER TEN

With Lieutenant Villa acting as the sniper's spotter and security man, the two Mexican soldiers crawled onto the golf course to a nearby depression in the green that gave the shooter adequate cover, as well as a good line of sight to his intended victims.

When going up against a machine gun position, a sniper always liked to take out the gunner first with a shot to the head before doing the security men. That would be easy this time since the gunner was standing in the truck next to his gun, his back turned to the wind. Had he been checking out his surroundings instead of focusing on trying to light a cigarette, he might have lived a little longer. Not much, but maybe a couple more seconds.

As it was, the sniper had a clear shot of the back of his target's head and squeezed it off. The 7.62 mm slug took the gunman at the base of the skull as he was taking his first drag on the smoke. He didn't get a second.

That done, the startled driver was next as he frantically cranked the engine of his vehicle. It had just caught when the shot sent him slumping over the wheel.

The third gunman dropped his AK in panic and made a run for it across the grass. But, as Paco knew, it was stupid to try to run from a sniper, you'd only die tired. This man went down, too, before he made it more than a few yards.

"First blood, Colonel," Villa reported to Mendez, who was with the troops of the bridge diversion unit in the village. "Three gunmen and a machine gun in an SUV on a golf course. So far that's all we've encountered, but we're not into the built-up area yet."

"Keep going," Mendez sent back. "We've found a way to cross the lagoon, and I need you to keep them busy up there."

"Can do, Sir."

Villa got on his radio and told his other hunter-killer teams to try to draw fire. "When you get a good fight started, though," he cautioned, "break contact, pull back and start another one somewhere else. I don't want anyone to get tied up with these bandits because I can't come and get you."

He put the radio back and turned to his sniper. "Let's go hunting."

"WE HAVE A REPORT of a force moving in from the north," Juan Gomez reported to Diego Garcia. "Somehow they got through that range of hills without a road."

The Matador leader's hand went to his temple. Damn those people! His plan was working so well, but he'd only expected to encounter small pockets of resistance, not an entire Mexican army unit that wouldn't obey their orders from Mexico City. He didn't have enough troops to fight an offensive battle against them, but he could mount a good defense. Plus, this was where the hostages would turn the battle in his favor no matter what the odds, and he had no shortage of them to expend. If he was forced to, he'd send truckloads of women and children to the hot spots to see if the Mexicans were willing to gun them down as they advanced.

"How many of them are up there?" he asked.

"We don't know at this time," Gomez said. "I sent a truck patrol up there to take a look, but I can't raise them on the radio so they might have gotten into trouble. The enemy also has another small group trying to come up the coastline, and we're engaging them now."

Garcia went to the map on the wall. "Pull a third

of the men from the hotels in the south and send them to the north. Have them take up defensive positions around the two hotels up there and tell Del Gato to use the hostages as shields. I don't want to lose any of our people in stupid gun battles."

"What about the men who have been shooting at our people downtown?"

Garcia knew that the unknown gunmen attacking within the built-up area weren't Mexican Army troops. They were hitting and running away like cowards, and that wasn't the way regular troops fought. More than likely, they were the same men who had escaped from the jail. And, if that were the case, they were being led by that Yankee bastard Brognola. It had been a mistake not to have killed him from the outset rather than trying to keep him as trade bait.

The Cuban had made relatively few mistakes during his career, and this one galled him. Had he done what he should have when he'd had the chance, he wouldn't be dealing with armed men operating inside his perimeter. More importantly, Elena wouldn't have gone out last night and would still be with him to help him fight.

"Tell everyone south of here to shoot on sight, kill anyone they see on the streets. Armed or not, Yankees or Mexicans, kill them."

"Sí, Jefe."

THE RISING WIND BROUGHT the sound of gunfire from the north and Bolan focused on it. "We've got company," he told Brognola. "And that's not just two or three guys lone-wolfing it. That's disciplined firing, and there's a couple dozen weapons involved."

De Lorenzo also heard the distant gunfight. "Maybe the bastards don't have complete control of our army, after all," he suggested. "I know that some of our Ranger units have been working counterterrorist ops in the border regions, and their officers aren't the kind who will give up without a fight. If they got word of what was happening here, they'd be sure to come and investigate."

"In another circumstance, that'd be good," Bolan said. "But it's going to make it difficult for us to move against Garcia as we'd planned. With your people attacking, the Cubans are going to be hunkering down and expecting trouble."

"Damn!" de Lorenzo said. "I hadn't thought of that."

"What size are these units that're working the border?" Brognola asked.

"Most of them are light battalions of jungle fighters," the Mexican replied. "Maybe five, six hundred men all told. But they usually only deploy a couple of companies at a time on routine patrols. If they get lucky and run into a concentration of guerrillas, they call for the rest of the unit to join them."

With this new addition to the mix, Bolan realized that it was time to rethink the program.

"Hal," he said, "why don't we head up that way to see if we can contact those Mexican troops? With

Hector being the senior government official on the scene, I think he can be of use to their commander. At the least, the army needs to know the extent of the hostage situation here, so they don't attack the hotels."

"Damn," Brognola said, "I hadn't thought of that. If they start lobbing shells into those buildings, the collateral damage issue isn't going to play well on TV back home."

"If you can get me close enough to them," de Lorenzo suggested, "I think that if I go in alone, I can get them to accept my surrender. Garcia has my wallet and ID card, but I'm wearing dogtags that give my rank and position in the government."

"Are you sure you want to risk that?" Brognola said. "You'll be moving into a free-fire zone."

The Mexican grinned. "If I recollect, I've already been shot at a couple of times."

"And, Hal," Bolan stated, "as soon as Hector makes contact, I want you to go with the Mexicans, too. Now that they're here, it's too dangerous for you to be playing commando with me. When the shooting starts getting serious, it'll be no place for freelancers."

"Including you," Brognola pointed out.

"As long as you let them know that I'm out here, I can still do something useful."

"He has a point, Hal," de Lorenzo said. "It won't look good if you're accidentally killed by Mexican troops. Your President will not be happy with us."

With the Mexican troops having dealt themselves a strong hand, the game had changed and Brognola realized that it was time for him to retire from the field. Someone else would have to take care of Garcia.

"Okay," he said. "I'll do it."

"Then we'd better get a move on," Bolan told them. "If you haven't noticed, the sky's not looking too good and the wind's picking up."

From horizon to horizon, the sky over Cancun had turned a dull lead gray. The usual gentle offshore breeze was starting to gust as the storm approached. The palms flanking the boulevard were swaying and discarded bits of paper and plastic bags were dancing in the air.

De Lorenzo took a weather gauge himself. "You're right, it's coming in. And it's going to be a good one."

VILLA HAD MOVED his hunter-killer team south a quarter mile and was set up between the golf course clubhouse and the first of the big resorts on the strip. This hotel apparently had been designed with some kind of jungle paradise theme and was surrounded by a lush, overgrown tropical garden on the three land sides. The foliage was a perfect place for terrorists to hide defensive positions.

The sniper was scoping the area directly in front of his position when he saw something white on a stick waving back and forth about three hundred yards to his left front.

"I think I've found a guy who wants to surrender," Paco radioed to Villa.

"Wait one," the officer sent back. "I'll be right up."

Villa crawled up to the sniper's hideout and took out his field glasses.

"Left front—" the sniper took the range through his scope "—a little less than three hundred meters."

"Got it."

Villa focused on the moving stick and saw the top of a man's head. Occasionally the man would pop up for a quick look. Taking a piece of note paper from his map case, he stuck it on the muzzle of his M-16 and raised it up high enough to be seen as a sign.

The would-be surrenderee spotted it and pumped his white flag up and down three times to acknowledge the return signal before stepping out in to the open.

"Cover him," Villa told Paco.

The man, a civilian by his clothing, emerged and started for them. "Hurry man!" Villa called, waving him forward. "Run!"

The man started running hunched over as if expecting a bullet in the back. He walked the final few steps, his hands high in the air. "God," he said in Spanish, "am I glad to see you people."

Villa pulled the man down under cover and held his pistol on him while Paco patted him down.

"Okay, who the hell are you?"

"I'm Hector de Lorenzo, the attorney general from Mexico City."

"Pleased to meet you." Villa laughed. "I'm General Santa Ana."

"I'm serious." De Lorenzo kept his voice calm. "Let me take out my dogtags. They're inside my shirt."

Villa backed off, but kept the muzzle of his pistol aimed at the man's head. "Real slowly. I'm not having a good day."

In deliberate slow motion, de Lorenzo reached his hand under his collar and pulled out his dogtag chain.

"Take them off and toss them to me."

De Lorenzo pulled to break the chain and tossed them underhanded. Rather than take his eyes off his prisoner to catch the chain, Villa let it fall at his feet before crouching to retrieve it. The metal tag read that this guy was who he was claiming to be, the attorney general of the Republic of Mexico. That's what the tag said, but Villa wasn't convinced. They could have been stolen.

"If you're who this says you are," he said, "what in the hell are you doing in Cancun?"

De Lorenzo shrugged. "Mexico City was hosting the bi-annual meeting of the Organization of the Justice Departments of the Americas at the Hotel Maya, and we were in the middle of dinner when the Cuban terrorists broke in and captured us. Me and my—"

That got Villa's undivided attention. If there was anyone the young officer really hated, it was the Cubans. Even though Castro was no longer a force in the region, he continued to arm and support any bandit and narco group he could find. "What Cubans?"

"The terrorists who are behind this outrage are led by Cubans." De Lorenzo gave him a brief rundown of the events of the past couple of days.

Villa listened to the story, but still wasn't buying it. "You say that you were with the American A.G. and were rescued from jail by some kind of American commando?"

"Not the A.G.," de Lorenzo replied, "but a special advisor to the American President. The commando was sent by their President to get him out and they decided to take me with them when they escaped."

"This sounds like a plot from some gringo movie with Bruce Willis or one of those guys."

De Lorenzo really didn't blame the young officer for being skeptical. It did sound a bit farfetched. But, he was tired, short on sleep, food and patience, and was weary of this game of twenty questions.

"I'll tell you what, Lieutenant," he said. "Why don't you put me in contact with your commanding officer so I can tell him what's going on in downtown Cancun? Something tells me that he'd really like to have some recent field intelligence. Then, when I'm done with that, you and I can go back to playing stupid games about which action-adventure movie this situation reminds you of."

Villa didn't hesitate, but whipped out his radio. After explaining the situation to Mendez, he handed it to de Lorenzo. "It's Colonel Pablo Mendez."

"This is Hector de Lorenzo," the A.G. said. "You're the CO of the Panther battalion, right?"

"I am," Mendez replied.

"Well, your predecessor, Raul Domingo, was a good friend of mine when I was in the National Police."

"Oh, you mean old Paco. Man, that guy sure loved his mescal, didn't he?"

"His nickname was Hot Dog," de Lorenzo corrected him. "And he never touched mescal because it made him puke."

"I'm sorry about that test, Mr. Attorney General," Mendez said. "But I'm sure you understand that I cannot afford to take chances."

"I completely understand," de Lorenzo said. "But how about telling this young stud here who I am."

"Put him on the radio."

Villa listened for a moment before answering, "Of course, sir."

"I'm sorry, sir," he told de Lorenzo. "But I have to be careful."

"I understand," de Lorenzo said. "Now, if we can get on with it, I have that American official I mentioned hiding back there, and he's also a close personal friend. I want to get him over here before he gets himself killed. Can you lend me a rifle so I can go back after him?"

"No, sir," Villa said, "I can't allow you to risk your life. My unit will all go get this man."

De Lorenzo had to bow to that reasoning. "But I still want a weapon."

Villa reached down and unbuckled his twin pistol rig and handed it over. "I'd be honored, sir, if you would use these guns."

"Thank you." De Lorenzo belted the brace of pistols around his waist. "And knock off all the 'sirs.' As long as I'm in the field, my name's Hector."

Villa smiled. "My men call me Pancho."

WHEN BOLAN and Brognola saw the Mexicans start a maneuver drill to bring them up to their position, Bolan patted the big Fed on the shoulder.

"I'm going to take off," he said. "I don't want to get involved with the Mexican army. If they come into town, though, let them know that I'm out there."

"Good luck."

"You, too."

Brognola knew the drill. He had his shotgun on the ground, the muzzle facing to the rear, and his hands up when the first Mexican soldier appeared. *"Buenos dias,"* he said.

"Don't move, *Señor*," the rifleman said in English.

"No problem."

After the soldier patted down Brognola, he motioned for him to follow. A few yards away, de Lorenzo was waiting with half a dozen Mexicans. "You okay, Hal?" he asked.

"I'm fine." Brognola put his hands down.

"Where's your friend?"

"He went hunting in town."

BEING IN THE TROPICS was the closest to living in paradise that most humans would ever experience. Memories of the Garden of Eden were so deeply embedded in the human psyche that it drove millions of sun-seeking tourists to Mexico and the Caribbean every year. But, as with most pleasure, being in the tropics wasn't without a corresponding, and equal, measure of pain. To keep those who lived in paradise from thinking that they had somehow been singularly blessed by a loving deity, the tropical latitudes also provided some of the most destructive weather known on the planet.

By the time Bolan got back to the main resort area, the winds had picked up. And with them came the rain. At first it was just torrential rain, water falling in never-ending bucketfuls, limiting one's vision to no more than fifty yards. Before long, though, the wind grew strong enough to start deflecting the rain, sending it slashing sideways like liquid bullets.

Bolan didn't mind the rain whipping his face and obscuring his vision. He could handle it, but it didn't look as though the opposition was dealing with it well. When a pair of gunmen running for cover from the deluge came into view, he simply shot them down one at a time. The second man didn't appear to have heard the first shot over the howl of the wind.

He revisited the defensive positions he and Brognola had spotted earlier. Some of the positions were no longer manned, the gunmen apparently having left to seek cover from the storm. In one such abandoned machine gun position, he found that the Russian RPD machine gun had been left behind, as well. He quickly removed the weapon's bolt and threw it far away. It never made sense to leave a usable enemy weapon at your back.

Moving on, he found one stouthearted terrorist still at his post braving the downpour. Bolan admired the gunman's fortitude, but that didn't grant him any slack on the battlefield. Using a little Kentucky windage in the face of the gale, Bolan put a bullet through the sentry's heart. The late sentry's position also had a machine gun, which he disabled, as well, before continuing.

This was where the lack of communication between him and Brognola was going to start hurting the operation. With no way to talk to him, Bolan had no way to find out what the Mexican commander's intentions were and didn't know where he could do the most good to help him. Even so, as long as he could find careless terrorists, he could take them out.

THE INFORMATION de Lorenzo passed on to Mendez made him only more determined to get his people onto the peninsula to start ridding it of terrorists. He had many concerns about that operation, but the storm wasn't one of them. The Panther battalion was accustomed to dealing with the weather in the tropics. Hurricanes were a way of life in the Yucatán, and the jungle war always went on, storm or no.

When Mendez saw that the gunmen at the end of the bridge seemed more interested in seeking cover from the slashing rain instead of defending the causeway, he quickly changed his battle plan. Rather than risk his men trying to cross the southern end of the lagoon in small boats, he'd take the bridge and cross his remaining units on one axis.

Calling over Captain Ortega, he pointed out the enemy positions. "Push them off that bridge, Captain," he ordered.

"Yes, Colonel."

CHAPTER ELEVEN

From his hotel office command post, Diego Garcia was closely following the firefight on the beach to the north. A shoreline wasn't a good place to mount an attack, and it didn't make sense that the enemy would try to come at him from that direction. When the firing stopped after a short time and the intruders withdrew, he suspected that the Mexicans had sent only a small patrol to test his defenses. When another small firefight broke out on the other side of the peninsula, it confirmed his suspicions. They were probing his positions, looking for his weak points.

Rather than attempt to defend the entire peninsula, the Cuban had gone to a strong-point defense posture. He had units positioned at each of the hotels guarding the hostages and the rest of his troops were scattered out in strong positions at the main avenues of approach throughout the area. That should have been adequate to deal with isolated attacks by anyone who hadn't been rounded up in the initial takeover. How his defenses would hold up against the Mexican troops depended on both their strength on the ground and their determination to attack.

"Comrade Colonel!" the Matador radio operator cried as he rushed into his office. "The Mexicans are attacking us at the bridge!"

He now saw that the probes from the north had been feints to draw his forces away from the bridge, and he'd fallen for it like an amateur. If he lost control of the bridge before he could move his men back in to defend it, he wouldn't be able to hold on to Cancun and his plan would fail.

"Tell them to blow the bridge," he commanded. "And to be prepared to beat back a major attack. I will send him reinforcements as fast as I can."

"Yes, Comrade Colonel."

COLONEL PABLO MENDEZ'S troops were barely onto the village end of the bridge when a thunderous explosion split the air, sending chunks of concrete and steel flying. Ortega's assault unit had been caught by surprise, but the demolition charges had been set off too soon and few of his men had been caught up in the blast.

The smoke and dust of the explosion barely had

time to rise in the air before the wind and rain beat it back down. When Mendez could see clearly again, he was relieved to find that the bridge hadn't been completely destroyed. Only one side of the roadway had been blown into the lagoon and, even then, only for about a third of the length of the span. The rest of it looked to be passable for his troops, at least for the moment. It could have suffered unseen damage to the under structure that might cause it to collapse beneath their weight, but that risk had to be taken.

"Push them across as fast as you can and secure the other side, Captain," Mendez ordered the commander of his assault units. "I don't want to lose the momentum."

"Yes, Colonel."

Under covering fire from his two M-60 machine guns and a brief 40 mm grenade fire, Ortega threw two squads across the shattered bridge as a point element. A full platoon followed them twenty-five yards behind.

"Let's go, men!" he shouted.

Rather than stand and fight for their end of the bridge, Ortega was surprised to see the terrorists abandon their barricades and fall back to secondary prepared positions farther inside the town. Whoever was running this bunch of bandits was no soldier, but Ortega wasn't complaining. He'd take a little good luck any time it showed up.

When the first of the Panthers reached the peninsula end of the bridge, they quickly took cover behind the abandoned sandbag barricades and engaged the fleeing enemy. Almost immediately, though, more gunmen appeared from inside the town and a fierce firefight broke out.

Mendez immediately committed the rest of his men to reinforce Ortega and sent them across the damaged span on the run. He had his bridge head now, but, like at Arnheim, it might prove to almost be more trouble than it was worth.

The only thing that was making it even possible was the fact that the enemy didn't have much in the line of heavy defensive weapons. He didn't, either, so it would be a fight between infantry rifles and light machine guns. With the storm increasing, weather was also going to become a serious consideration, but he was confident that his people could deal with it better than the terrorists.

As he always did, he moved forward himself to take command of the battle. The motto of his battalion was "Follow me" not "After you."

WHEN BOLAN HEARD the explosion at the bridge, he realized that the Mexicans were trying to cross and it sounded as though the Cubans had blown it up. He had no way of knowing if they had been successful, but it was worth a look. If nothing else, the terrorists would be congregated there and it should be a target-rich environment.

As he got closer, he heard the firefight intensify, which told him that whatever the explosion had been, the Mexicans had been able to cross the lagoon and establish a beachhead. With the Mexican assault holding the gunmen's attention, it provided a perfect opportunity for him to move in to create a second front.

Bolan had little trouble maneuvering behind the Cubans. When he came upon a sandbagged position blocking one of the streets leading to the bridge, he located a covered firing position well back so he wouldn't be easily spotted and pinned down.

The gusting winds were going to make his accuracy a bit tricky, but would also muffle the report and make it almost impossible for the Cubans to discover where he was firing from. Getting his first man in his sights, he compensated for the wind and squeezed off a round.

EVEN THOUGH most of the Panthers were fighting in the open, they had made some progress. Ortega had managed to slip a couple of hunter-killer teams down the shoreline and into the town behind the gunners. If he could put enough pressure on their flanks, he expected that they would fold as they had done at the bridge. Marxists could get themselves fired up well enough when they were brutalizing civilians, but he had rarely known them to dig in and fight to the death. He expected nothing different from this mob.

Mendez received a report from the hunter-killer teams that someone was attacking the terrorists from the rear, and he turned to his radio operator. "Get hold of Lieutenant Villa's team and have him ask the attorney general if he knows anything about this."

"At once, Colonel."

"Colonel," the radio operator came back quickly, "Mr. de Lorenzo says that the American commando who rescued him and the gringo official stayed behind when they linked up with Lieutenant Villa."

That was all Mendez needed to have to worry about right now, a friendly working freelance in his combat zone. "Tell all of our people," he told the radio man, "that there's a gringo commando working behind the enemy lines and not to shoot at him unless they have to."

"They will want to know what he looks like, Sir."

Mendez shrugged. "I have no idea except that he's a gringo and he'll be well armed. Make sure that if they see some guy shooting at the bandits, they let him continue to do it. Particularly if he's a good shot."

"If they can see him at all, Colonel," the radio operator replied. "The visibility is down to only fifty meters."

The storm was becoming more of a factor in the battle than Mendez had bargained for. But it was a factor he could use to his advantage. His men were suffering from it, but he was confident that the enemy was suffering even more. There was no way that these Cuban bastards were tougher than his men.

THE HOTEL MAYA had been designed to withstand the worst that a Caribbean storm could throw its way. Its walls were thick, its windows were reinforced glass and it had auxiliary generators to provide power for the sump pumps. Several times the staff and guests had ridden out a seasonal storm with little or no discomfort. In fact, the hotel had a tradition of holding raucous storm parties—fueled by free drinks and snacks—beside the sheltered pool.

This storm was no different than the ones that had passed this way before. The only damage the wind did to the pseudopyramid was to wipe out most of Diego Garcia's communications system. The antennas for his long-range radios had been placed on top of the building for the best reception, but they hadn't been designed to ride out a hundred-mile-an-hour wind gusts. Garcia could no longer communicate with the outside world.

If that wasn't bad enough, the news he was receiving from his short-range tactical radios forced him to concentrate on his local battle situation, which was getting worse.

Part of it was because of the storm. The winds were gusting up to a hundred miles an hour now and the blinding rain made it difficult for his troops to hold their positions. For some reason, though, the Mexicans weren't being affected as much as his men were. Not a man to denigrate his opposition, Garcia knew that the Mexican counterterrorist units were well trained. His men had been well trained, too, but few had the extensive combat experience the Mexicans had, and that additional experience was telling.

He was well aware of the classic military axiom that said no operations plan survived the initial contact with the enemy, and he had prepared his fallback plans for almost any contingency. But he hadn't expected to face an additional enemy in the form of a hurricane. He could fight the Mexican troops or he could fight the storm, but he couldn't fight both at the same time.

The storm would pass, but with the Mexicans now firmly established in the town, the initiative had been passed to them. He would soon be tied down and forced into fighting a series of defensive battles.

He wasn't, though, condemned to be trapped like a rat. One of his contingency plans gave him a way out. The storm would make it more difficult to pull off, but it still could be done.

Being a Cuban, Garcia was no stranger to Caribbean hurricanes. They slashed across his motherland on a regular basis. And, as every Cubano knew, a hurricane wasn't an unrelenting fury that lasted for days. It was a furious spiral of wind that whirled around a core of calm known as the eye of the storm. Within that eye, often as large as fifty miles in diameter, there was no fury and no destruction as there was no wind. When the eye passed over, the winds died to nothing, the sun reappeared and the birds took to the air once again. People left their shelters to marvel in the calm and to watch the wall of darkness that was the other side of the wheel of fury slowly approach.

"When is the eye of the storm supposed to pass over us?" he asked his radio operator.

"I don't know." The man shrugged. "We can't get through to the weather center anymore. But the last forecast I had before we lost the antennas was that it will be here in a little more than an hour."

"Can you repair the antennas?"

"If I could find them, Comrade. They're probably halfway across the Yucatán right now."

"Can you reach the ship with the little radios?"

"Yes, Comrade."

"Get Comrade Nguyen on the radio."

"At once, Comrade."

As HER NAME IMPLIED, the SS *Carib Princess* made her living plying the seaways of the Caribbean Sea. While primarily a fair-weather sailor, she had been fitted with stabilizers large enough to handle anything that Mother Nature could throw her way should she ever need them. But with modern satellites keeping track of the world's weather, a South Atlantic storm was barely able to even get started before someone spotted and reported it. When that occurred, the *Carib Princess* with her combination navigational and meteorological suite was always among the first to know in time to get out of the way of the storm.

As the cruise ship's de facto captain, Nguyen Cao Nguyen had kept a close eye on the hurricane as it approached. The South China Sea didn't get the number of typhoons that the Caribbean did, but they weren't unknown. As soon as the wind had picked up, he put out to sea a few miles to keep the ship from being battered at her mooring. He had no fear about being able to ride out the storm. The *Carib Princess* had been built to take a Force-Five Gale, and this was predicted to be only a Four.

He was watching the storm on the bridge radar screen when his radioman told him that Garcia was on the radio.

"Yes, Comrade," he replied.

"The situation has changed," the Cuban said. "The Mexicans are across the bridge, and I lost my long-range communications. I am going to transfer the Yankee doctors back to the ship and my operations staff, as well. I need to use the ship's radios so I can have communication, and having the doctors on board will protect us from the Yankee government.

They won't dare attack us when I'm holding so many of their prominent medical people hostage."

Nguyen wasn't happy to hear that. If Garcia transferred both the hostages and the operational staff to the ship, it would be easier for him to abandon Cancun if things got too hot. Holding the peninsula was critical to provide a beachhead if Beijing decided to land their forces in support of the "revolution." Without it, they would have to risk going into Guatemala or Panama.

"Have you cleared that with Havana, Comrade?" the Vietnamese asked.

"They have given me complete freedom of action," Garcia snapped. "This is my operation, and I will run it as I see fit."

The Vietnamese agent had been concerned about the mental stability of his leader for some time and knew that Havana was aware of it, as well. Right before they launched, Elena Martinez had shown him an encoded message from the DGI saying that she was to keep an eye on Garcia and to report back immediately if he appeared unable to handle the job. As the second in command of Matador Section, Nguyen knew that he would be ordered to step up to the number-one slot should the Cuban be forcefully retired.

He hadn't been in contact with the woman this day, though, and didn't know if she was as concerned about the situation as he was. He had heard something about her having gone downtown alone the previous night to try to track down one of the prisoners who had escaped from the jail. It wasn't like Garcia to have been so lax as to have allowed that.

That Elena had gone out alone to rectify the situation was in character, however. The woman was one of the most dangerous people he had ever known. That she was still out of communication wasn't a good sign, and it put him in a quandary.

Martinez was the Cuban president's personal representative in the Matador Section of his own DGI— spy was actually a better term. She had the man's ear, and her sleeping with Garcia meant that nothing he did or thought was kept secret from the Cuban leader. The president also used her as a conduit to make his wishes known without having to put them down on paper. When it came to Matador operations, nothing was ever committed to paper, or to a hard drive, either, for that matter. That was how the Matador Section had been able to plan and execute this operation without a word about it ever getting out.

That was the main strength of the Matador operations, but it was also their greatest weakness. Until he heard back from Martinez, he had to play ball with a man who was rapidly losing his mind.

"Of course, Comrade," Nguyen said smoothly. "You are correct. When do you want me to come back into the harbor for the pickup?"

"When the eye of the hurricane passes over us here. I will have the doctors waiting so they can be quickly boarded and we can put back out to sea."

"The radar is showing the eye coming on us quickly," Nguyen said. "I'd give it under an hour."

"Very good. We will be standing by, ready for you."

"I will be there."

HAL BROGNOLA and Hector de Lorenzo stayed with Lieutenant Simon Villa's team as they worked their way deeper down the peninsula into hotel row. Rather than engage the terrorists at each resort they passed, under de Lorenzo's orders they were acting more like a recon team gathering information. In particular, the A.G. wanted to know about the movements around the Hotel Maya in hopes of getting an idea what Garcia would be doing next. Mendez's Panthers were still hung up at the end of the bridge, and it didn't look as though they would be breaking out anytime soon.

When they reached the Maya, the grounds were swarming with Cuban troops. Trucks were lined up outside the entrance, and the Cubans were loading them.

"Something's sure as hell going on over there," Brognola said as he counted the third flatbed truck to pull up in front of the hotel.

When a large group of civilians was led out of the hotel under guard and put into the first truck, it was obvious what the Cuban was doing. Garcia was moving his pawns on the board.

"He's moving the hostages," de Lorenzo said.

"But where?" Brognola growled.

"Let's find out. There's only so many places he can move that many people. Oh shit!"

"What?" Brognola asked.

"I think he's taking them to the cruise ship pier. That's the only thing that makes any sense."

"Those two Americans we ran into said that their ship was docked there," Brognola said. "And if he's putting the hostages back on that ship, that means he's planning to pull out, doesn't it?"

"With the Panther battalion across the bridge, it might be the only move left for him."

"Can the ship survive in this kind of weather?"

"I'm sure that it already put to sea before the storm hit to ride it out far from shore. But…"

De Lorenzo cast an eye to the east. "I think he's going to try to bring the ship back in and make his break when the eye passes over."

"If you're right, he'll make a clean escape."

"I'm sorry," de Lorenzo said, "but when he's gone, it should be easier to free the rest of your countrymen being held here, and there's thousands of them."

Lieutenant Villa turned to the Mexican official, his eyes hard. "Do you want us to try to stop the trucks and rescue those people?" he asked.

"No," Brognola interjected. "We can't risk any shooting around the hostages."

The young officer wasn't quite clear what the relationship was between the two men. In his mind, being a Mexican government official, de Lorenzo should be calling the shots. But for some reason, he kept deferring to the gringo. This was well over his command level, so he'd just do what either one of them told him.

"We can go down to the docks and try to get a closer look at what he's doing," de Lorenzo suggested.

"Good idea," Brognola replied.

CHAPTER TWELVE

Juan Gomez didn't have to be a graduate of Cuba's military academy to know that Diego Garcia's elaborate scheme to change the political landscape of Latin America was swiftly coming unraveled. As far as he was concerned, the dream of a sudden strike to overthrow the Mexican government had been just that, a dream. Admittedly, it had been a good dream for a dedicated revolutionary, but even with the Chinese support that had been promised, it hadn't been very realistic. And after his long career, if there was anything that Gomez prided himself on, it was being realistic.

Nonetheless, he had gone along with the Matador leader because he had dedicated his life to being a soldier of the glorious revolution, and he always followed his orders. He was proud to have been able to fight the Yankees and their puppet allies in Latin

America, Africa and the Middle East for more than twenty years. He'd often lost those battles, but it was the only life he knew and the only one he wanted to know. He was a soldier, and he wouldn't run now that things had turned against him again. He would do his duty to the revolution as he had always done, and that meant killing as many of the enemies of the people as he could.

The Mexican troops didn't bother him; killing them was just a matter of doing business. They were just fighting for their own motherland. He could understand that and would kill them like the soldiers they were. His real enemies were the Yankees who had escaped and who were bushwhacking his men in the town. That was an old game to him, and he had learned to play it well in Africa. Cancun was far from the jungles of Angola, but the game was played the same, man to man, the hunter and the prey, and he was good at it.

Before he could face his enemies, though, he had to cover the withdrawal of Diego Garcia, the Matador command group and the loading of the hostages back onto the cruise ship. With the Mexican troops across the lagoon and gaining a foothold on the peninsula, it made good tactical sense for them to leave. Cancun couldn't be held indefinitely and the second part of the plan still needed to be carried out. If it were not, this would all have been a complete exercise in futility.

Even though he had been ordered to cover the withdrawal, Gomez didn't feel that he was being abandoned. Not only would his presence stiffen the spines of the Matador fighters, he'd had about all he could take of listening to Garcia's ravings. He didn't know what had gone wrong with the man he'd followed for so long, but he had changed.

Garcia had once been the most audacious fighter he had ever known, but something had been wrong about the handling of this operation from the start. Earlier he had felt that the Martinez woman had had something to do with the Matador leader's frame of mind, but after she'd been killed, he had become even more unfocused. The big question now was if he and the Vietnamese had the cajones to pull off the rest of the operation by themselves without him around to keep them focused. But that wasn't his worry now; he had a real man's work to do.

Gomez grabbed a full chestpack magazine carrier and headed out to take personal command of the rearguard fighters. It was fitting that the storm had come upon them because a storm always favored an experienced hunter. He had stood against storms of nature and man-made storms of fire and steel, and neither of them had ever slowed him. His prey would be cowering under cover shelter, but the hunter only concerned himself with making his kill.

Gomez's prey was out there cowering from nature when the most dangerous thing on the planet was after them.

THE NIGHT THEY'D BEEN rescued, Richard Spellman and Mary Hamilton had not come across any of the other people their rescuers had said would be in hiding. Maybe it was because they had been too frightened to approach them in the dark. As day broke, they continued their search, also with no results, but when the wind rose they became concerned for their safety from the storm. When they stumbled onto a small, isolated hut on the beach south of the resorts, they decided to take shelter in it to ride out the storm and to wait for the promised Marines to arrive.

Spellman figured that it would be difficult to miss a Marine amphibious landing force hitting the beach with their armored vehicles while gunships circled overhead. When they saw the Stars and Stripes waving proudly, they'd come out of hiding with their hands in the air and be safe at last.

"The storm might hold them up a little, though," Spellman told his companion. "I don't think their amphibs can swim through this kind of surf. But as long as our little house doesn't blow down, we should be okay."

Just then, a gust of wind shook the walls of the hut and Spellman wished he'd kept his mouth shut. He was doing his best to hide the fact that he was scared witless, which usually translated into him running his mouth.

He moved closer to Hamilton and put his arm around her. If he had to be trapped by a storm, at least he had a worthy companion to be trapped with. He really hoped that they survived all of this as he wanted to spend the rest of his life with her.

LIEUTENANT VILLA WAS UNDER orders to let de Lorenzo and the gringo call the shots, but that didn't mean that he was going to let them do something terminally stupid. Being the officer in command of the security unit that allowed the attorney general of Mexico to get himself killed wouldn't be a good career move, and he had plans to do well in the army. But they wanted to follow the trucks, so he led the two civilians down to the port.

As he had hoped, the port offered little in the way of close-in cover and concealment, but provided a hiding place a hundred yards away where they could safely watch for the cruise ship. They had just gotten undercover when the first of the trucks full of hostages pulled up at the pier.

"You called it right," de Lorenzo told Brognola.

"Damn. I wish to hell I'd been wrong this time."

"Now we wait for the break in the storm."

The sudden calm that came with the eye of the

storm passing over Cancun was as if the hand of God had swept down to still the wind and waters. First the winds died down to a light breeze and then the sun blindingly broke through. It was as if the hurricane had never been, and even the birds took to the air again. A glance at the eastern horizon, though, showed a wall of black shot through with lightning flashes as a reminder that this hiatus was just that.

"How long is this going to last?" Brognola asked.

"Half an hour to an hour."

"But where's the ship?"

"It should be coming out of the stormfront anytime now," de Lorenzo said. "She would have had to run for open water to keep from being battered against the dock."

"A ship that big can't ride it out at moorage?"

The Mexican pointed to the smaller yacht marina at the other end of the harbor. "See what happens when you try to ride out a storm like that in a harbor."

What had once been a nice collection of very expensive private boats had been reduced to mostly sunken wreckage. A few broken hulls had been thrown onto the beach, and the floating debris field stretched for several hundred yards. "Even the larger ships have to get out of the way so their hulls don't get crushed."

Villa had been watching the horizon through his

field glasses and was the first to spot the *Carib Princess*. "I think she's coming."

"Let me see," Brognola asked.

Villa handed over his field glasses and Brognola put them to his eyes. The bright sun made the vessel's white hull almost gleam. Were it not for the fact that the cruise ship was full of American hostages, it would have been a beautiful sight suitable for a TV commercial hawking a fun-in-the-sun cruise.

Four trucks loaded with drenched civilians were waiting by the time the SS *Carib Princess* tied up at the pier. The deck of the cruise ship was spotted with a couple dozen well-armed gunmen as the gangplank was put down. A wet, bedraggled collection of men, a few women and kids were taken off the trucks, hurried up the gangplank and taken belowdecks. As soon as a truck was offloaded, it returned to the hotel to collect more hostages.

Brognola burned with frustration at being helpless, but there was nothing he could do. De Lorenzo and their five-man escort wasn't enough to do anything useful. But even if the entire Panther battalion was on hand, the presence of the hostages would keep them from acting. He had devoted his life to trying to prevent things such as this, but now that he was actually witnessing American citizens being led into captivity, he could do nothing.

De Lorenzo heard his friend swearing under his breath, but said nothing. He knew what was bothering him, but this was a time when a man needed to be alone with his cursing.

NEITHER RICHARD SPELLMAN nor Mary Hamilton had ever been through a hurricane before so they had no idea how long it was supposed to last. When the fury seemed to diminish, it gave them hope that the worst was past.

"Richard," Hamilton said, "it sounds like the wind isn't blowing as strong as it was before."

"You're right," Spellman replied. "It sounds like it's dying down a bit."

Hamilton looked through a gap around the shutter covering the single window. "And it's getting lighter outside. Maybe we should try to find a better place to hide."

She had a good point. Their little shelter wouldn't have inspired confidence even had the wind not been blowing. Plus, it was in the open and would surely be searched if the terrorists spotted it.

"Good idea."

They opened the door and stepped out onto the sand. Spellman was stunned to see how quickly the sky was brightening. From what he had remembered from watching TV news coverage of hurricanes wiping out Florida, he'd thought that they usually lasted longer than this. But maybe a hurricane in the tropics was somehow different.

Since they'd jumped ship in the dark, he didn't have a good idea of where they were in relation to the center of town. He remembered that one of the Americans the previous night had told them to go south. Finding the sun through the thinning clouds, he took off in what he thought was the right direction.

When they reached the edge of the built-up area, Hamilton took over the lead again. Not only did she speak Spanish, anyone seeing a woman wouldn't automatically open fire. When they heard a vehicle approach in the street, they took no chances and ducked into an alley and waited for it to pass.

It turned out to be an SUV with black-clad gunmen on board, and when it stopped, the two fugitives slipped deeper into the alley. Looking for a way out, Hamilton went to the end and peered around the corner.

"Oh, God, Richard," she said. "There's more of them."

Spellman risked a peek himself and saw the sandbagged machine-gun emplacement manned by a couple dozen black-clad terrorists. They were blocked in.

Spellman was turning when he caught sight of a figure from the corner of his eye and a rifle butt slammed him in the side. Hamilton screamed.

When Spellman got to his feet, four men were

holding guns on them while an older man who looked to be the man in charge approached.

Gomez wasn't fooled by the now dirty cook whites the pair wore. The jackets had the name of the ship sewn on them, but there was no way these two were from the ship's crew. They were fat-faced Anglos.

"When did you escape?" he asked in accented English.

"The first night," Spellman gasped.

Gomez laughed. "You should have stayed hidden, Yankee. You might have lived longer."

Gomez pointed to four of his men. "Take them back to the ship," he said in Spanish. "See that's she's put with the other women and find a good place to hold him. I don't want him to get loose again."

"Yes, Comrade."

"I love you, Richard," Hamilton cried as two men led her away.

Another rifle butt to the belly kept Spellman from answering her.

WHEN THE GUNMEN started pulling up the gangplank, Brognola was ready to go back to the hotel to wait for Striker to catch up with him. The show was over, and a sorry-assed spectacle it had been. He was turning away when de Lorenzo grabbed his arm.

"Hal!" he said. "Look."

Brognola turned and saw two people in white uniforms being escorted onto the ship. "Ah, shit!"

"They didn't find a good enough place to hide," de Lorenzo said.

"Shit!"

As soon as the last truckload of hostages had been hurried aboard the *Carib Princess* and secured in the holding areas, Diego Garcia stormed into the bridge of the cruise ship with his headquarters staff.

"Get us under way immediately," he told Nguyen Cao Nguyen. "The Mexicans might have long-range weapons, and I can't risk the ship taking any damage."

"Where's Gomez?" Nguyen asked when he didn't see the old veteran fighter in the command group.

Garcia came to a position of attention. "Like a true Hero of the Revolution, he stayed behind to lead the men covering our escape."

Nguyen didn't like the sound of that. Gomez was an experienced military leader, and his vast expertise in combat operations had proved critical on more than one occasion. With both him and Martinez now gone, outside of Garcia, he was the only one left of the original Matador group that had planned this operation. That it hadn't gone as they had planned was an understatement.

While he was still optimistic about the outcome of the second phase, splinters of doubt had been driven deeply into his mind. He was far from the paddies of the village where he had grown up, but he would have given anything for a gray-haired old priest to make a sacrifice of salt and rice to the god of war and to light a couple of joss sticks to try to improve their chances.

He was a Marxist now and knew better than to slip into error of primitive superstition, so he turned to the helmsman. "Make for open water."

"Aye, Comrade."

THE CALM THAT FOLLOWED the appearance of the eye of the storm had a stunning effect on the combatants. For Colonel Pablo Mendez's Panthers, it was as if a veil had been lifted and they could now go to work. His counterterrorist platoons broke up into their hunter-killer Teams and started hunting their enemies in earnest.

Hunting bandits in a built-up area wasn't their trained specialty, but they were very good at improvising. The crackle and snap of small-arms fire sounded like a drumroll as they started probing the enemy's defenses. They were all aware that the eye would pass and the storm return, so they wanted to get as high a body count as they could before the wind and rain picked up again.

THE EMBATTLED Matador fighters could now look around and clearly see how many of their comrades were no longer among the living. It wasn't a reassuring assessment. Even worse, the Mexicans were on the offensive and pushing hard. Small units were attacking almost every one of their positions and inflicting casualties.

Juan Gomez was driving his SUV from one position to the next trying to rally his fighters and to assess the situation. The Cuban had been at his business long enough to know when the combat equation had turned against him. His fighters still outnumbered the Mexicans, but the battle wasn't going in their favor because their hearts weren't in it. He fondly remembered the men he had fought with in Angola all those years ago. They had been true fighters of the revolution. No matter what the odds, they would stand and die if need be to show their enemies how brave men died.

This generation, though, wasn't made of such stern stuff. To them, the Revolution was something they read about in books or heard stories of from their fathers. They didn't burn with a desire to give their all for the cause. Most of them were going to die anyway, and he laughed when he thought how it would surprise them. He had made his acquaintanceship with death a long time ago, and every day that he didn't die was a joy. His death would be an even greater joy, though, and he felt that it was coming to him this day.

Stepping out of his vehicle at one of his main blocking positions, he bent to take a fresh chestpack ammo carrier from the body of one of his dead. After looking around, he beckoned to the leader of the group.

"Yes, Comrade." The man saluted.

"Your orders are to stand and hold this position until I return," Gomez told him.

"And where are you going, Comrade Gomez?" the man asked suspiciously.

Without changing expression, Gomez pulled his pistol and shot the man in the head. Soldiers of the Revolution didn't question their leader's actions.

The Matador fighters pretended not to have noticed that their leader had just been shot to death, and Gomez pretended that they were going to do what they had been told as if they were brave. Beyond shooting half a dozen more of them to pump up the fear factor even more, there was little he could do to make them stand and fight.

As soon as his back was turned, he knew they would start to fade away. That was fine with him, though. Any man who abandoned his post under fire became an enemy of the people, and if he spotted him, he would kill him.

CHAPTER THIRTEEN

Even though Bolan had been doing well in his solitary venture against the terrorists, when the winds started to abate he disengaged from the main battle area. He'd been through a hurricane or two before and knew what was coming next. As long as the eye of the hurricane was overhead and the skies were clear, he intended to keep out of convenient rifle range of the Cubans.

He made his way back deep into the town to a small garden plaza and took cover inside a tourist information booth. He really didn't count himself as a tourist, but it seemed appropriate. He was surveying his front when a bullet hit the stuccoed wall beside his head.

Hitting the ground, he crawled across the walkway to the raised shrubbery beds bordering the plaza. He wasn't much of a botanist and didn't know what he was hiding behind, but the bushes were thick enough to conceal him. The low brick wall bordering the beds gave him some cover.

Since there hadn't been an immediate follow-up shot, whoever was out there was an experienced shooter and he knew that it wasn't one of the Mexicans thinking that he was one of the terrorists. There was no mistaking the sound of an AK, so it had to be a Cuban. The Kalashnikov wasn't a good long-range sniper piece, which meant that the guy had to be fairly close by. He hadn't had time to check the angle of the shot by the bullet hole in the wall, but he knew it had been fired from close to ground level.

Carefully parting the foliage in front of him so as to make little movement, Bolan peered through the greenery. Three broad streets entered the plaza, and he had a good line of sight to two of them. But if he had a line of sight to those locations, the sniper would, as well. He could be a hundred yards down either of those two streets in a concealed firing position.

A second shot rang out, and though he didn't see a muzzle-flash, he sent a snap shot down the street directly in front of him. He really didn't expect it to connect, but even a near miss would tell his opponent that he was still in the game. And a deadly game it was going to be.

He carefully rolled to the side and parted the foliage again. This time he thought he saw a flash of movement right before another shot rang out.

Taking a flash-bang grenade from his harness, Bolan thumbed the fuse and tossed the bomb into the middle of the plaza, which was bare earth. Even as wet as it was, the detonation should create a big enough mud spray for Bolan to duck into the alley behind him.

Crouching with his eyes closed, he counted down to the detonation.

With the flash he was on his feet, crouched low, sprinting for the alley. Two AK rounds sang past his head as he ducked around the side of the building.

JUAN GOMEZ'S CHAGRIN at having lost his prey was tempered with a savage joy at having found someone who apparently knew how the game was played. This Yankee, and he could only be a Yankee, hadn't panicked at being fired on, nor had he done the macho Mexican thing and charged. Even under sniper fire, this man had kept his head and had taken the time to make a clever escape from a bad situation.

The Cuban doubted that this Yankee would run for safety now that he was out of the line of fire. Not this one. This was a man, and he would take to the alleys himself and hunt for whoever had fired at him, which was what Gomez wanted more then anything. Even more than surviving this cockup, he wanted one more chance to go up against a worthy opponent, win or lose.

He rose from his position and slipped into the backyard of the neighboring two-story house. It had a ladder from the balcony to the roof and, like a stalking jungle cat, he wanted the high ground.

THE BUILDINGS in this particular part of town were mostly smaller two-story structures, many of them with Spanish-style balconies. They also had sunken doorways that could provide cover for a man on the ground level. As with all soldiers, Bolan liked the high ground and decided to use it to go after this guy. He was too dangerous to be left out there to try to kill someone else. There was also a good chance that his assailant would come after him, so he might as well get it over with.

A few yards into the alley, he went through a gate into a small backyard. As he had expected, the yard had stairs leading up to a balcony, then up to the flat roof. Moving quickly, he took the stairs. Once on the roof, he crossed to the side facing in the direction he had come. His building was one back from the open area, and the roof of the building facing the plaza was higher than the one he had chosen, but not so high that he couldn't pull himself onto it.

Once there, he stayed low as he crossed to the balustrade on the street side and took cover. Dismounting the optical scope from his H&K, he used it to scan the roofs and fronts of the buildings across the small square. As he had half expected, he didn't see anyone, but he doubted that they were empty. Everyone liked the high ground, and he settled in to wait.

After fifteen minutes, even though his combat instincts told him that the sniper was still out there, he was beginning to think that maybe the Cuban had moved on. Leaving his current position, though, wouldn't be a wise move right as yet.

He was dividing his time between watching the streets and the rooftops when he caught a flash of movement from a rooftop down the side street. He wasn't in a good position to take him under fire, so leaving his H&K on the balustrade with the muzzle exposed, he crawled to the other end of the roof. When he reached the side of the building facing the lower one he had come up from, he let himself down onto it. From there, he went down to the balcony and took the stairs to the ground.

Figuring that the Cuban would stay focused on the rooftops for a while, he would make his move on the ground level.

GOMEZ SPOTTED the rifle muzzle. A warrior knew the value of holding the high ground and the Yankee had it, but he could deal with it. Leaving his perch, he kept to the shadows as he slipped down to the garden. There was a building behind the gringo's hiding place and its roof was high enough for him to make his kill.

He was moving from walled garden to walled garden and was within one house of his planned assault point when he caught a flash of movement from the corner of his eye. He was diving for cover when he felt a blow to his chest and was slammed to the ground.

THOUGH HE HAD SEEN his man go down, Bolan waited for several minutes before breaking cover. When he did, he approached his downed opponent, his .44 trained on him and his finger on the trigger. He wasn't going to take a chance with a guy who was this good.

He wasn't surprised to see that the Cuban sniper was an older man, and from the scars on his face, a veteran soldier. For decades Cuba had exported thousands of her troops to fight surrogate wars for the Soviets in Africa and Latin America. This doomed expedition was like a leftover cold war scenario from the seventies or eighties, so it was fitting that a veteran of Cuba's foreign wars was taking part in it.

The Cuban painfully opened his eyes when he heard Bolan's footsteps, but was too badly wounded to try to reach for his assault rifle.

"Yankee," he said in accented English, "you tricked me."

"You should have stayed in Cuba, *compadre*," Bolan stated. "Didn't you hear that communism's dead?"

"Tu Madre," the Cuban said as he died.

BOLAN FINALLY LOCATED Hal Brognola outside the Hotel Maya with the Mexican army unit he and de

Lorenzo had surrendered to. Lieutenant Villa's team was still trying to keep their VIPs safe, and the hotel grounds were the most secure place in Cancun right now. Most of the remaining surviving terrorists were either on the run or surrendering, but the Panther hunter-killer teams were still cleaning up isolated pockets of die-hard resistance.

"You look like you've been busy, Striker," Brognola said by way of greeting.

"Just the usual," Bolan replied. "Scouting around and taking out the trash, but I think it's just about over around here. The Cubans don't seem to have the stomach to fight to the death over this."

"Not with their boss gone," Brognola said. "Garcia escaped on that ship."

"I was a little busy at the time, but I figured that's what was going on when I saw it come back into port."

"I saw him get on board," Brognola recounted, "but there wasn't anything I could do about it."

"Speaking of doing things," Bolan said, "don't you think it's about time that we got back in touch with the Man? He's probably got half the surveillance systems in the country looking for you right about now. I'm sure he's gotten over your not wanting to do what you were told."

"Don't you think we're doing okay without him? I mean, we managed to run Garcia out of here, didn't we?"

"With the help of a storm and the Mexican army," Bolan pointed out. "Someone needs to tell him that Garcia has put to sea with those hostages. We've got a real situation going on here, Hal, and those people need more help than we can give them no matter what we try to do. This is a major event, and some tough decisions are going to have to be made on a higher level than just the two of us. Let me put the radio back online, so we can get this squared away with him and get back on the road."

Brognola thought about that for a long moment. "Okay," he conceded. "But after I make my report, I'm going to ask if the Navy has something close enough to come and get us so we can still follow that bastard, but do it in style. I'm not going to let him get away with this."

Since it was obvious that Brognola had the bit firmly in his teeth and wasn't about to spit it out, Bolan could only go along for the ride wherever it went.

Bolan put the batteries back in his satcom radio, bounced a signal off a satellite to Stony Man Farm, told the techs in the com center that Brognola was on the line and had them patch him through to the Oval Office.

"It's Striker, Mr. President," he said. "Yes, I have Hal Brognola here… Yes, sir.

"I think he wants to talk to you." Bolan smiled.

"Okay." Brognola wore a big grin when he turned

the radio off. "He says that all is forgiven and we're back in business big-time. He's sending a nuke sub to pick us up, an attack boat. It's coming at flank speed and should be here in under three hours."

"And we're supposed to follow Garcia's ship and report on what we see him doing, right?"

"At a minimum," Brognola said. "But he left it open for suggestions for direct action. Let's go find Hector and tell him what's going down. He's set up a command post inside with the Mexican battalion commander."

NOW THAT Colonel Pablo Mendez's counterterrorist Panther battalion had the situation with the Cubans well in hand, the Mexican attorney general was acting as the local political commander. He and Mendez had set up a joint command post in the hotel manager's office recently vacated by Diego Garcia and his people. As a stockholder in the resort, de Lorenzo had been glad to see that the Cuban thugs hadn't trashed the place too badly on their way out. The same couldn't be said for the hotel's liquor stocks.

"Gentlemen," the Mexican said when Bolan and Brognola walked in, "good news from Mexico City. The presidential palace and the National Police headquarters have been freed, and they're working to bring key buildings and public service functions back under government control. This 'revolution' isn't going to last more than another day or two at the most."

"That's good to hear," Brognola said. "And I have a favor to ask of you."

"Anything, my friend."

"Do you think that Colonel Mendez and his men can take care of the American tourist hostages until someone can get in here to evacuate them?"

"That sounds like you're planning to go somewhere again," de Lorenzo said.

"We are. The President is sending a submarine to pick us up and we're going to follow Garcia. Do you want to come along?"

"I'd love to go with you." De Lorenzo sighed. "But my duty is to remain here and oversee getting things back to normal, whatever that's going to be, as quickly as I can. I want to see Garcia get his as much as you do, but we have a lot of very frightened people here who need to be reassured and evacuated as quickly as possible. I just got word that the airport is in friendly hands once again, and the airlines will start flying in as soon as the storm completely dies down and the runways can be cleared of debris."

"Do you need any help from Uncle Sam?" Brognola said. "I have friends in high places, and I'm sure that a word from me would get immediate results."

De Lorenzo laughed. "Tell your 'uncle' thanks, but this time the Mexican government owes the United States. The least we can do is to assist your stranded citizens and see that they're made as comfortable as we can until they can be evacuated. What you can really do to help all of us is to get that Cuban bastard."

"We'll get him," Brognola promised. "You can take that one to the bank."

"If you get him alive," de Lorenzo said dryly, "I'm sure that my government would love to put him on trial and prove that Castro was behind this so we can take a chunk out of that bastard, as well."

"I can't promise that," Brognola said honestly, "but I can assure you that my Justice Department will render all possible assistance to your department in getting to the bottom of this. I'll personally see to it that you get a full exchange of information and assistance should Mexico decide to take direct action against the perpetrators of this outrage."

De Lorenzo was fully aware that Brognola had just promised him that the United States would go to war alongside Mexico if that was deemed appropriate. He still wasn't sure how much pull his friend really had with the American President, but if he was serious, it was a major commitment. And with the stance the United States had taken against terrorism worldwide since the 9/11 attack, it might actually come to pass.

He bowed slightly. "I thank you, but until the situation in Mexico City is clarified, I'll have to wait before I pass on that offer. But give your President my heartfelt regards the next time you see him."

"Will do."

De Lorenzo whistled up an SUV to take the two Americans to the pier to meet their submarine before returning to his new duties. He'd never known just how much was involved in running a city. Even with the Panthers doing double duty as cops and medics, as well as soldiers, until the civilian authorities could be screened and put back to work, he was going to be a very busy man. Now he knew why he had gone into police work and not politics.

NGUYEN CAO NGUYEN stood on the *Carib Princess*'s bridge, his feet spread well apart to move easily with the roll of the deck. Less than half an hour after leaving Cancun harbor, the ship had sailed out of the calm eye of the hurricane and back into the full fury of the storm. The rain was slashing the bridge like liquid machine gun bullets and the howl of the wind was unrelenting.

Even though the ship was designed to ride out the worst the Caribbean and South Atlantic could deliver, she had her work cut out for her this time. She had been battened down for rough seas, so her exterior was weathering the storm well compared to what was going on inside. The stabilizers were supposed to keep the ship stable on all three axes, roll, pitch and yaw, and they were getting a real workout. Nguyen had the helmsman head her into the gale to minimize the effects of the waves.

"How much longer is it going to blow this hard?" Nguyen asked the Matador operative serving in the place of the ship's first officer.

"The Yankee National Weather Service is giving it the rest of the night," the man reported as he consulted his clipboard. "But they say it should slow to something like forty or fifty kilometers an hour by daybreak."

"How long before it's completely gone?"

"Hard to tell." The First Officer shrugged. "The radar plot shows that it's turning north and east over the Yucatán, so it's probably going to turn and come back into the northern Caribbean. We might have to endure this for at least another two days."

The Matador planning team hadn't included a hurricane in the operation, so they were reverting to Plan B. The problem was that Plan B wasn't comprehensive and wouldn't deliver the crushing blow to America that the original operation had envisioned. The Yankee economy would still be crippled, but the results wouldn't be as long-lasting as Nguyen had wanted so Beijing could make its move.

Nguyen was disappointed that they had been

forced to evacuate Cancun, and he knew the lords of Beijing wouldn't be pleased when they got his radioed report. They had depended on him to make this plan work for their ends, as well. China was poised to jump in to provide assistance to any of the Latin American nations that asked for it in the name of Revolution. Several treaties of mutual defense and assistance were ready and waiting to be signed by the victorious revolutionaries. Once inked, the pacts would be implemented immediately.

It was planned that most of that assistance would be in the form of military forces on the ground. Several older oil tankers had been converted to troop transports for the operation, and a hundred thousand men, their weapons, ammunition and equipment were on the high seas right now. More men and equipment were standing by at Chinese airfields ready to be flown in. At this point in time, though, those troops might just have to sit in their transports a little longer. There was still the off chance that they could prove useful in Panama or Guatemala, but the planned Cancun beachhead was off the table.

To make it worse, the news coming in from the Matador units in Mexico City wasn't good. Even with Cuba's proclamation of support for the revolutionary "uprising" in Mexico, it didn't look as if it was going to be successful, either. He had more hope, though, for the second phase of the plan. With the

American hostages on the ship as a shield against American attack, at least it could be accomplished.

They were scheduled to arrive at their resupply point at daybreak and, if the weather report was accurate, they could load the material and the helicopters they needed immediately. Once that was done, it was only half a day's sailing to the first of the Plan B targets.

CHAPTER FOURTEEN

Commander Douglas "Bulldog" Rawlings, captain of the nuclear submarine USS *Sandshark,* was a typical attack-boat skipper. Closing with and destroying enemy warships on the high seas was in his blood. Commanding a lumbering Boomer cruising around the oceans of the world waiting for a launch order that would probably never come would have driven him mad. At least in a fast-attack boat, he could lurk around the sea lanes and play bumper tag with the Russian and Chinese pigboats when he wasn't making practice torpedo attacks on unsuspecting cruise liners.

As the skipper of a United States warship, Rawlings had no idea why he'd been ordered to divert to a Mexican resort town at flank speed to pick up two stranded civilian VIPs. To him that sounded like a job for a garbage scow, not a nuke attack boat. On top of that, modern submarines didn't like to be on the surface of the ocean even in good weather. Their hull shapes had been maximized for underwater speed, and they were pigs on the surface in any kind of gale. Sailing into a hurricane and surfacing in a harbor was a good way to mess up his tidy little boat.

All that aside, though, when the Chief of Naval Operations got on the horn to personally order him to take his deep-sea boat into Cancun, he hadn't argued. It wouldn't have been a wise career move. He fully planned to be the first pigboat officer to be CNO himself, so he knew how to act when the admiral came asking for a favor.

That task was, however, turning out to be easier said than accomplished.

Deep under the waves at diving depth, the *Sandshark* wasn't at all affected by the storm raging on the surface. The problem was that he would have to surface to make it all the way into the harbor. It was too bad that he hadn't gotten the call an hour or two earlier when the eye of the storm had passed over Cancun. That would have been smooth sailing for him even on the surface. Now that the eye had passed, it was rather nasty up there again.

Rawlings knew better than to even try to dock his boat at the pier when he pulled into the harbor. He didn't need to have his outer hull plates stove in. Instead he held her half a mile offshore submerged up to the sail, under just enough power to hold her in position headed into the gale. He didn't have direct communication with his would-be passengers, but when CinClant informed him that the package was waiting, he launched a Zodiac raft to retrieve them.

He watched through the optical attack scope in the control room as the small rubber boat fought her way through the waves to the pier. And, as he had been informed, two men were waiting on the dock. They quickly climbed down into the raft for the rough trip back.

When they got closer, he turned the periscope over to the watch officer. "Bring them to my cabin before you dry them off," he ordered.

"Aye-aye, Sir."

RAWLINGS WASN'T impressed when the two men were shown to his quarters. One of them was notable to be sure, a tall dark-haired guy who looked like a professional hard case. If he turned out to be any kind of trouble, though, he'd put the SEALs on him. The other, older man looked like some kind of federal desk jockey. What in the hell he'd been doing in Cancun that required his being picked up in the middle of a hurricane, he had no idea.

"I'm Captain Doug Rawlings," he said, ignoring the puddles of water forming at their feet, "skipper of the *Sandshark*. Welcome aboard."

The bureaucrat put his hand out. "Hal Brognola," he said. "Thanks for picking us up."

"I have no idea who you two gentlemen are, but, my orders are to put my boat and my crew completely at your disposal."

He paused. "Except, of course, for my offensive armament. No offense, but if you ask me to shoot, I'm going to have to clear it with someone first."

"No problem, Captain," Brognola said smoothly. "I'd have to talk to the President myself before I asked you to do something like that."

That put Rawlings back a little. If this guy thought that he could pick up the phone, call the National Command Authority and ask for a hotshot, he obviously had a lot of pull somewhere. He'd best step lightly until he had a better understanding of who these two guys were and what in the hell was going on.

"But I really don't think that it's going to come to that," Brognola added quickly. "At least, I certainly hope not."

"I understand that you have a SEAL team on board?" Bolan asked.

Rawlings hesitated for a long moment. His six SEALs were on board to support a highly classified operation code-named Ever Last. Not too many people were cleared to know about it and beyond the President, the Secretary of Defense and of the Navy, to his knowledge none of them were civilians. That meant, of course, that the hard case was a spook of some kind.

Bolan caught the hesitation and understood the problem. "I assure you, Captain," he said, "that I'm cleared to know about Operation Ever Last."

"And you are?" Rawlings said. "If I might ask."

"Colonel Cooper, Jeff Cooper."

"Yes, I have a SEAL contingent on board, Colonel, but not a full team."

"Do they have a SDV?" Bolan asked. The SEAL Delivery Vehicle was one of the best underwater vehicles ever invented and might be useful.

"They do." Rawlings nodded.

"I might need to ask to borrow it later."

Again Rawlings hesitated, but for a shorter length of time. The CNO had made it clear to him that these guys could have anything they wanted. If this hard case wanted to borrow the SDV, he'd better let him have it. He would, though, make him sign for it. Army guys had a history of not returning the stuff they borrowed from the Navy.

"Gentlemen," the captain said, "I know we have much more to talk about, but can I offer you dry clothing and something to eat first? Maybe coffee?"

Since eating hadn't been very high on their priority list of things to do for the past couple of days, a meal sounded good. "A sandwich perhaps?" Brognola suggested. "And coffee, please."

Rawlings keyed his intercom. "Cookie, report to my cabin."

"Aye-aye, Sir," the speaker answered.

"And," Brognola added, "if I could ask, do you happen to have antacid tablets in your medical stores? I have a rather sensitive stomach, and I've been without anything to take for a couple of days now."

Rawlings kept a perfectly straight face as he keyed his intercom again. "Doc, bring a couple of rolls of burp pills to my cabin."

Bolan hid a grin, Brognola was known for never being without a stock of his trademark antacids. There was no crisis anywhere in the world that was so threatening that it couldn't be controlled by crunching a couple of tabs every couple of hours.

"Nausea or heartburn, Sir?" the medic asked.

"Antacids."

"Right away, Sir."

When the chief cook reported, the captain ordered a cold-cut plate with appropriate condiments and a coffee service. The sub's corpsman followed right on the cook's heels and handed over two rolls of industrial-strength antacid tablets.

"Thanks a lot." Brognola gratefully accepted them and immediately popped two.

The meal appeared quickly and little was said as Bolan and Brognola made sandwiches and wolfed them down.

"What can you tell me about your mission?" Rawlings asked. "It'll help if I know what we're heading into. And—" he locked eyes with Brognola "—my crew performs at their best when they know what it is they're supposed to be doing."

Brognola understood the unspoken message and agreed. "Needless to say, Captain, this all has to be on a strict 'need to know' basis, but I want you to shadow a cruise ship full of Americans. They're being held hostage by what we think is a Cuban terrorist group."

Now Rawlings understood the urgency of the mission and his unconventional passengers. In the War Against Terror, a ship full of American hostages was a nightmare.

"What's the ship?"

"The *Carib Princess*," Bolan replied. "It was hijacked as it passed through the canal."

Rawlings hit the intercom again. "Mr. Johnson, to my cabin, on the double."

Lieutenant Rob Johnson was the *Sandshark*'s intelligence officer and the man who kept track of the submarine's potential target list. "Yes, Sir?"

"Mr. Johnson," the captain said, "drag out the cruise ship recognition file and fire up the satellite downlink. I want the SS *Carib Princess* and as soon as you've located her position, have the officer of the deck make an intercept course on her at all speed."

This wasn't the usual kind of target that the sub

went after, but Johnson knew better than to question the order. There were, however, a couple of operational details he had to ask about.

"Captain," he said, "the wind's gusting better than sixty knots up there, and I don't know if I can tow the satcom array in that. I'd hate to lose it."

"It's either that or surface and use the antennas, Mr. Johnson," Rawlings said. "I need that ship's location War Emergency."

"Aye, Sir."

"He'll find her." The captain poured himself a cup of coffee. "He's a regular hound dog."

He took a sip, sat back and looked at his guests. "And what do you plan to do after we find her?"

Brognola smiled grimly. "We're still working on that, and we can use any input you might have."

Rawlings was beginning to like these two spooks. At least they didn't think they had the world by the balls and knew all the answers.

"And speaking of input," Brognola said, "it will speed things up quite a bit if I can have access to secure communications, so I can get in touch with my headquarters."

"No problem," Rawlings said. "I'll make a secure suite available and have coffee sent in."

BEING ON BOARD the USS *Sandshark* put Bolan and Hal Brognola back in real-time contact with the combined intelligence-gathering apparatus of the United States of America. Everything from NSA Carnivore E-mail intercepts to real-time imaging from the NRO's Keyhole series deep-space recon satellites was now available to them as it came in. Even better was that America's premier clearinghouse for such information, known as Stony Man Farm, was also hard at work on the situation. But even with Aaron Kurtzman and the Farm's computer room crew hard at work, they had little to show for their efforts.

The problem was that Diego Garcia had apparently planned and executed his operation completely off-line. The lessons learned from the dismantling of Bin Laden and his terrorist network seemed to have been taken seriously by the Cubans. In fact, nothing relating to the Matador Section of the Cuban DGI was on any computer anywhere in the world. Further, the use of cell phones by the operatives had been strictly limited. Instead they were using fifties technology against adversaries who were geared up to look for twenty-first century clues. There were some radio communications between the different elements that had been intercepted, but they were all encoded and were limited.

When Brognola returned to the small berth he and Bolan had been assigned as their quarters, he looked as if he were about ready to have a coronary. "I can't believe it," he said. "Hunt and the Bear haven't been able to come up with anything on those Cubans. We're still operating blind."

Brognola was beyond frustration and starting to edge into rage. He was never one to back down from a fight, but at least he had to know who to shoot at.

"Except that we now know exactly where they're at right now," Bolan informed him. "The sub's crew was able to access their link to the spy satellites and the ship's been spotted. Rawlings is on an intercept course for her at flank speed, and we should be in torpedo range within a few hours."

"That's even worse," Brognola. "We may have them spotted, but we can't do a damned thing about it."

"What's the deal?"

"The usual." Brognola sounded disgusted. "The *Carib Princess*'s passenger manifest reads like a Who's Who of the world's medical research community. He's got prominent scientists, including a couple of Nobel prize winners, from almost every industrialized nation in the world on board, and most of them have their families with them. When the Man informed the nations involved that the ship had been hijacked and that some of their citizens were being held hostage, the excrement hit the ventilation big-time. We've got ourselves a big problem here with no solution in sight."

"We've got to let the captain know."

Brognola shook his head. "I guess we have to."

CAPTAIN RAWLINGS WAS in the sub's control room personally supervising the pursuit. The *Carib Princess* was an older ship, but she was fast. Even with the storm, she was still running at better than twenty-five knots, and it was a stern chase. It would be a few hours before he could catch up with her.

"We've just heard from Washington," Brognola said.

Rawlings accurately read the expression on his face. "Let's take it to my cabin."

The captain listened grim-faced as Brognola briefed him on the nature of the hostages and the problems they posed for the President.

"Right now," Brognola said, "the President is conferring with the governments involved to try to work out the rules of engagement if we do have to start shooting."

"Christ!" the captain said. "Another multinational circle jerk."

Even with the much publicized allied coalition that was supposedly "assisting" the United States in the War Against Terrorism, working with other governments had rarely been in America's best interests. And there was little chance that this incident would prove to be any exception. Regardless of the nationalities of the hostages involved, history had shown that the best hope for success in any hijacking situation was swift, bold action against the hijackers, not endless conference calls while politicians desperately tried to cover their respective asses.

"While he's trying to get that sorted out," Brognola said, "we're to continue following the *Carib Princess* and to keep him updated on everything she does."

"That much we can do." Rawlings sounded disgusted. "But that's not the best use of this boat. They can do that from two hundred miles in space."

"I think you and your crew'll get your chance to do something useful before this thing plays out," Brognola predicted.

"I'll hold you to that."

ON THE BRIDGE of the SS *Carib Princess*, Nguyen Cao Nguyen and his first officer were keeping the ship out of the worst of the storm. As the weather service had predicted, the hurricane had rebounded after hitting land in the Yucatán and had turned northeast. That put the southern shore of the Caribbean out of the worst of it, but this was a big storm and even the fringes carried powerful winds. And at the speed he was making, the trip was still rough.

Diego Garcia was hard at work in his makeshift command post set up in what had previously been the cabin of the ship's captain. He had been forced off his timetable by both the storm and the Mexican army, but now that he was back in communication with his operatives, he could make the necessary adjustments and get back on track.

Some of the news he was receiving from his operatives, however, wasn't good, particularly the reports from those in Mexico City where the situation had collapsed. The success of the People's Revolution in Mexico had been a big gamble, but one that he'd thought would be worth taking. That it had long been a dream of his president to bring socialism to Mexico had also played large in his planning. That the revolution had apparently failed wasn't a complete surprise to him. The socialist fervor burned brightly in certain progressive segments of Mexican society, but too many of the common people had been seduced by living so close to the United States. Visions of quick riches through greed and capitalism had corrupted them beyond salvation.

The attempt, even though a failure, could still serve the Cuban president's long-range plans for the region. The Matador teams had driven a dagger deep into the heart of the privileged and corrupt elite elements who had ruled Mexico for so long, and maybe some reform would come from it. Maybe now the common people would be able to see the vulnerabilities of the ruling class that he had exposed and would start planning their own revolution.

The news from the United States was also pretty much as he had expected. The widespread invasion of the American border states that had captured so much media attention was finally being contained. This part of the operation had been designed to be a feint to cause a panic and to draw the Yankee forces away from Mexico and Panama to deal with it. The real strike against them, the one that would score the killing blow, was yet to come. By the time it was discovered, it would be too late to stop it.

Nguyen had said that they would reach their destination by daybreak. Transferring the material he needed for the second phase would take two hours at the most, so by midday he should be in position to launch.

AT DAWN, the SS *Carib Princess* arrived at her destination and dropped her anchors in deep water a mile offshore from Goat Island. With the storm not yet completely gone, Nguyen Cao Nguyen had ordered the Matador pilot to keep well offshore. He also kept the engine room online ready to make full turns at a moment's notice if they lost their anchors.

The weather was also a topic of great concern to Diego Garcia. "How much wind can those helicopters of yours take?" he asked the Matador operative in charge of the planned air operations.

"As you know, Comrade," the pilot pointed out before answering the question, "we are using old Russian machines. Anything over fifty kilometers an hour makes it difficult for them to take off and land, almost impossible."

One of the biggest problems Garcia had had to

overcome in planning the entire operation was that everything he needed to pull it off had been supplied by Cuba. That meant that it was Russian in origin and long obsolete. No one, not even the new capitalist Russians, were willing to sell more modern military equipment to Cuba. It was sad to see that the Russians had caved in to the pressure from Yankees as they had done, but it was a reality.

"The wind is blowing at forty klicks an hour right now," the pilot added, "with gusts up to fifty, so it's going to be tricky."

"We have to load the material now," Garcia said. "So put your best pilots in the machines. And if I have the ship faced into the wind so the landing pad will be shielded from the wind, do you think they can manage it?"

"They will try, Comrade."

"See that they do better than that," the Cuban replied. "We have to get that material on board while we still have the cover of the storm. I don't want to remain anchored here a moment longer than I have to."

The pilot stiffened under the rebuke. "They will do their best, Comrade."

"See that they do."

CHAPTER FIFTEEN

The USS *Sandshark*'s pursuit of the SS *Carib Princess* had continued throughout the night, but by daybreak the submarine had caught up with the cruise ship as she dropped her anchor close to a small island. Since nuke submarines weren't equipped with anchors, the captain had been forced to cut power so the boat could lay motionless in the water at her periscope depth of sixty feet while stationed three thousand yards away from the *Carib Princess*. Sixty feet sounded like a lot of water, but it wasn't enough to shield the sub from the effect of the waves above.

Being a round-hulled submarine, the attack boat didn't take well to sitting idle, especially when there were strong winds topside. Early submariners had once taken pride in calling their primitive undersea craft pigboats. Deep-running, modern subs had banished that nickname, but dead in the water as she was, the *Sandshark* wallowed like a pig in a distillery slop.

In the control room, Rawlings braced his feet against the roll of the submarine deck and watched the *Carib Princess* through the attack periscope.

"What in the hell is that bastard up to?" he muttered to himself.

"What's he doing?" Hal Brognola asked.

"He's just sitting there and nothing's going on," the captain replied. "No boats are coming out from the island and none are leaving the ship. There's also no one up on deck. I can see crew on the bridge, but that's it."

"I have engineering contact," the sonar man reported. "She's making enough turns to keep her bow into the waves."

"Rotary Wing contact," the radar man called from his console in the attack center. "Fifteen hundred meters, bearing one-nine-six and closing fast."

"Contact, aye."

"Permission to go defensive, Sir," the weapons officer requested from his firing console.

"Permission granted," Rawlings snapped.

"Going defensive, aye."

In modern antisubmarine warfare, the greatest sub killers weren't the charging destroyers of WWII fame dropping depth charges off of their fantails. In the twenty-first century, enemy subs were killed by helicopters carrying ASROCs and other antisub missiles. And a motionless sub was dead meat to an air-borne killer. When Rawlings had come up to periscope depth, he had also raised the sub's search radar antennas to keep an electronic watch on skies above.

With the skipper's permission to go to a defensive posture, the weapons officer turned the launch key and had his finger poised over the button for the *Sandshark*'s air defense missile system.

"Weapons hot," he called.

"Weapons hot, aye," Rawlings confirmed. "Wait for target conformation."

Rawlings swiveled the periscope up to take in the horizon. "It's a Russian bird," he called as he IDed the chopper. "An old Mi-8 Hip, and it's heading for the *Princess*. No ASW gear spotted, go to weapons hold. Relax."

"Weapons hold, aye."

The tension in the combat control center eased off a bit.

"The chopper's turning into the wind to land on the *Princess*'s fantail," Rawlings said, keeping up a running commentary about what he was seeing.

"Can you make out its markings?" Bolan asked.

"It's unmarked, but it's wearing brown and green camo."

"That's Cuban paint," Bolan said.

"Which fits with the rest of this program," Brognola growled.

"He's touched down on her fantail," Rawlings reported, "and armed men are getting out and offloading something in small canisters."

"Second aerial contact," the radar operator called again. "Same bearing."

"Weapons still hot, Sir," the weapons officer reminded his skipper.

"Maintain weapons hold," Rawlings commanded. As much as he'd like to splash those guys, his rules of engagement didn't cover that option. He wasn't quite sure what they did cover and strongly suspected that Brognola was making them up as he went along. Sooner or later, he was going to have to get something through approved channels before he really screwed the pooch on this bastard operation.

"The first chopper is lifting off," Rawlings reported, "and the second one is moving in to land."

As he watched, the choppers made several more trips before landing again and being tied down at the *Carib Princess*'s aft deck.

"Okay," Rawlings said. "All the birds are down and are being secured on deck."

Diego Garcia having his own little air force now put this whole program in a different light. He'd seen no weapons on the choppers, but that, too, could change.

"Okay," Rawlings announced. "She's pulling up her anchor chain."

"I have increased screw noise," the *Sandshark*'s

sonar man reported. "She's making eighteen turns and increasing."

"She's putting back out to sea," the skipper announced.

"With the choppers on board?" Brognola asked.

"Three of them."

"I need to use the secure communications again," Brognola said.

"Cooper and I will be in my cabin," Rawlings replied.

BOLAN AND RAWLINGS were having coffee in the captain's cabin when Brognola joined them.

"The political shit storm's amped up even more." Brognola looked disgusted as he poured himself a cup from the captain's pot, "and we're kind of redundant out here. Everybody with a two-bit satellite in a suicide orbit is keeping a close eye on that damned thing, hoping that the terrorists will 'see reason' and turn the hostages loose. The only problem is that while everyone's trying to communicate with the ship, it's not responding."

Brognola shook his head. "And of course, most of the flak is coming from the Europeans. For all their lip service to helping us in the War Against Terrorism, they haven't been mugged enough yet and they still don't understand what's really going on or how to deal with it."

"Sounds like the crap we always used to hear from them before 9/11," Rawlings commented. "You'd think they'd understand by now."

"Bottom line," Brognola said, "is that until further notice, the President wants us to continue following them and see what develops."

"How about a private party?" Bolan asked.

"I suggested that," Brognola replied, "and he said he'll take it under advisement."

Brognola shook his head. "I hate it when he starts talking like that. All it means is that by the time the shit hits the fan and he gives me the 'go,' it'll be too late and people will be dying."

"Do you want me to go ahead anyway?"

Brognola thought for a moment, and Rawlings couldn't believe what he was hearing. Whoever these two guys were, they acted as if the wishes of the President and national policy were simply obstacles to be gotten around. He knew what his orders read, but he couldn't let this one go unchallenged.

"Gentlemen," Rawlings said, "I know that I've been ordered to cooperate with you guys in any way I can, but I can't sit here and listen to the two of you trying to find a way to disobey the orders of the President of the United States. In my book that's a little too much like treason, and I won't be a party to it."

"If you'll just calm down and listen for a minute, Captain—" Brognola put steel in his eyes "—I'd like to suggest that you don't really understand what Cooper and I do for a living."

"Maybe not," Rawlings replied, meeting his gaze, "but I know that I don't like what I'm hearing."

Brognola chose to ignore that and continued. "In my line of work," he said, "I'm almost required to go against the President's wishes all the time. It's part of my job description and necessary to get the job done. And, on occasion, I even tell him to his face that I'm going to do it. Unlike him, see, I don't have to play 'cover your ass' games when the lives of Americans are on the line, because I don't have to run for election."

He leaned forward. "You know, Rawlings, sometimes I really wish I did have to be elected to do what I do. Then maybe I'd be defeated this November and not have to do this anymore. Then I'd get turned out to pasture, and then when shit like this comes down, someone else would have to try to find a way through the political minefield to get the job done before the body count gets too high."

"Is there any way you can use your weapons to disable that ship?" Bolan asked, purposefully changing the subject.

"Not without putting the passengers in danger." Rawlings was glad to be back on a topic he knew something about. This shadow terrorist war was being played by rules he'd never even known existed and it was a bit unnerving for a simple sailor like himself.

"Remember, that to a submariner, there are only two kinds of ships—subs and targets. All of our weapons are lethal to a ship like that."

"Can you fire a torpedo with the warhead disabled?"

Rawlings shook his head. "Even without the warhead, our MK 48s move so fast that they would probably penetrate the hull of that damned thing and go all the way through it. Since she's not a warship, she doesn't have any kind of armor belt to protect her. If I try that, I'll sink her for sure."

"There's another thing to consider," Bolan stated.

"What's that?" Brognola asked.

"Right now, Garcia's in the driver's seat," Bolan said. "He's got the human shields he needs to protect him while he does whatever it is he's planning to do. And, right now, we don't know what that is. He's got those choppers, and whatever they ferried over from that island, so his plans include an aerial delivery of some kind, somewhere."

"You're saying that we just follow him and wait?"

"I'm saying that for the time being, those people on the *Princess* probably aren't in any imminent danger of being killed. He needs those people alive not dead. He'll only kill the hostages to make a point or to protect himself."

"That's cold, Striker," Brognola said. "Real cold."

"We've been here before, Hal. This might be one of those times when the 'good of the many...'"

"Dammit, Striker..."

"Hal, let's get real," Bolan said. "This guy was a part of a widespread operation apparently designed to overthrow several Latin America governments while we were tied up trying to stop an invasion across our borders. And from what you said about Garcia, he's probably the man in charge of the whole thing. And now that he's been driven out of his base of operations in Cancun, we don't have any idea where he's planning to go next or what he's planning to do.

"But," Bolan continued, "considering that he just had cargo and choppers loaded onto the ship, I don't think he's finished yet. That doesn't look to me like the actions of a man who's running for cover. He's got another operation planned, and it's going to be delivered by chopper."

As was usually the case, Brognola took Bolan's assessment of the situation seriously. The man had more time on the sharp end of the stick than anyone in the President's entire lineup of generals, special operators and advisers.

"Okay," he said, capitulating, "we'll do what the Man wants and follow them."

"We already are," Rawlings said.

NOW THAT the canisters and the helicopters were safely on board the *Carib Princess,* Diego Garcia's mood picked up dramatically. An uncertain fate had intervened against him at Cancun, but he wasn't defeated and wouldn't be. In fact, he now would make the strikes that would damage the Yankees the most and bring them to their knees. Best of all, unlike the earlier strike against the Trade Center Towers, it wasn't something they would ever be able to recover from.

The clever Yankees had cleared away the rubble from the so-called ground zero in New York and were starting to rebuild. But his strike was one that would remain forever visible to all, or at least for a thousand years, whichever came first.

The first target of Phase Two was a few hours' sail away, the Sonoco oil platform Delta 39. D-39 was one of the largest drilling rigs in the Caribbean–South Atlantic oil field region and a good place to start.

"Make for Delta 39," he told the Matador helmsman.

"As you command, Comrade."'

AS HE HAD TOLD Mary, Dr. Richard Spellman wasn't an action-adventure kind of guy. In fact, his favorite pastimes were reading and watching old movies. The last time he'd been involved in sports of any kind had been in high school when he'd been second string on the baseball team for his first two years. He was, though, fairly fit.

And as an M.D., he knew what fear and stress did to the body and brain. But until he had set foot on this cruise, he'd never been in many fearful or stressful situations.

In the past couple of days he had learned that he could take more than he thought he ever could. Even the shock of being recaptured in Cancun hadn't put him down. Having Mary Hamilton taken away had raised his concern, but his dying wasn't going to help her. Instead, he had docilely allowed himself to be led away and locked in a laundry closet.

They had taken his watch, so he lost time in his new lockup. From his use of the bucket he had found and the level of his hunger pains, he figured he had been locked up for a day or longer when he heard a key in the lock and the door opened to reveal two scowling gunmen.

"Come," the first gunman snapped.

"No problem," Spellman said as he stepped out of his makeshift cell. When the gunman motioned for him to walk down the passageway, he moved out between the two.

Spellman was shocked when the lead gunman said something to his partner and split off up one of the ladders, evening the odds.

The physician looked back over his shoulder past the gunman and mugged surprise. *"¡Hola!"* he said loudly.

When the gunman turned to see who was behind them, Spellman brought his fists together and hammered them on the back of the gunman's neck. He heard an audible crack and the man slumped to the floor like a puppet with its strings cut.

Being a doctor, he couldn't stop himself from automatically kneeling to check for a pulse, but there was none. From the way the man's head lolled on his neck, it was obvious that he had broken it. He was surprised how easy it had been, but the man'd had his back turned.

Grabbing the body by the feet, Spellman dragged it back into the laundry closet and closed the door behind them. The first thing he needed was a change of clothing. The cook's whites he'd worn since the night of the hijacking had outlived their usefulness. The gunman was a little larger man than he was, but that was better than his being smaller.

He stripped the corpse of its pants and black fatigue jacket, but kept his own shoes. After belting the gunman's black leather belt and holster over the jacket, he took the pistol from the holster and looked it over. The safety switch on the left side of the receiver had two positions: one marked with a green dot and one with red. Since the lettering on the side of the slide wasn't in English, he couldn't count on the U.S. tradition of green meaning go and red meaning stop working here. Red could also mean danger, ready to fire.

Spellman wasn't very familiar with firearms. He knew enough from the movies that he thought he could change the magazines if it came to that, but he didn't know how to test the safety switch. Taking a couple of pillows from the shelf, he flicked the pistol's safety to the red position. Pressing the muzzle tight against a pile of sheets, he held the pillows over it and pulled the trigger. He smiled as the pistol bucked in his hand; he had guessed right the first time. The report had been well muffled, and no one could have heard it from the passageway.

He had a gun now, but how he was going to find Mary was still a problem. Without speaking Spanish, there was no way that he would be able to pass for one of the terrorists. But he was hoping that dressed in black, anyone seeing him from a distance would take him for one of the gunmen and not raise the alarm.

He opened the door a crack and, finding the passageway empty, stepped out. Until he got this ship figured out, he decided to go down to the machinery decks to look for a better place to hide until nightfall.

Now that the *Sandshark* had caught up with the *Carib Princess*, Captain Rawlings had no trouble maintaining station a few miles behind her. Trailing his satcom array, he sent an hourly position report to CinClant. He received nothing in reply, so figured that his earlier orders from the CNO were still in force.

"If he keeps on this course," the officer of the deck stated, "he's heading for one of the oil platforms."

"Aw, shit!" Brognola muttered.

Garcia and an oil rig could mean only one thing, and he didn't need an environmental disaster added to an already overly complicated situation. There was nothing like a little environmental hysteria to really screw up an operation.

"You can use the radio if you need to." Rawlings nodded toward the commo room.

"I know he's got the information already," Brognola said, "but I want to bounce something off of him."

"Good luck."

CHAPTER SIXTEEN

As the submarine stalked the *Carib Princess* on her way to the oil rig, Brognola prowled the control room muttering under his breath. Being forced to sit and wait was killing him. Thanks to the sub's corpsman, at least he had something to take to keep his stomach in place. Even though Captain Rawlings was making hourly reports to his superiors, he, too, was keeping the White House Chief of Staff updated. Each time he called, though, he was told that the President was still in conference on the matter and had made no decision. If this kept up much longer, antacid tabs or not, he wasn't going to have any stomach lining left. The pots of coffee he was washing the tabs down with would make sure of that.

"She's reducing turns, sir," the sonar man called from the other side of the room.

The sub had been cruising at periscope depth, and Rawlings sent the scope up again for a quick look. "He's hull down," he announced, "and coming to a stop."

When the *Carib Princess* went dead in the water fifteen miles from the oil platform, Rawlings ordered the *Sandshark* into a protective position between it and the oil rig and sent up the scope to look at what the Cuban was doing. Whatever he had in mind, it wouldn't be good. This time Rawlings also deployed the Mk-18 scope, which had video imaging capability, and piped the images it captured to a monitor at one of the attack stations so Brognola and Striker could watch.

TO KEEP FROM ATTRACTING undue attention, when the *Carib Princess* arrived in the vicinity of the oil platform, Garcia stopped the ship well below the horizon. He wasn't unaware that the ship was being tracked by the Yankees' recon satellites and by their high-flying spy planes. As long as he had the passengers, though, he didn't care if his position was known to them. He did, however, want to catch the crew of the oil rig by surprise.

The rigs had large crews, sometimes up to a hundred men, and, while his assault teams were well armed, they were relatively small. But with the oil workers reportedly not being armed, his fighters shouldn't have much trouble with them.

The Matador air operations leader walked onto the bridge. "The men and the canisters are ready to launch, Comrade," he reported.

"Well done, Comrade." Garcia smiled. "Tell them to take off."

The first Mi-8 Hip lifted off with twenty-two Matador fighters inside for the ten-minute flight to the oil rig. As soon as the platform was pacified, the second aircraft with the canisters would join it. An hour after that, America would start paying for her crimes against the people.

THE VIDEO from the *Sandshark*'s periscope showed movement on the rear deck of the cruise ship as one of the helicopters was readied for takeoff.

"I've got rotary-wing contact Romeo Six, Sir," the radar man announced when it launched. "It's bearing directly for the platform."

Rawlings turned the scope to catch the chopper when it flew past.

"My guess is that he's sending an assault force to the platform," Bolan said.

"I can take that chopper out, Sir," the weapons officer suggested.

"Weapons on hold, Guns," Rawlings snapped.

"Aye, Sir, weapons on hold."

"Can you contact the rig and warn them?" Brognola asked the captain.

"I doubt if they're armed," Bolan interjected. "And it might be better if they don't try to resist armed gunmen. We don't know what he's planing to do yet."

Bolan had a bad habit of pointing out the obvious, so Brognola backed off. It was a bitch having to wait for the enemy to make his move. It was worse having to ask Washington to do what needed to be done.

IF YOU WERE TO ASK HIM, Bud Miller probably wouldn't call himself a patriot. That was too fancy a word and he would have shied away from it. Sure he loved his country, but like most Americans, he bitched about everything from taxes to scumbag fat cats and politicians, and he didn't think a real "patriot" would do that. He also wasn't much for what was touted as American family values. He'd never known his dad, his mom was a royal pain in the ass and he was currently between ex-wife number three and whoever was in the running to become number four. Working on oil rigs wasn't conducive to marital bliss, but he'd never had any trouble getting hitched. The women liked the fat paychecks, but the extended tours on the rig were another matter.

Miller was, though, a man who was fiercely loyal to his friends, and the crew of Sonoco Delta 39 were as close to a family as he'd ever really had. On shore, his door was always open and his couch available for any roughneck who needed to sober up or who had just been thrown out of his trailer by a pissed-off, soon-to-be ex-wife. He was also known as a soft touch for a small loan until payday, a never-ending point of contention with his ex-wives all of whom thought that their alimony payments should always come first.

So, when the unmarked chopper touched down on the rig's landing pad unannounced and started disgorging black-clad gunmen, Miller became angry.

One of the reasons Miller was never short of feminine companionship and was so well respected among his peers was that he was a big man. Not big as in John Belushi, but as in Arnold Schwarzenegger. Being six-six and two hundred and forty pounds made him a man to be reckoned with in almost any situation. Even so, he was an easygoing kind of guy as if to compensate for his bulk. That's the thing that drew women to him like flies to a ham sandwich at a Fourth of July picnic and accounted for his string of serial marriages.

He was laid-back and hard to ruffle, but when he was angry, everyone sat up and took notice. When that happened, and it was only rarely, those who could, evacuated the premises. Those who couldn't, quickly said "Yes, sir."

"Hey, Bud!" Rick Fraser, company man and shift supervisor, stuck his head out of the office. "Who the hell are those guys in that chopper?"

"Fucked if I know," Miller said. "But they sure as hell don't look friendly to me. Those are AKs they're packin' not M-16s."

"I'd better go down there."

"I wouldn't do it, Rick. You got the key to the gun rack?"

There wasn't much need for guns on an oil rig, but if someone went overboard, a rifle would keep the sharks away until they could get the boat to him. Plus, in the wake of 9/11, some guy in Washington had woken up to the fact that oil rigs could be hijacked and had made surplus military rifles available if the oil companies wanted to arm their rigs.

Miller's bosses had taken a dozen of the offered rifles and pistols and a small supply of ammunition, but kept them under lock and key in the main office.

"Let me go down and talk to them," Fraser said. "I'm sure there's some reason they're here."

Miller wasn't one of those die-hard union guys who thought that every company man was a moron. Granted a lot of them couldn't pour piss out of a boot unless the instructions were printed on the bottom of the heel, but he'd also known some damned good men in the higher ranks of the company. Unfortunately, Fraser wasn't one of them.

Miller turned back and walked over to a tool

locker. Taking out a three-foot titanium pry bar, he headed for the main office on the next deck up.

Jim Simmons, the shift crew boss, was parked behind his desk, as he usually was, drinking a cup of coffee. "Who the hell's in that chopper?" he asked. "We aren't scheduled for any resupply today."

"They're packing guns." Miller headed for the arms locker. "AKs, I think."

"You're shitting me!"

"Nope." Miller fitted the end of the pry bar to the lock hasp and applied pressure. "And Fraser's gone down there to talk to them."

"What the hell are you doing?" Simmons frowned.

"I'm buying the company a new lock," Miller replied as he popped the hasp free. "Put it on my tab."

Simmons was a good man who had come up through the company the hard way, but he could be a bit slow on the uptake at times. Worrying too much about a fat pension he'd be getting at the end of the year could do that to a man.

Miller reached in, pulled out an AR-15, the civilian, semiauto version of the M-16, and cracked the bolt. "We're gonna need these when your boy gets his ass blown away."

As if on command, the rattle of an AK on full-auto sounded. Grabbing a handful of loaded magazines, Miller headed for the door.

Simmons stared after him, his jaw slack, his coffee cup halfway to his mouth.

THE CREW at the drill head heard the firing over the cacophony of the working drill. An oil rig wasn't the place for quiet solitude, but gunfire, particularly full-auto fire, was a first. Without being told, the driller started to pull the bit out of the hole to shut down.

"Yo, Jack!" Miller leaned over the railing of the upper desk and shouted to the drill head foreman, "Get your guys up to the office and get some guns."

"What's going on?" Jack Dawson asked.

"I don't know," Miller shouted. "But those guys from that chopper have AKs, and I think they're trying to take over the rig."

"The hell they are!" Dawson waved to the rest of his crew. "Let's go, guys!"

As Dawson and his men ran for the office, Miller worked his way around, searching for a covered position to try his luck. The superstructure of the platform got in the way of his line of sight to the landing pad, so he ended up in the open on one of the catwalks above the water. It wasn't the best place in the world for a would-be sniper, but it was all he could find.

He'd never fired an AR-15, and the straight-line stock and sight placement were a little strange to him. But he got a sight picture on a guy about seventy-five yards away who looked to be in charge and squeezed off a round.

The guy didn't go down, and Miller lined up on him again. He was squeezing when a blow to his left arm spun him and he slipped off his perch. The rifle slipped from his hands as he fell toward the waves below.

JACK DAWSON, the drill head foreman, made it to the office with only three of his eight-man crew left. The rest had fallen back along the way. Thanks to someone's artistic use of a pry bar, the arms locker was open. The four men snatched AR-15s from the rack and stuffed their pockets with loaded magazines.

"How do you use this damned thing?" one of the younger men asked, frowning.

"Here." An older man stuck out his hand. "Gimme that fuckin' thing."

Flipping the rifle upside down, he took a magazine and stuffed it into the well. "That's how you load it. To drop the empty mag, you just hit this button."

Rolling the rifle right side up again, he pulled on the charging handle and let it fly forward. "That puts a round in the chamber. The safety's simple enough for even a dumb shit like you."

"Thanks, old-timer." The kid grinned.

"If you'd been in the Army, you'd know simple shit like that."

"Okay, boys," Dawson said. "Let's go."

RAWLINGS HAD MANEUVERED the *Sandshark* to within five hundred yards of the Delta 39 for a better look at what was going on. With his optical scope up to full power, he could see the figures on the platform and the firefight that was taking place. It looked to be pretty much one-sided, but it showed that the roughnecks had access to weapons.

Brognola and Bolan were also watching on the video relay as the scene played out. "If he can sabotage the drill head," Brognola said, "he can put that well out of action for quite some time."

"But that would just be temporary," Bolan said. "Even if it catches fire, it can be put out and restored fairly quickly."

"What if he opens the valves on the holding tanks and releases the oil?"

"Then we'd have a problem," Bolan admitted. "But that, too, can be contained."

"So what the hell's he doing?"

Bolan shrugged.

BUD MILLER surfaced above the waves under the platform and spit out a mouthful of water. His arm was throbbing, but when he looked at the wound, he saw that the bullet had just torn a furrow through the muscle. He could move it okay. It didn't hurt much yet, but he knew that was only temporary. If he was going to save himself, he needed to do it now while he still could.

The platform's three massive sea legs were hollow steel tubes with ladders inside for the convenience of the maintenance crew. Six feet above the waterline, there was a hatch that could be opened from the outside. The thought was that if someone fell into the water, he could swim to one of the legs, climb up the rescue rungs welded on the outside, open the hatch and make his way inside. From there, the maintenance ladder would take him up to the main deck. As far as Miller knew, this rescue system had yet to be used, but he was glad it was there and would save him.

Keeping as low in the water as he could, he paddled to the closest leg. The rescue rungs were on the inside curve of the leg, so he would be hidden in case anyone looked down to see if he had survived. Favoring his wounded arm, Miller went up the rungs one-handed. The dog on the hatch was properly greased, but stiff, and it took a moment for him to get it open.

Inside the leg, he left the hatch open a bit to give him some light as he took a look at his wound. The salt water had washed it clean, but it was still bleeding. Taking off his T-shirt, he used his teeth to tear a strip off of the bottom. The makeshift bandage would slow the bleeding, which he figured would clot sooner or later. Right now, though, he had other things to worry about.

He started up the maintenance ladder, knowing

that the first exit hatch he came to would open onto the lowest of the rig decks: the loading dock below the main deck. He thought it might be a better idea to exit there to take a look at what was going on before he went further up. Cracking the hatch, he peered out and found that the deck was empty.

Miller stepped out and had started for the ladder that led to the main deck when he heard boot heels coming down the metal steps. He ducked behind the platform leg for cover and waited. When he heard the footsteps stop, he risked a peek. The gunman was a Latino, who didn't seem to be very comfortable about the prospect of walking around on open-mesh deck plates. It took a while before a guy got comfortable with seeing the waves below his feet.

When the gunman headed in the direction of Miller's pillar, he ducked back behind it. But knowing the guy was concentrating on where he put his feet gave him an idea. He listened to the hesitant steps and waited until it sounded as though the man was right on top of him.

Stepping out from behind the pillar, Miller clotheslined the gunman, smashing his forearm into his Adam's apple and crushing his larynx. The gunman gagged and his hands clawed at his throat as if he were trying to open his smashed airway. No such luck. He went unconscious in seconds, slumping to the deck. A few more seconds and he was dead.

Being a man who never liked to see garbage littering his oil rig, Miller grabbed the corpse by the ankles, dragged it over to the side and tossed it into the sea. The body sank beneath the waves.

After snatching up the fallen assault rifle, Miller took cover behind the pillar again to examine his prize. He wasn't a dedicated gun nut like some of his buddies, but he wasn't a complete firearms novice, either. He knew what an AK looked like and roughly how it worked; he'd just never had a chance to fire one. But if these bastards were able to use them, he figured he could do it, as well.

Taking out the magazine, he cracked the bolt to empty the chamber and let it go forward. Pulling the trigger, he found that the weapon was on safe. Seeing the big flat lever on the left side of the receiver, he flicked it up one notch and pulled the trigger again. This time, the hammer fell with a click. That was the fire position.

Resetting the magazine, he chambered a round. Rather than put the weapon back on safety and having to fumble around if he needed it, he left it hot and kept his finger outside the trigger guard. Now that he was armed, he realized that he should have stripped the gunman's body of his extra magazines, but it was too late now.

Instead of taking the ladder the gunman had used, Miller went to the other side of the deck and took the other ladder up to the main deck. He had work to do.

"WE HAVE A SECOND rotary wing contact Romeo Seven bearing for the platform, Sir," the radar man announced.

Rawlings turned the scopes to pick up the second machine, and both Brognola and Bolan watched it on the video monitor. "Probably carrying explosives," Bolan commented. "Better give the Coast Guard a heads up so they can start notifying the company to get their fire-fighting crews going."

"Do it," Rawlings told his radioman.

"Aye, Sir."

WHEN MILLER GOT up to the main deck, he saw that he wasn't the only roughneck who had struck back. More than one black-clad body lay in a pool of blood. Several drillers had been killed, as well, but the firing had completely died down. If that made him the Lone Ranger still defending the rig, so be it. This time, though, he was going to find a better place to do it from. Getting shot hurt.

He'd found a great place: the cage holding the welding gas bottles. The sides were quarter-inch plate, which he figured would give him a little protection. Before he got started, though, he needed to know how much ammunition he had so he snapped the magazine out of the AK. To his disappointment, he counted only four rounds, which wasn't much.

With one in the chamber, though, he should be able to cause some damage if he took careful shots.

He was replacing the magazine when he heard the rotor sounds of a second chopper. The riggers had more gunmen than they could deal with right now and didn't need any more. Poking only his head and the rifle above his makeshift armor, Miller took a deep breath and sighted in on the approaching chopper.

Not knowing that in a chopper the pilot sat on the opposite side than a fixed-wing aircraft pilot, Miller sighted the man in the right-hand seat. He took up the slack on the trigger and fired slow aimed shots until his magazine went empty.

By the second shot, the chopper seemed to wobble in the air. The Mi-8 rolled a few degrees, her left gear wheel dropping low enough to hit the edge of the main deck. The chopper slammed onto the deck hard, snapping off her tail boom. The spinning rotor slammed against the steel deck, shattering the blades and sending them flying.

As soon as the fuselage came to a halt, several men staggered out of the wreckage and took off running. Miller didn't see any flames, but knew that fuel might be leaking. His AK was empty now, but he was pleased with the job he had done with it. Now he had to find a place to hide.

CHAPTER SEVENTEEN

Diego Garcia was in the captain's cabin off the bridge when the Matador Air Ops officers rushed in. "The helicopter carrying the material crashed on the platform," he reported. "There was firing right as it was landing. The copilot was killed outright, and the pilot lost control of his machine and crashed."

"And the material it was carrying, Comrade?" the Matador leader asked.

"Some of it was lost in the sea, but a few of the canisters were damaged on impact and the material leaked onto the platform."

A flash of pain hit Garcia behind the eyes and he blinked. This wasn't the time for him to show weakness, so he bit down. He could still make the plan work, but he would have to move quickly.

"Leave the material there," he said. "Don't try to

salvage it. Recover our fighters immediately in the other machine and we'll move on to the second target."

Garcia hit the intercom to the bridge. "Helmsman, as soon as the helicopter is recovered, make a course for Bravo 108," he ordered.

"As you command, Comrade."

"And—" he turned back to his air officer "—when we hit it, I want twice as many men to make the assault and I want them to completely eliminate the workers. Launch both of the helicopters together and when the site is secure, one of the machines will fly back here to pick up the material."

"Yes, Comrade."

As soon as the man left, Garcia took two of his dwindling supplies of pain pills. No man in the history of socialism had been tested as he was being tested. But no matter what obstacles were put in his way, he wouldn't quit.

WHEN THE CUBANS reacted to the crash of the chopper by loading back into the remaining helicopter and evacuating the platform, Bolan's suspicion that the Cubans had planned to destroy it were confirmed.

"But with what?" Hal Brognola thought out loud.

"My hunch is that whatever it was, it got lost when that second chopper crashed."

"You think they're going back for more?"

"Not when they pulled their fighters out," Bolan said. "I'd say they're leaving."

"She's making turns to get under way, Sir," the sonar man reported.

Captain Rawlings turned to Brognola. "What now?"

"Just keep tailing her," Brognola replied wearily, "and I'll try once more to get some definitive guidance out of the Puzzle Palace. Someone up there's got to know what the Man wants us to do."

A HALF HOUR LATER Brognola walked into Rawlings's cabin, poured himself a cup of coffee and took his place at the table.

"The Man was in a meeting I couldn't break into again," he said, "so I patched into the Farm and ran this incident past them. They were following it by satellite, and it's worse than we thought. Those weren't explosives that were being transferred to that oil platform. It was nuclear waste of some kind, probably from nuclear power plants. When that chopper crashed, the nuclear detection satellites picked up what it was carrying and it's real hot. Hunt thinks that they were going to try to contaminate the wells by pumping it down into the oil bearing strata."

"Would that work?" Rawlings frowned.

"Apparently only too well," Brognola replied. "While the underground pools of oil beneath the wells are more or less separate, there's still a slight connection between the different pockets. If he can contaminate half a dozen wells with the stuff, it'll spread from one strata to the others and poison the oil in the entire Caribbean region. Hunt says that if he can pull this off, no one will be able to use the oil for a thousand years or more."

"There goes the President's plan to become self-sufficient in oil by 2010," Rawlings commented dryly.

"I think Garcia's trying to strike at the heart of our national economy," Brognola said. "First the hordes of illegals storming across the fence and now this. And if Cuba is working in conjunction with the OPEC nations on this, I think we can expect a repeat of the '73 oil embargo on top of it. But this time, it might work."

"Our radar plot," Rawlings said, "indicates that he's steaming toward one of the other oil rigs in the vicinity. ETA a couple of hours."

"How about launching the SEALs," Bolan asked Rawlings, "at least to cripple the ship?"

"If you can get your boss to sign off on it," the captain said. "I'm sure they'd be glad to swim over and put a charge on her rudder to put her out of commission so he can't try this again. But to do that, and no offense meant, I'll have to get clearance from someone in the chain of command whose name I've heard before."

"No offense taken," Brognola said. "I'll see if I can get through to him again."

Gulping down the rest of his coffee, he left for the commo room again.

BROGNOLA DIDN'T LOOK quite so grim-faced this time when he returned to the makeshift war room in Rawlings's cabin. "I didn't get everything I wanted," he said, "but even a slice is better than no pie at all."

He handed a faxed hard copy to Rawlings. "Here's your firing orders," he said. "If Garcia launches those choppers again, you have the National Command Authority's permission to engage and blow them out of the sky. A copy's been sent to CinClant to cover your ass with them."

"'Bout fucking time." The Skipper grinned broadly. As a fighting man, it rankled that he wasn't able to do anything about the Americans being held hostage on that ship. But he could sure as hell blast those choppers out of the air before they did any more damage to oil rigs.

"How about the SEALs?" Bolan asked.

Brognola sat at the small table and reached into his pocket for an antacid tab. "The SEALs aren't officially authorized," he said. "He's still having trouble with the Europeans, particularly since the nuke alert satellites are going off like a string of cheap Christmas tree lights. Everyone's screaming and waving their hands like a bunch of old women, and they've convened an emergency session of the UN Security Council to discuss this 'new' emergency."

In another circumstance, the Stony Man action teams would be all over this, both for the sake of the hostages and to take care of the nuclear material before it got out of hand. But as it was, both of the Farm's teams were engaged half a world away and Bolan was the only Stony Man operative in a position to act right now.

"The good news, if you want to call it that," Brognola told Bolan, "is that when I asked, he didn't outright forbid you to go in and take care of business. He didn't authorize it, but then he didn't make any of his usual threats if you go, either. He's leaving it completely up to you."

That was the way Bolan liked to operate anyway. "I'll opt in."

Rawlings couldn't believe what he was hearing. "You're trying to tell me that you don't have specific authorization from the President to take action on this, but that he still wants it done?"

Brognola mugged his best innocent look. "Like I tried to explain before, that's how it usually works."

The sub captain shook his head. "Man, this has gone from James Bond all the way to *Alice in Wonderland,* and it hasn't gotten any better as it's gone along."

He held up a hand to keep Brognola from going

into his rap about the nature of his "job," if it could be called that, again. He had no way to confirm any of this and it was making his head ache. He also knew that if he called CinClant for clarification, though, it'd be like putting a gun to his own head.

"Look, Captain," Bolan said, turning to Rawlings, "you're the boss here. We both know the law of the sea, and I know how it works. So before this goes too much further and everyone gets wrapped around the axle, how about coming up to the surface alongside the *Princess* just long enough to let me off this boat. You and Hal can then go on your way and argue about who's going to do what to whom and when."

"You've got to be out of your mind, mister," Rawlings growled. "It's still blowing up there, and you wouldn't last five minutes in that water."

"That's kind of my concern, isn't it?" Bolan locked eyes with him. "And if I remember, Captain, your original orders were to pick me up and take me where I said I wanted to go, right? Well, this is where the bus stops for me. I'm getting off as close to that ship as you can get me."

"Striker," Brognola jumped in, "you can't help those people if you drown."

"Someone has to help them," he replied, "and I seem to be the guy who has the best chance right about now. We don't know what Garcia's ultimate plans are, but I'm not willing to risk all those people's lives in the hopes that he turns them loose sometime in the future."

He leaned closer to his old friend. "You know how these things work, Hal. This isn't the first time we've come up against this scenario and if we don't take this guy out, he'll start killing those people, and you know it. Regardless of what the Man's going through with the Europeans and the UN, the ball's in our court and I'm the only one in place who can make a play.

"Plus—" he glanced up at the clock on the wall "—time isn't on our side. This storm impeded him as much as it has us, but it's dying down. Once it's blown past, we have no idea what he's going to do next. What if he has a nuke weapon on board, as well as that waste material and he decides to sail it into a major harbor? With the hostages on board, we won't be able to stop him."

"Okay, you two," Rawlings said in capitulation. "I've got to be out of my mind, but I'll go along with this. You know, I've had a great career so far in this man's Navy. I've gotten my ticket punched all the way through, I've made a few above-the-zone promotions and had some choice assignments where I did quite well, thank you, and got my required brownie points. I'd really like to be the CNO someday because I think that I could do a lot for the fleet.

"But…" Rawlings added, a strange look on his

face, "I'm not sure that I want to wear the gold braid if it's covered with American blood. So, since you two crazies seem to be determined to trash your careers, as well as risk your lives, the very least I can do is help you do it. Promise me, though, that if you survive, you'll come and see me when I'm permanently beached in the old sailors' home."

Brognola laughed. "If I remember, it's right down the street from the old disgraced federal bureaucrats home, so we'll be neighbors."

"I take it that you know how to use underwater gear?" Rawlings asked the man he knew as Cooper.

Bolan nodded.

"Okay, I'll go along with this dog-and-pony show, but there's one problem. Even in good weather, you can't swim fast enough to catch up with him when he's under way. You get suited up and the next time he stops, I'll release you as close to the ship on the lee side as I can. I can't get too close, 'cause I can't risk a collision in winds like this. If we take any hull damage, we'll go under. But I can put you within a couple hundred yards of her."

"That should do it."

"And while you're getting suited up," Brognola said, "I'll get hold of the Farm to see if the Bear can come up with a blueprint for that thing. I'm sure that the builder kept something for the archives."

"If your man can't find anything in the builder's

records," Rawlings offered, "tell him to try the Coast Guard. They're likely have a deck plan in their data banks because they use them for their contraband searches."

"Good tip."

THE SEALs HAD THEIR own small compartment by the torpedo room in the forward end of the sub. In times of underwater war, they would assist the ordnance men in keeping the tubes fed with Mk-48 ship killers and tube-launched cruise missiles. At other times, they provided security for the sub in foreign ports or were available to undertake their signature ops on land.

Rawlings led Bolan into the SEALs' berth and walked up to an older man with a buzz cut and master chief petty officer's chevrons pinned on the collars of his Marine-style OD combat fatigues.

"Master Chief Duffy," Rawlings said, "this is Colonel Cooper. I need you to help him get suited up with some of your spare gear. We're going to be dropping him off soon."

The SEAL didn't comment on the absurdity of launching a swimmer in this kind of weather, particularly someone who wasn't a fin. But he'd heard the scuttlebutt that they had a pair of high-level spooks on board, so he kept his thoughts to himself. He just extended his hand. "Pleased to meet you, Sir," he said.

Bolan shook his hand. "Master Chief."

"The chief'll take care of what you need," Rawlings said. "When you're ready, let me know."

Duffy led Bolan over to the SEALs' lockers and started to break out a full set of underwater gear. Bolan stripped to his shorts and donned the wet suit as soon as it was laid out.

"You've worn this gear before, Sir," the chief said as he watched Bolan suit up.

"On occasion, Chief," Bolan admitted, "but it's been a while. So, how about running me through all the checks to make sure I don't miss anything."

The SEAL watched closely as Bolan made the connections for the scuba gear and adjusted the wet suit. "Is it true, Sir, that there's a bunch of terrorists holding Americans hostage on that ship?"

"That's classified information, Chief," Bolan said. "And if I told you, I'd have to kill you."

The SEAL started to bristle before he realized that Bolan was playing the old Spec Ops game with him. He couldn't reveal classified information outright, but from one professional to another, he could give him the pieces and let him put them together himself.

"There are Americans on the ship, Chief," Bolan admitted, "and right now we're not too sure about the status of the regular crew."

That was all the SEAL needed to hear. He was an

expert at the game and could read everything he needed to know into that one innocent statement.

"Well, Colonel," he said, "I'm glad that you're going over there to have a little look-see then. And—" he reached into his own locker to pull out his wet suit "—I'm honored to be able to help you."

"This is supposed to be a solo trip, Chief."

"Oh, I understand fully, Sir," the SEAL said as he started to pull on his wet suit. "But it's real easy to get hung up in the escape hatch on this tub. And if that occurs, someone has to go up there and get you free or we can't dive again. I'll have to go through the hatch with you to make sure you clear the tube."

Bolan watched the SEAL strap his waterproof weapons case to his chest. "And the hardware?"

"Sharks, sir." The SEAL grinned. "There's a lot of sharks in these waters. Every time we surface, we put a diver in the water to keep them off."

Bolan smiled. "Do you have a compass I can borrow?"

"This is better." The SEAL brought out what looked like a wrist compass, but wasn't. "It's a magnetic mass detector. It'll guide you to that thing blindfolded.

"Also—" he clipped a gadget onto the hood of Bolan's wet suit "—this's a beacon that'll let us know where you are at all times. That way, if you get lost, me and my boys'll be able to find you."

"You're going to get your ass in big trouble for this, Chief, you know that."

The SEAL smiled. "You know something, Sir? I've got over twenty-eight years fin time in this man's Navy, and I'm about ready for a well-earned retirement. In fact, I've got the papers sitting in my desk right now. On my way to the escape trunk, I think I'll just stop by the old man's office and drop them on his desk."

Bolan wasn't adverse to having a little professional help, but he wanted to make sure that the SEAL knew what he was getting himself into.

"Before you do that, Chief," he said, "you need to be advised that we're not going to have any backup on any level. If we're able to free those people, we're not going to get a medal for it. If we screw up and get killed, all hell's going to break loose and your family won't ever learn how you died or where you're buried."

The SEAL lost the smile in his eyes. "Been there, Sir, and I've done that," he said. "I've been on my own before with all that political deniability bullshit. I used to swim with SEAL Six."

SEAL Team Six was the Navy's premier dirty-little-jobs organization. Moamar Khaddafi lost what he had claimed was a fertilizer factory hidden inside a fortified mountain complex courtesy of SEAL Six. The chemical samples the team recovered, however, had identified the "fertilizer" as nerve gas. As far as volunteers went, he could do a lot worse than a SEAL from Team Six.

"Were you on the Libyan thing?"

The SEAL winked. "Libya, Sir?"

Bolan grinned. "That's what I thought."

"And I don't even want to know who you learned to swim with, Sir," the chief said. "I learned to recognize you guys years ago when I was working in the Delta."

If the SEAL wanted to think that he was a Company man, Bolan wasn't about to enlighten him. He'd been accused of being much worse than a CIA officer. And, recently, the Company had been winning back the hearts and minds of the public.

"How're you fixed for hardware?" Duffy asked.

"I'm covered for handguns, but could use one of those waterproof H&Ks you guys use."

"Sound suppressor and laser sight, right?"

Bolan nodded. He put his 93-R and Desert Eagle in the waterproof weapons bag, followed by the borrowed SEAL H&K MP-5 SD-3.

When the two were ready, the other SEALs went with them to the escape trunk to assist.

CHAPTER EIGHTEEN

Richard Spellman hadn't made much progress in finding where the women were being held captive on the *Carib Princess*. Initially, after he'd freed himself, he thought that he might be able to locate a clue by noting how many terrorists stood guard on each deck. His thought that there would be more guards watching over the decks holding the men rather than the women hadn't proved to be true.

One thing he hadn't expected was how few of the ship's original crew were still on board. From his short sojourn on the *Princess* before the hijacking, it had seemed as if there had been at least one crew member for every two guests. Now, though, the only crewmen he had seen were those working in the galley and the engine room, and there weren't many there, either. Where the rest of them had gone, he didn't have a clue. The up side was that with so few crewmen, there were fewer eyes to spot him as he tried to learn his way around.

As the *CARIB PRINCESS* had drawn closer to the Bravo 108 platform, Captain Rawlings had brought the *Sandshark* to within five hundred yards of the cruise ship. When it went dead in the water again, he wanted to waste no time getting into position to launch Colonel Cooper.

"She's reducing turns, Sir," the sonar man stated. "Coming to a stop."

Rawlings turned to his com. "Bring us along the lee side, about two hundred yards out."

"Aye, Sir," the com answered. "Two hundred yards on the lee."

"Chief Duffy," Rawlings said over the intercom, "we're coming alongside. Prepare to launch. Mr. Brognola, report to the control room."

Brognola reached the com right as the sub maneuvered into position close enough to the *Carib Princess* to launch the divers.

"We're in position, Sir," the helmsman reported. "And all stop, but for steerage."

Rawlings picked up the ship's intercom. "You ready to go back there, Cooper?"

"We're ready to go, Captain," Bolan sent back.

"We're 196 yards from the target on the lee side,"

Rawlings said. "I have to keep the boat at two knots
for steerage, but you need to get clear of the hull as
soon as you can. If I have to get under way suddenly,
I don't want you to get caught up in the screw wash."

"I understand," Bolan sent back.

"Good luck."

"Thanks."

THE INSIDE HATCH to the escape trunk could only ac-
commodate one man at a time, so the SEAL went in
first. Bolan followed and joined the chief under the
air bubble flange. As soon as the inner hatch was
closed, the SEAL reached over to give Bolan's scuba
gear a final check. "You ready, sir?"

Bolan put his mask in place and said, "Let's do it,
Chief."

"Roger. And remember, I want you to exit first."

"Got it."

Duffy turned a valve and opened the outer hatch.
As soon as the trunk was flooded, the SEAL tapped
Bolan on the head. He ducked out from under the air
bubble flange and pulled himself up through the
trunk. Once outside, the current was strong enough
that he held on to the open hatch to keep from drift-
ing away. As soon as the SEAL joined him, Bolan let
him lead the way.

Even sixty feet under the surface, the waves felt like
hammer blows. The current, though, was working
with them and the swim took less time than expected.

Duffy signaled a halt a few yards from the ship's stern and motioned for Bolan to stay put while he went up to take a closer look. When he came back down, he took a speargun with a grapple head from his harness and motioned for Bolan to join him on the surface.

The two men swam to a point along the side where the ship's superstructure met the fantail. Duffy aimed his CO_2 speargun at the railing and fired. With the waves tossing them around like corks, the spear missed and fell back into the water. Duffy loaded another, aimed again and fired.

This time the grapple head caught on the railing and the SEAL tugged on the spear's line to lock it in place. Duffy motioned for Bolan to go up first.

Using the grips tied into the line, Bolan went up hand over hand, rolled over the railing and freed his Beretta from his weapons bag before signaling for the SEAL to join him.

The SEAL moved up the line and was coming over the railing when a sudden wave knocked him off balance. He slipped on the wet deck and fell back against one of the railing posts.

"You okay, Chief?"

"You know," the SEAL said with a grimace, pain showing in his eyes, "I think I just broke my fucking arm."

"Can you swim back to the sub?"

The SEAL shook his head. "No way, man." He tugged at the H&K subgun strapped to his chest. "I'm staying here. I can still shoot."

"Look, Chief," Bolan said, "you got me on board and that's what I needed. But I'm not going to be able to do what has to be done if I'm working with a one-armed man. You know the drill. I've got to leave you behind and I want you back in the water. If you get captured, you're just one more guy I'm going to have to rescue."

"I'm really sorry about this, Sir." The SEAL shook his head.

"It's not your fault, Chief, but I want you back on that boat."

"I'll send one of my other men over."

"No, I don't want anyone else going to the wall for me. Believe me, there's a good chance of some big-time political shit rolling downhill over this, and you don't want any of your people to get caught up in it. Save them for an occasion when they can do their job and not have to pay a price for it."

Swimming back to the sub one-handed would not be much of a problem for the SEAL, but getting back into the water was another story. If he hit the water with the arm unsecured he could pass out and drown. Taking the sling from Duffy's H&K, Bolan helped the SEAL strap his arm to his side.

"That should hold it in place."

The SEAL nodded. "It'll do."

Bolan helped the man to his feet and over to the railing. The SEAL stiffened and saluted with his left hand. "Good luck, Sir."

"You, too, Chief."

The SEAL turned and dived over the rail into the storm-lashed waves below.

BOLAN SLIPPED off his fins and tossed them over the side with the rest of his scuba gear. On this expedition, he'd either win or die on the *Carib Princess* and, whichever happened, he wouldn't be swimming away until his business was concluded. Picking up the SEAL's ammo carrier, he slung it over his back and hooked the extra subgun onto his harness.

The hatch into the superstructure was unlocked, and once inside the passageway, he saw a ladder that would take him down to the lower decks. Fortunately the vessel was an older cruise ship, not one of the floating palaces featured in all the vacation adds on TV. That was both good and bad for what he had in mind. The good part was that he wouldn't have so much space to work his way through. The bad part was that he wouldn't have as much space to hide in, either.

As a first step, he had to make sure that the diagram the Farm had faxed to the sub matched the reality of steel. The ship was old enough that it could have gone through any number of refittings and relying on the original blueprints could be fatal.

The first change he ran into was the compartment that had been labeled Linen Supplies on the blueprints. The sign on the door now read Deck Chairs. He wasn't concerned with the supply of towels, but it showed that the blueprints were outdated.

That meant that he'd have to do a complete recon before he could start getting serious.

CAPTAIN RAWLINGS planned to maintain his position off the cruise ship for as long as he could in case something went wrong out there and the two men had to return to the sub. While his two guests talked a good talk and sure had a lot of pull with powerful men in high places, pirating a ship on the high seas was a lot different than a land operation. The plan sounded good, but he half expected it to fail.

His expectations were realized when he saw the indicator light for the escape trunk outer hatch flash on. When that indicator glowed, it meant that the trunk was being opened from outside the hull.

"Aw shit," he muttered.

"What is it?" Brognola asked.

"They're coming back."

"What happened?" Brognola couldn't keep himself from asking.

Before Rawlings could tell him that he would have to wait until the men were inside, the intercom clicked in. "Captain to the sick bay, please."

"Let's go," Rawlings told Brognola.

As everything else on the *Sandshark,* the sub's medical facility gave new meaning to the word compact. It had one operating table and room for a gurney. Rawlings was surprised to see Master Chief Bill Duffy lying on the gurney having his wet suit cut off of his upper body.

"Where's Colonel Cooper?" he asked. "Did you reach the ship?"

"We did, Skipper." The SEAL winced as a corpsman nudged his arm. "For a spook, he's a hell of a swimmer."

"What happened?"

"I'm sorry, Skipper," the SEAL said, looking thoroughly disgusted with himself. "I slipped on the fuckin' deck plates and broke my fuckin' arm."

"Where's Cooper now?" Brognola asked.

"The last I saw, he was on board and getting ready to do his thing."

Brognola relaxed.

Having the chief go with Cooper had been the only thing Rawlings could think to do to give the spook a little more of a chance. Now the man was alone on a ship with an unknown number of terrorists.

Rawlings turned to Brognola. "What do we do

now?" he asked, surprised to see that his guest was smiling.

"We wait for Striker to get settled in over there and go to work."

"Do we keep station here," the captain asked, "in case he wants to come back?"

"No, he'll be staying there until the job's over."

Rawlings shook his head and sent up a quick prayer, knowing that he'd never see Cooper alive again.

CAPTAIN RAWLINGS had the helmsman take the *Sandshark* out halfway between the *Carib Princess* and the oil rig again. Now that he had his rules of engagement sorted out, he was anxious to go to work if the opportunity presented itself. He didn't need his radar operator to alert him to the choppers this time. He was close enough to the hijacked cruise ship to clearly see through the scope as the terrorists boarded the helicopters and got ready to take off.

"Guns," Rawlings ordered as the rotors on the terrorists' aircraft started to turn over, "prepare to engage two enemy rotary wing targets."

"Prepare to engage, aye," the weapons officers replied. "Weapons hot."

"They're lifting off now," Rawlings said. "Fire when you have the targets."

"Aye, Sir."

"Target One acquired," the weapons officer said. "Fox One."

The sub shuddered as the Sea Sparrow missile left its launch tube.

"Target Two locked on and Fox Two."

Again the rumble of a launch sounded.

With the range as short as it was, there was hardly any time lag before the missiles impacted.

"I have Splash One," the weapons officer announced. "and Splash Two."

Rawlings watched through the periscope as the flaming wreckage of the two Mi-8s crashed into the sea. "Good shooting, Guns."

"Thank you, Sir."

NGUYEN CAO NGUYEN was alone on the bridge of the *Carib Princess* when the helicopters were launched. As he had done before, after issuing his orders, Diego Garcia had gone back to his cabin. The Vietnamese was watching their flight through his binoculars and was stunned to see an explosion on the first helicopter blossom in midair.

Something had shot it down!

He hadn't seen any high-flying jets, but he also hadn't been specifically looking for them, either. He was reaching for the intercom to Garcia's cabin when the second aircraft exploded, as well.

One of the bridge crew said that he thought he had

seen a launch plume rising from the sea, but that couldn't be. The radar didn't show anything anywhere near them on the sea. The missile had to have come from some kind of high-flying aircraft they couldn't spot.

The choppers had launched into the wind and the explosions were so close that the smell of burning jet fuel hit him. The odor also carried a stench of charred flesh he remembered well from his homeland.

The sound of the explosions brought Garcia back onto the bridge. He stood silent for a long moment, staring at the fuel burning on the wave tops.

"Bring a hundred of the passengers up on deck," the Cuban suddenly snapped. "Half of them men and half women, and tie them to the railings facing outward. I want the Yankees to understand that any further moves they make against us will result in their deaths."

"But what are we going to do now?" Nguyen asked.

"We will continue on," Garcia said. "They have not defeated us yet and they will not."

"But where do you want me to go?" Nguyen asked. "Without the helicopters, we can't attack the oil platforms."

"We have one more weapon in our arsenal—" the Cuban's eyes glittered "—and it will more than make up for the platforms we did not get a chance to destroy. In fact, this weapon will make up for everything the Yankees have done to the Mother Country for the last fifty years."

Nguyen frowned. The Matador plan had been carefully thought out to bring enough pressure on the American economy that it would collapse of its own weight. The aftermath of the Islamic attacks on 9/11 had shown the world just how fragile the Yankees really were. The expensive government bailouts of failing industries, the unprecedented jobless rates and business bankruptcies had shown the world their real weakness.

The vaunted strength of the American people depended solely on their buying and selling goods that no one really needed to have. For them to maintain their position in the world market, they had to constantly keep expanding their economy by producing more and more every year. Anything that could halt that process would bring a collapse they might never recover from. Cutting oil supplies had been seen as the best way to start.

"Set a course for Miami," Garcia said. "And once we are on the way, come into my Operations Room and I will tell you how I will deliver the crushing blow."

Nguyen sorely missed Elena Martinez and Juan Gomez right now. Garcia was obviously insane, and he didn't think he could take out the Cuban by himself. In fact, he had no choice but to do as he had been ordered.

WHEN RICHARD SPELLMAN heard the terrorists come out onto the rear deck to board their choppers, he had gone down to the utilities deck to keep out of the way. He had left his hiding place and was moving through a dimly lit section when he heard a slight noise.

"Don't move," a low voice behind him said in English, "and slowly put your hands out where I can see them and then turn around."

Spellman did as he was told and was surprised to see one of the men who had rescued him and Mary that first night in Cancun. "What are you doing here?" he asked.

"I was just about to ask you the same thing," Bolan said. "You didn't do what we told you back in Cancun, did you?"

"We tried." Spellman shrugged. "But we didn't pick a good place to hide and ended up in a little beach shack when the storm hit. Then, when the winds calmed down a little, we tried to find a better place to hide."

"How did you end up back on board?"

Spellman shook his head. "We were in the downtown area looking for another place to hide when we were spotted by a patrol and they grabbed us. They put me in a closet and took Mary away. I was able to get away later and I've been looking for her."

"Have you found where they're holding her?"

"Not yet." Spellman sounded grim. "The passengers are being held on two of the decks, and I can't get past the guards."

"How many terrorists are on board?"

"I don't really know," Spellman said, "but I'd say there's at least fifty or sixty."

That was close to Bolan's own estimate.

"I take it that you've made yourself acquainted with the ship?"

"More or less." Spellman nodded.

"Before I get started, then," Bolan said, "how about giving me a tour?"

Spellman didn't quite see himself as the commando type, but was pleased that this walking arsenal was trusting him this much. "Sure."

"First," Bolan said, "do you know how to shoot?"

"I've done a little target practice with hunting rifles and pistols," he said. "But that's about it. I don't consider myself a gun expert."

The SEAL hadn't had a pistol, and Bolan wasn't going to give up one of his own, so he unslung his extra silenced H&K. "Think you can use this?"

"It's full automatic, right?"

"Yeah," Bolan said, "but I can set it on burst mode for you. Every time you pull the trigger, it'll fire just three rounds instead of full-auto. It's easier to control that way."

Being a fan of action-adventure movies, Spellman recognized the thick sleeve on the subgun's barrel. "It's silenced, right?"

"That's right. It's not completely silent, but it'll make very little noise.

"And you'll need this," Bolan added as he shrugged out of the SEAL's magazine carrier. "Do you know how to change a magazine?"

"I've seen it done in the movies."

In spite of the situation, Bolan repressed a smile. At least the guy had some idea of what needed doing. He handed the subgun over. "Try it."

Spellman checked to see that the H&K was on safe before punching the magazine release. Once it was out, he popped it back in.

"Okay," Bolan said. "Let's put that thing on 3-round-burst mode and let's get started. I have a deck plan of this tub, but it's from back when it was built and I'm finding that things have been changed. I need you to take me to every place you've been."

CHAPTER NINETEEN

Now that the terrorists' choppers had been destroyed, Captain Rawlings ordered his sub to a greater depth to try to lessen the effect of the waves as they continued to track the *Carib Princess*. He was, however, still trailing an antenna on the surface to keep in communication. In military terms, the situation was still fluid, which was putting it mildly. As far as he was concerned, it was more like quicksilver: try to put your finger on it and it would slip away. He still was following the cruise ship, but knowing where the target was wasn't a tactical solution. You also had to know how to deal with it.

Unknown to Hal Brognola, the sub skipper was also in periodic contact with his headquarters in Washington, seeking guidance. It wasn't that he didn't really trust his unorthodox guest or disbelieved his credentials, but his adult life had been spent following orders that came down from the top of the military structure. But for the first time in his long career as a naval officer, he wasn't getting anything from his chain of command. As far as CinClant was concerned, he and his attack boat were on extended detached duty to the White House. Not since World War II had an individual naval vessel been under the direct guidance of the President of the United States, but those were his orders.

He hadn't been told, though, exactly what those orders meant or how he was supposed to carry them out. Since Hal Brognola was the only man on board talking to the President, he and his nuclear submarine were effectively being commanded by a civilian.

"Just got a hot flash from the NRO," Brognola said as he walked into the control room waving a handful of hard copy. "Their satellites are showing that Garcia has put some of the passengers on deck as shields."

"That bastard," Rawlings growled. As a professional naval officer, he was ready to go head-to-head with the armed enemies of his nation, to kill them in a military manner and to take his chances on being killed in return. He wouldn't, however, purposefully target civilians as terrorists routinely did. To him that was what made him a warrior and terrorists the scum of the earth.

"It's typical for those assholes," Brognola replied. "But, thankfully, he's a little too late. Had he brought them out on deck earlier, I don't think I'd have gotten permission to let you splash those choppers."

"So," Rawlings asked, "does that mean that there's going to be a change in our orders?"

"Sorry. We're just to continue following her. I'm to check in with the President's National Security Adviser every half hour, but I don't anticipate any real change soon."

IN HIS OPERATIONS ROOM, once the *Princess*'s captain's cabin, Diego Garcia went over his next move as he waited for Nguyen to join him.

As would any great commander, when he'd proposed this operation to his president, he'd had more than just a Plan B ready to back up his main effort in case it failed. He also had a Plan C ready to go and it was more than a just a secondary fallback position. It had been designed to be the grand finale and the master stroke of the entire Matador operation. It had also been kept a secret from the rest of the Matador leadership. Not even Elena Martinez had known about it.

Nor, sadly, did his president.

Garcia had never openly criticized his president— the man was a towering god of the revolution and the savior of his people. But, unfortunately, he was also a mortal, an aging mortal.

There had once been a time when the man would have welcomed a plan like the one Garcia had devised as his coup de grâce, welcomed it and backed it enthusiastically, but that day was long in the past. Being fully aware of that, Garcia hadn't even proposed his Plan C to his leader. Instead, he had presented the Matador plan for the Mexican revolution and the contamination of the oil wells, and the Cuban leader had willingly signed off on those operations.

The effects of the radioactively contaminated offshore oil fields would have delivered a crushing blow to the capitalistic Yankee economy since they were so petroleum dependent. But he also knew how clever those devils were. Cutting America's oil supplies would merely have spurred its government to faster development of alternative fuel sources. The science needed to make oil from biomass had been known since the Germans had invented it during World War II. It wasn't widely used because it was too expensive.

His strike would have made natural oil so expensive that the Capitalists could then make a profit by manufacturing oil, and they would have had oil production plants in operation as soon as they could be built. And, within a couple of years, they would have recovered fully from the oil shortage and would be back to spreading their fast-food culture all over the world again.

He could have caused a temporary dip in the march of Yankee globalism by hitting the oil fields. But destroying Miami would have an even greater effect than the attacks on New York City had produced. For one thing, Miami was a central point of the Yankee economic domination of Latin America. More goods moved in and out of the port than from any other city in the region. If it was shut down, American economic domination of the Southern Hemisphere would be seriously crippled.

On top of that, Miami was the home of the anti-revolutionary Cuban terrorist cartels that had relentlessly waged an almost fifty-year-long war against the socialist motherland. It was true that the Yankee government had encouraged their activities and in many circumstances had even armed and paid for their terrorist operations. But were it not for those traitors who had fled the motherland, life for the Cuban people wouldn't have been as difficult as it had been for these past decades.

Perhaps the most important factor in his choosing his ultimate target was that Miami was where his mother had been degraded and humiliated as a young woman merely for being Cuban. Her family had immigrated to Florida in the days of the thug Bastista when she had been just a young girl, and her experience growing up in America hadn't been a good one. Even though she had eventually learned to speak very good English, her teachers had treated her as if she had been mentally retarded. Her Anglo classmates had treated her worse, though.

He had been going through his mother's file in the DGI before retiring it to the archives when he learned that he had been born a year earlier than he had thought, and seven months before she had married the man he had always known as his father. In Castro's Cuba, being born a bastard didn't carry the disgrace that it did in other, reactionary, Latin countries. Nonetheless, he was a Latino and felt the shame, but not for himself alone. He had felt it for his mother, because she had been forced to hide it from him.

Making sure that the Anglo Cubans of Miami would never again abuse real Cubans or harbor traitors would be the crowning achievement of his operation. The lesson he would teach would ensure that arrogant Yankees would never again look down upon any Latino as being less than human. His were a proud people with a long history of greatness. And if given a chance through socialism, they would once again become a major force in the world.

After all, it was the Spanish who had discovered the New World and had opened it up to civilization and development. The Anglos, all of them, had only come as pirates and looters of the thriving old Hispanic empire. That they had triumphed over the

Spanish was a cruel twist of fate, but history didn't stand still. He was seeing to that.

More than just punishing Miami, though, his last effort would strike fear into the hearts and minds of the Yankees. They would be fittingly punished as no people had been punished since God had destroyed Sodom and Gomorrah.

NGUYEN CAO NGUYEN didn't think of himself as being a stupid man. There was no way that a stupid man could have overcome what he had to become what he was. Being a double agent spying on one Marxist government for yet another wasn't for the dull-witted, nor for the faint of heart. But for all of his well-practiced intelligence, he had somehow completely overlooked one critical part of the Matador plan. Admittedly, it was a minor point, which was easy to overlook against the backdrop of regional revolution leading to a major change in the power politics of Latin America. It was, however, a telling minor point.

What was Diego Garcia ultimately planning to do with the hostages on the *Carib Princess*?

It was only now that the plan to contaminate the oil fields had been foiled that he had given more than a passing thought to the seven hundred odd hostages on the ship, American and others. It was obvious that sailing to Miami had to be somehow tied to them, but he couldn't imagine how.

Those people were foremost on his mind when he entered Garcia's command post. "What are we going to do now, Comrade?" he asked. "Without the helicopters, we cannot proceed as we had planned."

The Cuban allowed a rare smile to cross his face. "Ah, but we can, Comrade. The fight is not over."

"The fight is never over, Comrade," Nguyen replied, automatically parroting the old Party slogan he had learned as a child. "But we have run out of options and have to find a way to escape and continue the fight somewhere else."

"Options, Comrade?" Garcia leaned forward, his voice rising. "Options? We still have an option for those who are brave and devoted to the cause. And this is an option that will strike a harder blow to the Yankee Imperialists than our other plans would have done."

Nguyen frowned. He knew of no other plan to attack the United States and, as the number two man in the Matador operation, if there were such a plan, he should know about it. If Garcia had been hatching plots on his own, there was bound to be trouble.

"But I don't understand, Comrade."

"I am not surprised," the Cuban replied. "No one understands the need to bring the Yankees to their knees as much as I do. Since I was a young boy, every waking moment of my life has been dedicated to their ultimate destruction. You are an Asian, Comrade, and your people have also suffered the predations of the Yankees, but not as my people have. The debt they owe us is beyond payment."

Nguyen doubted that the Cuban people had suffered from the Americans as much as the Vietnamese people had over the course of the long war in Southeast Asia. But this wasn't the time or the place to get into an argument about whose cause was more just and whose people had suffered the most. His earlier belief that the Cuban wasn't sane was proving to be true. The man was stark raving mad and that made him dangerous.

"What is this plan, Comrade Colonel?"

Garcia smiled. "When we loaded the nuclear power plant waste on board, I had a shipment of another special material loaded, as well, and several rockets I can use to deliver it."

"But I don't understand." Nguyen frowned. "What special material?"

"Radioactive cobalt."

Nguyen was stunned. He was no scientist by any means, but even he knew that cobalt was a dangerous material.

"The cobalt has been ground into submicron-size particles," Garcia explained. "Tests with similar molecular weight, but nonradioactive material of the same grain size showed that it will be picked up by the offshore winds and dispersed inland for miles. It will be a thousand years or more before southern Florida will be anything other than a dead wasteland. In fact, the effect on the city will be far more destructive and longer lasting than even a fifty-megaton nuclear weapon would be if it detonated in the harbor."

Nguyen was shocked speechless. A nuclear terrorist attack against an American city was unthinkable! Not even the strongest hard-liners in Beijing were willing to even consider such a move. The retirement of a large part of the Yankee's nuclear arsenal since the demise of the Soviet Union had lessened their retaliatory strength, but they were still so strong that no one wanted to play the nuke card against them.

"I see that I have your attention, Comrade," the Cuban said.

"But you are inviting a nuclear strike against at least Cuba, if not China, as well."

Garcia smiled. "I am confident that they would not retaliate in that manner unless I were to detonate a regular nuclear device. Which, of course—" he shrugged "—I am not planning to do. And, even if I had such a device, I wouldn't use it."

"But I don't understand."

"Everyone fears the destructive effects of nuclear weapons," Garcia continued, "and the hysteria has always been amusing to me. They have all forgotten that the first two nuclear weapon targets, Hiroshima and Nagasaki, were not eradicated by the attacks. The buildings were destroyed as well as much of the population, yes. But the survivors were not forced to abandon their cities and flee forever. In fact, the Japanese have continued to live in those two cities uninterrupted until today."

Nguyen was no military historian, but he recognized the truth of that statement. The threat of American nuclear domination had hung over the heads of the world for so long that people had forgotten the reality of those history-making events. Nonetheless, Garcia's plan was horrifying.

"What I am planning to do to Miami will leave the buildings intact for the entire world to see. In fact, there will be no signs of what had occurred at all except that all higher life in the affected area will have ceased to exist."

The Cuban shrugged. "Most of the plants and trees will continue to live as will much insect life. But all higher animals—mammals, birds and fish—will have died along with the Yankees, and no one will be able to live there for a thousand years."

Garcia sneered. "The Yankees are pathetically involved in an endless debate about what kind of monument they think should be built in New York to memorialize the attack on the World Trade Center towers. They will never need to do that for what I am going to do. The memorial for my attack on Miami will be Miami itself."

AFTER RICHARD SPELLMAN conducted a slow, methodical hour-and-a-half tour of the lower decks of the *Carib Princess* for his companion, Bolan had tossed his faxed deck plan. He had learned that even the stairwells had been changed over the years.

"That's all of it I know about," Spellman said when they were back in their hiding place. "I haven't been unable to get into the upper decks much."

"You've done well," Bolan said.

"What are we going to do now?" he asked.

Bolan smiled thinly. "We're going to start cleaning this place up one piece of dirt at a time."

That sounded like a real good idea on paper, and it was Bolan's usual response to this kind of situation. But the circumstances he was dealing with this time were going to require some fancy footwork. For starters, being on shipboard severely limited his freedom of movement. He had told Spellman that he was going on a rat hunt, but more to the point, he and the doctor were more like the rats in a trap. Also, with the hostages onboard he couldn't go into a full-bore slash-and-burn operation.

In addition, although he had armed Spellman, he knew that the man had zero experience with what was coming. The fact that the doctor had been able to hide out for so long was a good indicator of his worth, but he knew not to put too much into that. The man was a medical researcher, not a dedicated outdoors type, and he had no military training.

"To do that, though," Bolan said, "we're going to have to keep ourselves hidden as long as we can. As soon as they figure out that we're on board, we won't be able to help anyone."

Spellman knew the numbers they were facing and could only agree. He was beginning to think that the arrival of the commando was more of a two-edged sword than a solution. But he hadn't been able to do anything on his own and maybe at least he'd be able to get some payback now before he was hunted down and killed.

"You lead off," he said, meeting Bolan's eyes, "and just tell me what you want me to do."

THE SUBMARINE continued to follow the *Carib Princess* as she headed in a northerly direction, but the tension level had lessened significantly since the splashing of the choppers. The waning of the hurricane had also added to the sense of normalcy in the sub's control-room crew. Hal Brognola had taken up residence in the control room whenever the captain was at the com, leaving only to visit the communications suite periodically.

"It looks like he's making for Miami," Brognola announced when he returned from his half-hourly check in with Stony Man Farm.

"That's confirms what we're getting from his sonar plot," Rawlings replied.

The sub crew didn't need to use radar to tell them where their target vessel was heading. The *Sandshark* was an underwater hunter, and her sonar returns worked just as well and had a greater range than surface radar.

"I don't like it," Brognola growled. "He sure as hell isn't just going to let those people off the ship as a gesture of goodwill or some feel-good horseshit like that. His only chance now is to try to set up some kind of exchange, and I don't think that's going to fly. The President isn't going to cave in to European concerns and let those assholes off the hook no matter what."

Hal Brognola was probably the nation's most experienced counterterrorist operations officer. The list of incidents he had overseen would be the size of a small phone book, but he was more of a coordinator and didn't consider himself a skilled tactical analyst. For that kind of information, he used the sharply honed minds of people like Striker.

At the present time, though, Striker was out of communication. That left him dependent on the more conventional thinking of the State Department and the Oval Office, which didn't give him much confidence.

It took a certain kind of man to be a good skipper for a nuke attack boat. Like a hunting cat, Doug Rawlings always had to work alone and his sole thought was to kill. No matter what the odds, no matter what the defenses, he had to get in close enough to his target to loose his weapons and kill. With that mind-set, he was predisposed to look for the counterattack options of every man he went up against.

This wasn't the usual tactical situation Rawlings was accustomed to working with, but the man who had taken over the *Carib Princess* was as cunning an enemy as he had ever faced. And if he were in the Cuban's position, he'd be planning yet another attack.

"What if he has an actual hot weapon on board?" he asked Brognola.

The big Fed frowned. "A hot weapon?"

"Along with the nuclear waste we know he had, maybe he has some kind of nuclear device, as well," Rawlings said.

"Jesus!"

"That's the one threat," Rawlings continued, "that we've never had a defense against—a nuke detonating in a harbor. If I was in his situation, that's what I'd do, and Miami harbor is a real good place to do it."

CHAPTER TWENTY

Once the destination of the *Carib Princess* had been clearly established, the *Sandshark* came to the surface and was running in plain sight a thousand yards behind the hostage-laden cruise ship. Hal Brognola had been invited to join the captain in the small bridge in the sail to watch the continuing pursuit. Rarely was a nuke boat commed from the sail bridge for longer than an entry or exit from a port, but nothing about this mission was normal, so running on the surface made a weird kind of sense.

Watching through his borrowed high-powered field glasses, Brognola could see the hostages spotted along the ship's railing and the dozen or so gunmen who kept them there. Beyond that, no other activities could be observed. He lowered the glasses and rubbed his eyes.

"Do you think your man's still alive?" Rawlings asked him.

Brognola paused before answering. "I do. He's still alive, and you can take that to the bank. Not only is he alive, he's pissed off, and doing everything one man alone can do to try to get that thing turned around."

"I'll give you that he's good," Rawlings said. "Chief Duffy can't stop talking about him, and I know I sure as hell wouldn't want to run into him in a dark alley. But he's still only one guy, you know. Do you really think that he can take on those people all by himself and bring that situation under any kind of control?"

"I do." Brognola nodded. "I've known him for a long time and he's a truly remarkable man. Every time something goes wrong and I've given him up for dead, he's come back still breathing and ready to go. He's not immortal, God only knows. But I don't think that this is the time that I'm finally going have to bury him."

"I sure hope not." Rawlings smiled. "That man's got more balls than a ten-lane bowling alley and he deserves to pull this one off."

"That he does." Brognola chuckled as he brought the field glasses back up to his eyes.

He hadn't overstated the confidence he had in the man he called Striker, but rarely had Bolan put himself in a situation such as this. He was a trapped like a rat in a coffee can, and once the Cubans discovered that he had joined them, the game would be over.

Though he knew the reality of what Striker was facing, he still had hope.

AFTER RUNNING Richard Spellman through a couple more weapons and tactics drills, Bolan decided that it was time to take their act on the road. He was going to start slow, though, to see how many of these people he could eliminate silently. This was no time for a Banzai exhibition with both hands blazing fire. Once things got too noisy the best weapon in his arsenal—surprise—would be lost and so would his chances. Ninjalike stealth was his only option.

The Executioner's first victim literally walked into them, or almost. The man came down a darkened passageway completely unconcerned about what might be hiding in the shadows. In other circumstances he could be excused for his inattentiveness. The terrorists had absolutely no idea that they weren't alone on their purloined ship, but Bolan wasn't cutting anyone any slack today.

He and Spellman had come up to the third deck and were moving toward the stern when they heard the man's footsteps and ducked into an alcove. Bolan pushed Spellman behind him, drew his Tanto fighting knife and put his finger to his lips. The Executioner pressed against the bulkhead and his black combat clothing made him almost invisible in the dim light. But death was almost always invisible.

When the unsuspecting terrorist walked past his hiding place, Bolan stepped out behind him and took him down.

His knee went into the small of the man's back, his left hand clamping around the man's mouth at the same instant, and he pulled him backwards. The knife slid into his lower back and twisted, ruining his right kidney. The shock of the assault and the massive blood loss that ensued quickly ended the terrorist's life.

Bolan caught the man's slumping body under the arms and dragged him into the alcove.

Spellman wasn't a cutter, but he remembered all of the anatomy he had hammered into his head to pass the required examinations. However, he had never cut into a live body. And beyond the occasional household mishap involving a sharp kitchen implement, he hadn't had much to do with blood. That had just changed big-time.

Bolan led Spellman down the passageway toward the galley. As their recon had shown, the galley and the engine room were the only two places still manned by members of the original crew. And to keep them on the job, a Cuban with a gun was keeping an eye on them.

When they had passed the gallery on the recon, the guard had been lounging in the coffee-break room right off of the main galley. The cooks were so cowed by what they had been put through that the Cuban had little to do. That was about to change.

Down on the galley deck, Bolan found a different terrorist on guard duty. This was an older guy, but no smarter. He, too, was sitting in the break room, his AK lying against the wall while he sucked down a cup of black coffee and smoked a thick Havana cigar as he cruised through an American skin mag.

Walking into the break room and knifing the guy probably wasn't going to work well this time, so Bolan freed the Beretta 93-R from his shoulder leather. He flicked the fire selector switch to single shot, then stepped through the open door. The Cuban looked up just in time to get a subsonic 9 mm round right through his left eye.

The guard fell face-first onto his skin magazine, leaking blood onto the blond centerfold.

To keep from leaving too much of a mess behind, Bolan and Spellman eased the body into a locker and cleaned up the table. The skin mag went into the locker with its late owner.

Once the place was tided up, the pair left. Bolan decided to go down to the engine room to try his luck there.

DIEGO GARCIA, on the bridge in personal command of the SS *Carib Princess* as they sailed into Miami harbor, smiled thinly when he saw that the harbor had been evacuated in honor of his arrival. On a normal day the port would have been brimmingly full of merchant and cruise ships of all descriptions, as well as swarms of smaller working craft and pleasure boats. This day, though, except for a couple of small military and police patrol craft, he had the harbor all to himself.

He felt as if he were commanding the Yankee battleship *Missouri* when it had sailed into Tokyo Bay at the end of World War II. But he was bringing war to this country, not putting an end to it.

Though the harbor and waterways were clear, the sky overhead wasn't. It was apparent that civilian air traffic had been banned, so all those helicopters and fixed-wing aircraft had to be military and police. The barrage of chatter on the aviation and marine frequencies the *Princess*'s radioman was picking up was all military and police. Garcia also knew that federal SWAT teams, Army counterterrorist commandos and every kind of local police were waiting just out of sight ready to pounce at the first sign of weakness or lack of vigilance he showed. But that wasn't going to happen.

These units had run hundreds of hours of simulated hostage war games and thought that they were ready for anything. In the exercises they had run, though, the "terrorists" had always been portrayed as common criminals who were hoping to buy their miserable lives with those of their captives.

He laughed when he thought of the incredible stupidity of both the cops and the crooks involved in those types of scenarios. The end was always the same. Sometimes a few hostages were killed, and sometimes the criminals were shot instead. But rarely did taking hostages ever result in the captors going free. That's why the police always spent so much time in "negotiations" with the hostage-takers. And that's what would happen this time. Both Florida and federal authorities would spend endless hours, even days, trying to talk him out of doing whatever he was going to do.

Garcia didn't mind at all, though. The longer the Yankees spent with their stupid little games designed to confuse the minds of even more stupid common criminals, the better. He was an avenger, not a criminal. If there were any criminals in this scenario, it was those in power in the United States who had inflicted so much damage on the Cuban people for so many years. Unlike the victims in common criminal acts, he didn't see his "hostages" as being guiltless of the crimes of the United States. They'd had a duty to vote leaders into office who wouldn't act as criminals against the lesser people of the world, and they hadn't done so.

When he got tired of playing stupid games with these people, he would take his long overdue vengeance.

A jagged shaft of pure pain lanced through his head right behind his eyes and he fumbled at the lid of the bottle in his pocket. Finally getting it open, he downed two pills, swallowing them dry. He was running low on his medication again, but this time he wouldn't need a refill.

As soon as he could focus again, he saw a police helicopter make a high-speed pass across his bow. The doors were open and he could see marksmen with high-powered rifles laid across their laps.

"Get some of the children up on deck," he ordered one of his men on the bridge. "Leave them up there long enough for the Yankees to see them and then take them down below again."

The man looked at him strangely. "Yes, Comrade Colonel."

"Do it!" the Cuban snapped as he placed the butt of his hand on the pistol holstered at his waist.

The man turned and left.

"Where do you want us to stop, Comrade Colonel?" the helmsman asked.

Garcia looked around the expanse of water. "Anywhere around here, but stay in midchannel."

"All engines stop," the helmsmen called down to the engine room.

With her engines at stop, the ship slowly came to a halt in the middle of the harbor.

"Put the anchors down, Comrade," Garcia ordered.

"Aye, Comrade."

CAPTAIN RAWLINGS kept the *Sandshark* in position behind the *Carib Princess* as she entered the Miami harbor. When he saw the vessel slow in midchannel, he keyed his intercom. "Full stop," he ordered. "Maintain steerage."

"Full stop, aye." The loud speaker repeated the command. "Maintaining steerage."

Brognola looked up to see that the *Carib Princess* was slowing in the middle of the harbor. "What do you think he's going to do now?" he asked.

"Well—" Rawlings took his field glasses from his eyes "—he's dropping anchor, so it looks like he's going to park there for a while. As to what he's going to do while he's there, I'll be damned if I know. I'm sure you know more about that than I do, but I still think a nuke's a viable option considering the target."

Brognola didn't remind the captain that neither Stony Man Farm nor the NRO had detected neutrino emissions from the *Carib Princess* or the vicinity. And no neutrinos meant no nuclear weapons. That fact, if it was in fact a fact, hadn't changed Rawlings's mind one iota. The skipper was a warrior to the bone and to be a warrior meant to always be on the lookout for a way to attack his enemies. He was convinced that Garcia hadn't come to Miami to surrender.

Even though he had no proof, Brognola was inclined to agree with Rawlings. He was also convinced that they hadn't seen the last of the atrocities committed by the Cuban. And, speaking of, the time had come for him to get off this tub and to get his feet on dry land and in contact with the Farm.

"Since everyone now knows where that bastard is going to be for a while," Brognola said, "I think it's time that I left and went back to work the way I usually do it."

"I can't say I'll be sorry to see you go." Rawlings laughed. "But now maybe I'll be able to get back to doing what I do best. Chasing around the oceans of the world looking for someone to shoot at."

Brognola chuckled. "Good luck with that, all the action seems to be here today."

HAL BROGNOLA had the Navy chopper put him down on the landing pad at the emergency command center that had been set up in the Miami Dolphins' football stadium. His biometric ID Justice Department card got him through the layers of security into the tent containing the communications center. Flashing the card again, he got a direct secure line to the President and made his report.

After leaving his name and ID number with the

Justice Department desk in the command center, he walked outside the tent into the sun. After having been in a hurricane and a submarine for too many days, he was glad to feel the warmth and light soak into his skin.

The entire stadium was boiling with humanity, official and freelance, and there was no shortage of units ready to do battle. Starting at the lowest level, there were Miami Police SWAT teams and, at the very top, Delta Force Hostage Rescue Teams. In between, every police unit in the southern half of the nation was represented with every federal agency from the Red Cross to FEMA.

And, of course, the American media was smelling blood and was out in full force.

The only human Brognola wanted to see was someone he could talk to, but that was highly unlikely in this mob. He also wanted a cleaning team on hand in case things went very bad for Striker. Going back into the tent, he flashed his card to bully a cell phone away from some lower-ranking Fed and walked outside to make his second call.

"I'm on an unsecured line," he said when the other end picked up. "I'm at the Miami command center, and I need cleanup for Striker. Send me Buck, a dozen of his people and a full commo setup for me."

Walking back into the tent, he returned the phone.

Now if something horrific did happen, he could get Bolan out dead or alive.

Above the adrenaline and sweat of overanxious humanity, he could smell coffee on the breeze. He followed his nose to the nearby Red Cross tent and poured himself a cup. He took a tentative sip and wished he'd passed on it. But his need for caffeine overruled his protesting taste buds and he choked it down. It was so weak, though, that he had to go for a refill to bring his blood values up to operating levels. As bad as it was, after finishing the second cup, he was charged up and ready to do whatever he could.

Exactly what that was going to be, though, remained to be seen.

CHAPTER TWENTY-ONE

Bolan had only been able to work his way through four more solitary terrorists before he'd noticed that the background noises of the *Carib Princess* were lessening as if the ship were slowing. On a vessel as large as a cruise ship, it was difficult to determine actual speed unless one had a visual frame of reference to judge by. Being deep inside the hull as they were, he needed to get to a porthole to see what was happening. That meant going up to one of the higher decks, thus increasing their risk of being spotted.

"Something's going on," he told Spellman. "We need to go up a deck or two to find a porthole."

"That's okay by me."

Spellman was ready for anything that would give him a break from the heart-pounding stalking of the Cubans. He had never been a hunter and had known nothing of stalking prey before this, to say nothing of stalking humans. Each time they spotted a victim he hung back as rear guard while the commando moved in on him and took him out. He wasn't making the attacks himself, but it was nerve-racking nonetheless.

Using the routes they'd reconned, the men made their way up to the C Deck and to a storage room off the movie theater. As with all of the doors on board, it was unlocked. Spellman kept watch by the door, his finger on the trigger of his borrowed MP-5 SD while Bolan slipped inside for a look.

"We're pulling into Miami harbor," he announced. "I recognize the city's skyline."

Just then they both heard the muted vibrations of the ship's engine die down. "And I'd say that he's coming to a stop."

The water served as a good brake and the *Carib Princess* finally slowed to a stop.

"Okay," Bolan said. "We've stopped a couple of hundred yards from the docks."

"Do you think he came here so he can release the hostages?" Spellman asked expectantly. If that happened, he and Mary could get out of this nightmare alive and go on to be the people they wanted to be together.

Bolan turned back from the porthole, his face set.

"Not a chance, I'm afraid, Dick," he said. "That

guy's a terrorist, and the last thing in the world I expect him to do is turn anyone loose and hold his hands out for the cuffs. Men like him have a track record of not letting their hostages go until they have what they want."

Spellman frowned. Even with the events since 9/11 he hadn't paid much attention to the lame excuses given as the motivations for terrorist attacks, so none of this entire incident made any sense to him. This latest move, though, was totally baffling. The Cuban had been foiled at every turn, so what more could he have in mind?

"But what could he want now?"

"From what he's tried to do so far," Bolan speculated, "I'd say that he wants nothing less than for the United States of America to cease to exist. Barring that, I think he wants to hurt us like the Arabs did on 9/11."

"But how?"

Bolan shook his head. "That's what's bothering me. Considering the situation, there are only a few options he can use, and none of them is very good."

"I don't understand."

"These guys are into making grandiose statements," Bolan explained. "They use grand gestures to make their point, no matter how illogical and twisted they may be, and most of these gestures involve killing people. Garcia already has all of the people on board the ship to expend, and now he has a cityful right in front of him to add to his body count. He's got something in mind, and we've got to try to find out what it is."

"So what do we do different, then?"

"We get even more cautious, because now that they've stopped, they're likely to move around even more."

Spellman didn't know how he could be more cautious than they had been, but if the commando said that they could, he'd at least try his best.

BUCK GREENE, the Stony Man Farm security chief, arrived at the Miami emergency command center with a contingent of twenty-four of his blacksuit commandos, a communication suite complete with com techs, tentage and supplies for the crew and Barbara Price, Brognola's SOG mission controller.

"Jesus!" Brognola growled when he saw his people empty out of the convoy of trucks Greene had borrowed from the Florida National Guard to ferry them all from the Miami airport. "Who the hell's looking after the Farm?"

Price walked up on his blind side. "When I heard you were in so deep that you needed help," she said, "I went down to the Dew Drop Inn right outside of town, grabbed the first dozen guys I could find, gave them some guns, showed them our perimeter and told them to be on the look out for idiots asking dumb questions."

For a second Brognola almost wished that he had stayed safely on board the *Sandshark*. At least there he'd had a chance to escape the woman he couldn't run his SOG without.

When Price saw Brognola's hand reach into his pocket, she opened her shoulder bag and handed him a fistful of antacid tablet rolls. "I figured you'd be running a little low on these by now."

"Thanks. And thanks for coming."

"I wouldn't have missed it for the world."

"What's the cover?"

She smiled. "Everyone's carrying J.D. Protective Security Detachment paperwork so we'll blend in with the rest of these Feds."

"What the hell is the Protective Security Detachment?" he asked. "Did you make that up?"

"Actually, Aaron did. He felt that if the State Department could have their own commando units, Justice could, as well."

Brognola shook his head. He just knew that he was going to catch flak for that before this was over. "Did you at least clear coming down here with the Man?"

"I guess you could say that," she replied with the glimmer of a smile.

Brognola knew what her enigmatic smile meant. She had simply told the President of the United States that she was coming south with the rest of the Stony Man crew and that he could like it or lump it;

she didn't care. Price had never learned how to be politic, nor did she have the slightest desire to learn.

He almost envied her.

BUCK GREENE reverted to his roots to get Brognola's Stony Man command post in operation as soon as possible. Since he had been a U.S. Marine for years, it wasn't difficult for him to revert to type. Much of his ranting was unneeded because his blacksuits were all consummate professionals. Stony Man didn't often locate to the field, but when they did, they did it with the same practiced professionalism that marked everything they did.

Brognola was astounded at how quickly it had all come together. His communications were in action in less than an hour, before the tent was even erected. A collection of satellite disks and portable generators made it possible to operate without hooking up to the thick bundle of cables that snaked across the stadium.

"We have established secure commo with the White House," Barbara Price reported.

"Please tell the Chief of Staff that we're operational," he said, "but that we have nothing to report at this time."

"Done."

Greene walked up next to report, his old Colt M-1911 .45 openly riding in his shoulder rig. His blacksuits were in full combat kit and had a mix of

M-16s and H&K MP-5s slung over their shoulders as they worked. The Stony Man crew was ready to go to war at a moment's notice, all they needed was a go sign.

"We're all set up," Greene said. "You have anything for my guys do to right now?"

"Not yet," Brognola admitted. "But I want to have half of them standing by suited up at all times. Work up some kind of schedule so they can launch on a sixty-second notice."

"How are they going to be transported?"

"I borrowed a Black Hawk from the Army and it's due in five minutes."

"Where're the pilots from?"

"Spec Ops out of McDill."

Greene smiled slowly. "They should do."

Brognola went to the commo tent to tell the President that his clandestine strike force was ready to go to work.

NGUYEN CAO NGUYEN returned to the captain's cabin after a brief inspection of the human shields Garcia had ordered. He had no real concern for the lives of those people, but he had doubts about the effectiveness of the tactic. As he knew from experience, the Americans tended to get frantic when their citizens' lives were threatened. Since they were moored in enemy territory, as it were, he didn't need to have to deal with the unexpected.

"We're well protected, Comrade," he reported. "I doubt that the Yankees will dare attack us here. When do we make our next move?"

"Our next move?" Garcia leaned back in his chair and smiled broadly. "We don't have a 'next' move."

"Comrade, I don't understand."

The Cuban leaned forward. "As I said before, we have a final move and it will take place right here. Once it is accomplished, we will have the victory that was denied us because of the storm."

The Vietnamese knew full well that the hurricane wasn't the entire reason that the Matador plan had failed, but kept his tongue. His disappointment was no less than the Cuban's, but his goals were more than personal gratification. Much more.

"When do we make this attack?" Nguyen asked.

"When I see that the time is right. The longer we wait, the more people the Yankees will bring in to deal with me."

He laughed. "And the more that are here, the more that will die.

"Come with me, Comrade." Garcia got out of his chair. "It is time for you to see what I have prepared for the Yankees of Miami."

Nguyen was very curious about what the Cuban had brought on board to use for his final strike. Since the storm hadn't yet completely abated, his duties had kept him on the bridge and he hadn't been able to oversee the loading of the material that had been flown from the island.

Garcia walked down the passageway on the main deck and entered the main swimming pool complex. The last time the *Carib Princess* had gone through a rebuild, the pool had been sunk into the top deck to give the water frolickers full access to the tropical sun they had paid to enjoy. On those rare days when the weather didn't cooperate, such as during the hurricane season, there was a retractable roof that could be extended to cover the pool. After withdrawing from the last oil platform, Garcia had ordered the pool pumped dry and the roof extended to cover it before their arrival in Miami.

Since the roof was covering the pool, the floodlights had been turned on to illuminate it. A few Matador gunners were taking a break in one of the poolside cafés while another squad worked in the bottom of the pool.

Five metal frames that looked as though they were made of welded-up water pipes had been erected in a line from one end of the pool to the other. To Nguyen's eyes, they looked a lot like the improvised rocket launchers the People's Army of Vietnam had used as mobile artillery launchers.

"Here it is." The Cuban almost beamed as the first

of a long line of his "ultimate" weapons was brought out, carried by two men. It was a rocket, about five inches in diameter and three feet long. The warhead wasn't attached.

"These are standard 122 mm rockets from the Army's BM-21 rocket launchers," Garcia hurried to explain. "When they are fired against ground targets, they have a range of twelve miles, but I will fire them at a high angle over the city, so the warheads will burst high in the sky and will have the best effect."

Nguyen instantly recognized the rockets and was surprised, as they were nothing special at all. The 122 mms had been a standard artillery weapon of the People's Army of Vietnam, as well as their Vietcong allies. Simple to set up and fire, they had a greater range than a mortar and had worked well for hit-and-run attacks against Yankee basecamps.

But these were just the rocket-engine sections, the warheads hadn't yet been attached. If what the Cuban had said earlier was true, the absent warheads were the heart of his plan.

Another squad of fighters entered the pool bearing metal boxes they placed carefully beside the rocket motors on the bottom of the pool. At Garcia's command, one of the boxes was opened and a warhead taken out.

The warheads were about the length of the standard high-explosive warheads he remembered from his days as a young Vietcong helper. What was different was that these warheads appeared to have some kind of plastic sleeve fitted over the explosive case, which went from the base of the warhead all the way up to the fuse section, and was about four inches thick.

The sleeves carried no markings, but Nguyen knew that they had to contain the radioactive cobalt Garcia had bragged of having. He had heard these kinds of weapons being called "dirty bombs" and the "poor man's nuclear weapon" in the Yankee media. The high explosive would detonate, pulverize the plastic sleeves and spread the cobalt on the wind just as Garcia had predicted.

As a method of attacking the Yankees, it was crude, but it would be effective, and Nguyen had no problem with them being used. What he had a problem with was that the Cuban had yet to mention how he, or any of the other Matador operatives, were going to escape the devastation they would cause.

He had dedicated his life to the People's struggle to free the world from the clutches of Yankee Imperialism, but he wasn't a fanatic, like the Cuban. Should it come his time to die for his cause, he had no problem with that. But he had no intention of throwing his life away when he could do more for the struggle by staying alive.

"And I assume that we escape in the panic that follows the attack?"

Garcia's eyes glittered. "You might say that."

Nguyen decided to examine the survival gear on board the ship more closely and to start planning his own escape. He had no intention of going down with the mad Cuban.

BOLAN WAS RIGHT about there being more terrorists on the move now that the cruise ship had halted. In fact, they were trapped in their storage room by the foot traffic in the passageway as more hostages were moved onto the deck to reinforce the ring of human shields as Garcia had ordered.

Spellman was taking a turn at peering around the side of the porthole when he spotted a familiar figure. "Oh, God!" he pointed. "That's Mary!"

Bolan looked and saw the pleasant-looking woman who had been with Spellman in Cancun. She was standing at the railing looking outward.

"Can she swim?" he asked.

"I don't know," Spellman admitted. "We weren't together that long before the terrorists took over and…" He paused. "After that happened we kind of didn't have a chance to talk about anything but that."

Bolan understood completely. Since their relationship was a shipboard romance, it was understandable that he didn't know all that much about her. It was a relatively short swim to the docks, but the swimmer would need to do most of it under water to keep from getting shot.

"Just an idea."

When Spellman started for the porthole, Bolan took his arm. "Don't," he cautioned. "Even if you can get her attention, it's not going to do either of you any good right now."

Spellman slumped and pulled back. "We've got to do something to help those people."

"We will," Bolan promised.

BOLAN AND SPELLMAN were heading back down to D Deck when they heard a scuffle ahead of them in the dimly lit passageway. They raced to a corner, peered around it and spied a terrorist screaming in Spanish at a man against the wall as he slammed his rifle butt into him. The hostage slumped to the floor, and the terrorist lifted his AK to deliver a blow to the man's head.

A round from Bolan's silenced 93-R took the Cuban in the side of the head. The terrorist slumped to the deck, half covering the body of the passenger.

The American abruptly shoved the corpse off him with a snarled, "Asshole!"

"You okay?" Bolan asked as he helped the ex-hostage to his feet.

"I'm fine." The man wiped the blood from his mouth and forehead. "Who are you two guys, anyway?"

Bolan met his eyes squarely. "Let's just say that we got trapped in here and decided to see if there was anything we could do to get this situation changed around."

The man eyeballed Bolan's hardware and combat suit, not quite the sort of thing a man who just happened to get trapped on a hijacked ship would wear. But he wasn't going to complain about the deception. He was alive and this guy, whoever he was, had saved his life.

"Can you get us off of this ship?"

"Not right now," Bolan replied.

"If I'm not going to be leaving anytime soon," the man said as he pointed to the dead Cuban's AK-47, "can I have that? I know how to use it."

When Bolan hesitated, the man continued. "I was an Army doctor back when they still made sure that we knew how to defend ourselves and our patients."

Bolan handed the AK to him. "Do you remember where the safety is?"

"Sure do." The doctor pointed to the flat lever on the right side of the receiver. "All the way up for safe, down one for single fire, down two for rock and roll. Right?"

"That's it."

The doctor reached down, took the magazines from the Cuban's ammo pouches and stuffed them into his pants' pockets. "As the man said, 'Let's roll.'"

"Let's do it," Bolan said. "But I take point. Keep behind me and Dick, and don't shoot unless it really starts hitting the fan."

"I've got it," the doctor said.

CHAPTER TWENTY-TWO

Now that Bolan had two comrades-in-arms, moving around the passageways without being seen was going to be a bit more of a problem. His new recruit, though another medical type, looked as if he knew how to carry his own load, but his experience was limited and far in the past.

Bolan had an idea. "Can you swim?" he asked to the doctor.

"Like a freaking fish," he answered. "Why?"

"If I can create a diversion to draw the guard's attention, can you dive off the ship and swim under water long enough to get out of small-arms range?"

The doctor took a deep breath and shrugged. "I can sure as hell try."

"Let's go to the stern of the ship," Bolan said.

As Bolan had expected, only half a dozen terrorists guarded twenty or so hostages on the stern of the *Carib Princess*. Most of the guards had their AKs slung over their shoulders, and they looked extremely bored. That was going to change real quick, but first he had to brief his pickup team on the game plan.

"Okay," he told the doctor, "here's what we're going to do. My partner and I will clear the terrorists off the deck for you. When we've thinned them out, I'll give you the go. Run straight out, dive off the deck and start swimming. The guards along the sides will try to shoot at you, so stay under water as long as you can. Got it?"

The doctor nodded. "Let me get out of these shoes," he said.

After stripping down to his pants, he picked up his AK again. "Let's do it."

"You remember the contact name I gave you?"

"Hal Brognola, Department of Justice."

"Okay," Bolan said. "On my count." He flashed his fingers out. "One…two…three!"

Bolan's first silenced 9 mm round sang right past a hostage and drilled a guard in the side of the head. Changing his aim point before the Cuban even had time to fall to the deck, he fired again.

Spellman's H&K was thumbed down to 3-round burst as the commando had told him to do and he took careful aim at a terrorist standing well away from the passengers. Of the three rounds of the short burst, the first one took his target in the lower back, the second high in the chest and the third went over his head.

Spellman froze for a second as he watched the Cuban collapse to the deck. Before, he had been a spectator when he'd watched the commando's back. Now he'd proved that he, too, could do what had to be done. It was a strange feeling, but he liked it.

Even the designated swimmer managed to get off a couple of well-aimed single shots before Bolan slapped him on the butt and shouted, "Go!"

The doctor dropped his AK and sprinted for the railing at the stern. He barely slowed as he hit the rail, vaulted over it and twisted into a swan dive into the harbor.

As soon as he was over the side, Bolan and Spellman retreated back into the ship.

THE FLURRY of full autofire on deck sent Diego Garcia racing for the bridge. "What's going on out there!" he shouted.

Nguyen Cao Nguyen had a portable radio to his ear and held his hand up to silence his commander so he could hear.

"There's been some kind of revolt among the prisoners," he said at the end of the call. "Apparently one of them managed to get an AK and shoot his way free. After killing several of our men, he jumped off the ship."

Garcia glared. "Did he get to shore?"

"They do not know," Nguyen replied. "He was under fire, but they have not seen a body."

"Get more of my fighters up on deck," the Cuban said. "And tell them that they are to shoot to kill at the slightest provocation. I will not have incidents like that happening right now. My plan is working, and I will not have it disrupted for any reason."

"If the passengers are all killed," Nguyen carefully pointed out, "we will lose our shield and the Yankees will storm the ship."

"You are right, of course, Comrade. And, to keep that from happening, gather all of the women and children together in the main dining room and put them under guard."

Nguyen hesitated. Americans were sensitive enough about hostage taking without segregating the women and children from the men. That would drive them into a frenzy and make it even more difficult for him to escape when this was over. His only chance was to have most of the hostages still alive after the rockets were launched. It would take the Yankees a while to discover what was in the warheads, and he planned to use that confusion to cover his escape.

"May I ask what you plan to do with them after the attack?" he asked.

Garcia's eyes narrowed and his hand went to the

side of his head. "What do I plan to do with them? Is that what you want to know?" His hands waved in the air. "They are going to die along with the rest of the Yankees. I want all of these animals out there dead, and I'm not going to exempt the females so they can breed even more enemies of the people. The motherland has too many enemies as it is."

These was absolutely no doubt in Nguyen's mind now that Garcia was totally, completely irrational and a clear danger to everyone around him. Rather than stick around to see the rockets launched as he had originally intended to do so he could report their effectiveness to Beijing, he needed to get off the ship as soon he could.

"Of course, Comrade." He smiled. "That is the only fitting punishment for Yankee Imperialists."

NOW THAT THE Stony Man tent was fully rigged and the floor laid, Hal Brognola found himself hanging around the com center. The fact that they had the best coffeepot made it a prime location. Until he'd had his first cup of radio room coffee, he hadn't realized how much he really loathed the foul brew that Kurtzman made in the Farm's Computer Room where he usually filled his cup. When he got back, he was going to assign one of the com techs the responsibility for coffee service.

"There's been firing on the ship." One of the com

techs turned to Brognola. "After a firefight on the stern, someone dived overboard."

"Jumped, not fell?" Brognola asked.

"That's the report," the blacksuit replied. "The bad guys were firing into the water after him, but no word yet if he was able to swim free."

Brognola was certain that whoever it was who had tried to escape hadn't been Bolan. Striker didn't run when there was work still to be done. Exactly what that work was, however, remained unclear this time. Radio communications with the ship had been established, but the terrorists weren't talking beyond making the usual threats against the hostages. He always felt better about a hostage situation when the perps were talking. It didn't matter what kind of hysterical, irrational garbage they were spewing just as long as they were talking and not killing their captives.

"Let me know when he's recovered, dead or alive."

"Yes, sir," the com tech replied. "I'll put in a call to the medical units and the people down on the docks to give us an immediate call back."

"Do that."

Brognola walked back to the coffeepot for a refill. It was going to be a long wait.

AFTER THE SHOOT-OUT, Bolan and Spellman managed to get back to one of their hiding places without being spotted. Needless to say, the terrorists were swarming the open deck now, their casual attitude in the wind. Their AKs were in their hands, and several passengers took a butt in a kidney to hurry them along.

"It looks like they're taking the women back inside," Spellman reported, taking his turn at the porthole.

Bolan joined him and saw half a dozen women being herded inside by a pair of Cubans, the guards had their weapons on them. If the women were being taken away from the human shield wall, it could be a reaction to their little action that got the doctor off the ship. That changed the location of the pieces on the battle board, but it might work to their advantage as it might be taking the women out of the direct line of fire.

LEAVING THE SHIP'S bridge in charge of the helmsman, Nguyen headed belowdecks to look for a way out while he still could. As with all commercial vessels, the cruise ship was equipped with the mandatory lifeboats. But a large, slow-moving life boat wasn't his first choice for making a quick getaway.

As a last resort, he'd simply jump ship and, if he was caught, he would shed his uniform and pretend to be one of the ex-hostages who had somehow managed to escape. That would only last long enough for his name to be checked on the passenger manifest, but it should be easy enough for him to slip away during the process. The problem was that he wasn't a very good swimmer, so a boat of some kind was his first choice.

He remembered seeing a flyer on the bulletin board outside the main dining room announcing that the ship now had personal watercraft rentals available in the recreation equipment area. One of those swift, small craft would be a perfect solution to his problem.

The recreational equipment storage area was on D Deck, back in the stern, and he made it there without running into any of the fighters on guard. The door was unlocked, so he slipped inside to find a dozen two-man Jet Skis lined up along one wall. If he could get one of them down to the excursion platform on the stern, he'd be home free.

Leaning over one of the craft on the rack, taking the cap off of the gas tank to check the fuel level, he heard a voice behind him. "What do you think you are doing in here, Comrade?"

The Vietnamese turned to see one of the Cuban fighters holding an AK on him. He was old enough to be one of the Army veterans, and that wasn't good.

Nguyen looked surprised. "Comrade Garcia asked me to look into the availability of these small craft in case we might need them to make our escape."

"That's not what he told me." The Cuban frowned. "He sent me down here to keep anyone from using them."

Nguyen looked honestly puzzled. "When did you last talk to him?" he asked.

When the Cuban glanced down at his watch, the Vietnamese drew his Makarov and shot him while his head was turned. The shot echoed in the empty compartment like a shotgun blast.

Nguyen put his pistol back in his holster and looked around to see where he could hide the body for a couple of hours. Spotting a pile of table canopies, he reached down to take the corpse by the legs when he heard boots pounding down the passageway. Realizing that he hadn't locked the compartment door behind him, he dropped the body.

A fighter slammed the door open and charged into the compartment, his AK at the ready.

"He was trying to escape," Nguyen said.

"Pablo was doing that?" The fighter frowned. "That is not like him, and we have been comrades since Angola."

"He said that Comrade Garcia has been acting irrational and he no longer had faith in him."

"I want to see the Comrade Colonel about this." The fighter shifted his AK to cover Nguyen. "Pablo was the most faithful fighter I have ever known, and I can't believe that he lost his nerve."

"I don't think that we need to bother the leader with something as trivial as this," the Vietnamese said smoothly. "This is the hour of his greatest triumph over the Yankees, and he needs to keep his mind clear."

When the Cuban backed away a couple of steps, but still kept his weapon trained, Nguyen knew that he might not be able to talk his way out of this one. One of the biggest problems he'd had working with the Cubans had been trying to overcome the pervasive racism of Hispanic culture. While the Cubans always loudly accused the Americans of being racists, they were inbred racists to the bone themselves. The color of a Cuban's skin often determined how high he could rise in the "People's" government. The real power always rested with the lighter skinned Cubans.

When it came to their relations with their so-called Asian comrades, the Cubans could be openly and brutally racist. Since this was another of the older fighters, he wasn't likely to cut him any slack in the name of international socialism.

"Take your pistol out carefully, Comrade," the Cuban said, "and drop it on the deck."

Watching the unwavering muzzle of the AK, Nguyen carefully removed the Makarov with two fingers and let it fall to the deck.

"Put your hands behind your head and march." The Cuban motioned with the muzzle of this AK.

Nguyen obeyed and headed for the door.

BOLAN AND SPELLMAN had gone down to D Deck to get out of the way of the increased traffic on the upper levels. Even so, there was no great hue and cry or pounding of booted feet searching passageways for them. That meant that they hadn't been spotted when they'd cleared the decks for their swimming messenger and could continue picking off the Cubans one by one.

They were heading toward the stern when they heard the thudding of boots. The two men ducked into a darkened stairwell. Bolan was surprised to see one man in Cuban uniform with his hands on his head being herded by a terrorist with his AK in his prisoner's back.

This was his day for rescuing prisoners so, as soon as the pair passed, he simply put a bullet in the trailing Cuban's head.

Nguyen heard the faint chug of the silenced pistol and the impact in his captor's head and the thud of his body hitting the deck. When he turned, he saw two men in black step out. He had no idea where these two had come from, but it looked as if he had gone from the fire into maybe just the cook pot. Garcia would have killed him on the spot when he learned where he had been, but he might be able to get past these two.

"Man, am I glad to see you guys," he said in American English. His years working for USAID in Saigon and his subsequent years as a "refugee" in the States gave him a perfect California accent.

Bolan wasn't impressed by this Asian's English.

The fact that he was wearing Cuban black fatigues and had an empty Makarov holster on his officer's-style belt belied his smile. The muzzle of the Executioner's silenced H&K didn't waver from its target, this guy's center body mass.

"He's one of them," Spellman said softly from behind him. "I saw him on the dock in Cancun."

"Who are you?" Bolan asked.

"I'm Jim Wong," Nguyen replied, "from the Directorate of Operations at Langley, working out of CTC opcon to the Cuban Desk."

This guy had the jargon down pat, but anyone could get the Company buzz words from any spy thriller. He'd always been surprised that the CIA didn't scrap their in-house language and start all over.

"Who has the Cuban Desk now?"

"Winston Clarington," Nguyen answered without hesitation. "He came over from DEA liaison in Bogotá last year."

With Bolan not having his com link to the Farm, he took the answer as being true. No one would make up a name like Clarington on a moment's notice. However, he was well aware that the Cuban DGI also knew who their "opposite number" was at Langley. Even so, there was a faint chance that this guy was legit, so he'd play out a little more line.

"And you're undercover with these people, right?"

Nguyen nodded. "I got 'sheep dipped' as a Vietnamese refugee unsatisfied with life in the States and worked my way into the DGI in Florida."

That was a plausible story, so Bolan continued. "What's Garcia planning to do with these people he's holding?"

Thinking that he was getting away with his "cover" story, Nguyen continued. "To be honest, I don't really know. He keeps his plans to himself and we don't usually know what's happening next until he gives us our orders."

"What were your orders when you came here?"

Nguyen shrugged. "Only that we were coming here and that we would strike a great blow against the Yankees."

Bolan had been expecting that was the plan, but he still didn't like it. "What kind of blow?"

Now that these two Yankees seemed to be buying his story, Nguyen had the time to notice that they didn't seem to have any kind of communications gear on them. That they didn't told him that they weren't exactly who they seemed to be. Without communications, they wouldn't be able to call in any information they got from him or call for reinforcements.

"All I know is that he's got Russian artillery rockets fitted with some kind of modified warhead," he said. "I don't know if they're biological or what, but he's got a dozen or so of them."

Deep in his mind, Bolan knew that statement was

the truth and it was the last piece of the puzzle needed to click everything into place. Miami's size and population density made it a perfect place to attack with a "weapon of mass destruction." Also since the city was the home of the anti-Castro Cuban exiles, there was an emotional reason, as well, for it being picked as a target.

The media always talked about the cunning and sophistication of terrorists' attacks as if they had been planned to purposefully inflict the greatest damage to their targets. But nothing could be further from the truth. Almost without exception, like all amateurs, terrorists of all stripes planned their attacks for purely symbolic or emotional impacts. The body count was always a secondary consideration. He didn't mind, though. If the religious and political fanatics ever stopped being hysterically crazed and actually tried to win their ideological wars, men like him would have a much harder job on their hands.

"Where does he have these rockets with the modified war heads set up?" Bolan asked.

"He drained the main pool on the top deck," Nguyen replied, "and plans to launch them from there. Right now the weather cover is on place over the pool so the police helicopters can't spot them."

"When's he going to launch?"

"He hasn't said, but I think he wants to suck as many Feds in as he can before he kicks off."

"What's his move going to be after he launches?"

Nguyen shrugged. "That's the problem, he hasn't said anything about that yet."

That also had the ring of truth to it, but Bolan knew that it wasn't the whole story. Something was dead wrong here. If Garcia hadn't planned for a withdrawal, he was planning a suicide attack on a grand scale.

"I can take you up there," Nguyen offered, "and show you where the rockets are. Now that you guys're here, you can help me stop him."

"Let's go," Bolan said.

"Do you believe that bullshit story?" Spellman whispered.

"We'll see how it plays out."

CHAPTER TWENTY-THREE

"Hal," Barbara Price said as she walked up to Brognola with a hard copy in her hand, "we just got a message from the trauma unit. The medics down at the dock pulled a guy out of the water carrying medical ID, and they think he's the one who jumped off the *Princess*."

"Is he dead?"

"Almost," she said. "He took a couple rounds and he's in the ICU, so we won't be talking to him for a while."

"Damn!"

Whoever this man was, Brognola had a hunch that Striker had had a hand in getting him off the ship. From the reports, there had been too much firing right before the man jumped for him to have done it all by himself. That evidence was so circumstantial that it would never even make it up the courthouse steps, much less in front of the judge. But it was all he had to work with and he was counting on it being true.

BOLAN DIDN'T TRUST this self-identified CIA guy Jim Wong any farther than he could keep a sight picture on him. He had the Company rap down, but his story was too pat and something felt very wrong about him. Even so, if he could lead him to where Garcia was planning to launch his attack, he could be useful. That he was following his lead, however, didn't mean that he trusted him.

"It's one more deck up," Nguyen said quietly, pointing to a stairwell. "But we'll have to be careful. They'll have it guarded."

"You'd better lead the way then." Bolan motioned with the muzzle of his H&K subgun.

With a gun at his back, Nguyen had no choice but to start up the carpeted steps. When he reached the top, he knew that he would break into the lounge area around the main pool. He expected that Garcia was deep enough into his paranoia to have posted a strong guard over his doomsday weapons. If there were enough fighters up there, it might give him a chance to make a break.

Nguyen was mounting the last two steps when he

realized that the big American was close behind him. "Keep going," he heard the man say as he felt the muzzle of his subgun nudge him. "And don't make any sudden moves."

When Nguyen came out of the stairwell, the Cuban fighter nearest the stair turned, but when he saw who it was, lowered his AK. Bolan stepped past Nguyen and shot the Cuban in the head before sweeping the room with well-aimed bursts.

As his fighters fell, Garcia snatched up one of the rocket warheads and turned to flee.

"That's the guy behind this!" Spellman yelled. "Don't let him get away!"

As Bolan turned to see what Spellman was shouting about, Nguyen saw his chance. Spotting an AK on the deck, he snatched it up and spun on Spellman, who was closest to him.

The doctor caught the movement from the corner of his eye and turned just in time to escape most of the short burst of AK fire. He felt two blows in the side that sent him crumpling to the deck.

Bolan spun to face the new threat and saw Wong swing his AK toward him. He dropped flat as a burst of fire cut through the air over his head. Rolling over onto his back, he snapped a short burst at the "CIA" man.

Nguyen staggered as the slugs tore through him.

Shock and surprise showed on his face. He tried to raise his AK again, but another burst tore through him and he fell.

Bolan kneeled beside Spellman and opened his fatigue jacket. He'd taken one round through the side of his abdomen and another one farther up had broken a rib. Both would be painful once the shock wore off, but neither was life-threatening for the next few hours.

"I'm okay," Spellman gasped as Bolan felt for further damage. "Go after Garcia."

"After I patch you up." Bolan reached for the battle dressing on his assault harness. "I don't want you to bleed to death before I can get some help on board."

Doctors were infamous for not being good patients, but Spellman was willing to leave his care to the commando's experienced hands. He knew he wasn't the first gunshot casualty this guy had patched up.

"When you see Mary," he said, "tell her—"

"I'll be telling her that you're going to be okay." Bolan cut him off. Spellman was in shock, and he needed to have his mind focused on surviving, not on what would happen if he died.

He tied off the ends of the dressing and took two pills from his med pouch. "Take these."

Spellman didn't even ask what they were.

"Here's your AK." Bolan handed him the assault rifle. "Keep an eye on this place."

"Go after Garcia," Spellman gasped. "He took one of the bombs."

"I'll get him."

BOLAN WENT in pursuit of Garcia. When he saw the sign directing passengers to the main dining room, he had a hunch and decided to check it out. The passageway covered his approach right up to the entrance. Through the glass doors, he saw that the dining room was crowded with what looked to be a hundred women and children. Beyond the rigors of their extended captivity, they didn't appear to have been mistreated. They were, though, obviously scared. At least five terrorists were holding AKs on the group while an older man shouted at them and waved his arms in the air. On the table in front of him sat one of the warheads he had seen on the rockets.

When the women started moving up against the wall at the side of the room, Bolan had seen enough. He didn't have to know what the leader was saying to know that a massacre was in the offing. With the women moving to one side of the dining area, though, the guards were now in the open. The stage was set and the play could begin.

Bolan flicked the selector on his MP-5 SD-3 down to 3-round-burst mode. His booted foot slammed the door open and all heads turned his way. It takes a split second for a human to focus and then react to the unexpected, but Bolan didn't give the guards a break.

The MP-5 in his right hand whispered silent death while the Desert Eagle that filled his left bellowed. With only five targets to work with, Bolan cleared the room before the last .44 shot had time to echo away.

The women and children were screaming and crying, but Bolan ignored them as he walked up to the older man he had figured to be the Cuban boss man. "It's over," he told him, the muzzle of his Desert Eagle unwavering.

"Yankee bastard!" Garcia roared as he lunged for the warhead.

The .44 slug exploded the back of the Cuban's head, ending his migraines for all time.

"Just stay here," Bolan told the hysterical women. "Block the door after I leave and don't let anyone in unless you know they are Americans. I'm going to try to get us some help, but I don't know how long it'll take."

BOLAN FOUND only one terrorist on the ship's bridge and dispatched him with a single silenced shot from the 93-R. The Cuban in the radio room looked up in time to receive the same treatment. Bolan pried the microphone out of his hand, switched the radio to the Coast Guard Marine Emergency Channel and keyed the mike.

"Any station," he said, "any station. This is the cruise ship SS *Carib Princess* presently in Miami harbor. Mayday. Mayday. Mayday. Any station, come in please."

"*Carib Princess,*" the Coast Guard radio operator replied, "this is Group Miami, what is your emergency? Over."

"We need emergency medical assistance on board as soon as you can get it here. Over."

"Who are you? Over."

"Let's just say," Bolan replied, "that I'm a concerned American citizen trapped on this tub. And I'm telling you that there's a ship full of people here including women and children who need help immediately. I need some medical teams and a military HazMat unit on board ASAP. Over."

"Where are the terrorists? Over."

"Most of them are dead," Bolan replied, "but there's enough still alive that the medics will need a SWAT team or two with them for protection. If you've got any Delta Force Hostage Rescue Team people out there, send them. Over."

"Mister, whoever you are," the radioman said, "I can't just take your word on this. I'm not sending medics onto a trap to become hostages themselves. Over."

"I'll tell you what," Bolan said wearily. "Get hold of the Justice Department element. I know they're hanging around somewhere, and ask to talk to Hal Brognola. Tell him that Striker needs some help over here. Over."

"Who? Over."

"Hal Brognola of the Justice Department. He knows who I am. Over."

"But who the hell are you? Over."

"I'm Striker. Over."

"Stay on the radio until I can confirm this. Over."

"I'm a little busy right now trying to stay alive," Bolan snapped. "So get your ass moving. Over and out."

Bolan pulled the radio mike from the socket and put it in his pocket in case he needed it later. Right now, he had to keep working on the opposition to keep them off balance so the reinforcements wouldn't have to face hot landing zones.

HAL BROGNOLA was in the barely controlled chaos of the Justice Department tent waiting to make another report to the Oval Office. The Man wanted updates every half hour even if there was nothing to report. And he had insisted that Brognola make the report in person instead of having one of his com techs do it. Each occupant of the White House had his idiosyncrasies, and this was just one that came with this particular incumbent.

From the corner of his eye, he caught something

going on at the entrance and looked up to see a Coast Guard Lieutenant Commander rushing into the tent. "Is there a Hal Brognola of the Justice Department around here?"

"I'm Brognola," he called. "What's up?"

The officer rushed over to him, waving a hard-copy printout in his hand. "Are you Brognola of the Justice Department?"

Brognola nodded. "I said I was, why?"

"May I see your ID, please."

Brognola dug his wallet out of his coat pocket, flipped his badge case open and displayed his ID.

The lieutenant peered and relaxed. "I've got a message from someone who calls himself Striker. He says he needs medics and a military SWAT team on board that ship."

"Give me that—" he reached for the fax "—and get ready to transport the people he wants."

"I'll need to get that from my higher command."

"Is the President high enough in the chain of command for you?" Brognola snapped, putting his hand on the secure hotline to the White House. "If you want, I can get the Man on the phone right now."

The officer didn't feel like trying his luck today. This was such a rat screw that it just wasn't worth it. "No, Sir," he said. "I'll arrange immediate transport."

"Thank you."

As soon as the man cleared out of earshot, Brognola clicked in his com link to the Stony Man command center. "Barbara," he said, "he's still alive. He called the Coast Guard and requested Delta Force and medics."

"Thank God. What can we do to get him out of there?"

"Right now, nothing," Brognola replied. "He only asked for medics and the Delta Force."

"I'll have Buck get some of his people down to the dock," she said.

Brognola hesitated for an instant. He, too, realized that things were moving too fast to keep to any preconceived plan for how to handle the situation. "Go ahead," he said. "But tell him to wait for me."

"You'd better hurry."

The Man was expecting a call in ten minutes, but this time he was the one who was going to have to wait.

The rotor blades were spinning on Stony Man's borrowed Black Hawk chopper when Brognola ran onto the makeshift landing pad.

"Get it in gear, Hal," Buck Greene shouted from the open door.

Hands reached to grab him and drag him inside right as the pilot pulled pitch and the Black Hawk lifted off. It was a very short flight to the docks opposite where the *Carib Princess* was anchored, but no one had time the time to waste taking a motor vehicle trip.

The Black Hawk had no sooner touched down than the blacksuits were out the door and taking up a perimeter around it. Brognola stepped onto the tarmac and saw that the Coast Guard already had several smaller craft standing by at the dock, and the wail of approaching ambulances could be heard. There was no sign yet of a SWAT team or the Delta Force guys, but he knew they'd be coming fast.

Exactly what they would do once they got here was yet to be seen, but he was tired of hanging back and he knew that Greene and his men were champing at the bit, as well. He took out his secure cell phone and put in a call to the White House.

"Okay," he told the Stony Man security chief, "the Man gave us the word to go to work and give the medics cover."

That wasn't exactly what the President had said, but taking a page from Price's playbook, he was putting his spin on it and hearing only the part that he wanted to.

Greene glanced over at the Black Hawk. "How do you want us to do it?"

"How about a fast repel onto the top deck?"

Greene nodded. "If our pilot is from McDill, he should know how to do that."

"Get them going," Brognola said.

Greene let out a shout and two of his squads sprinted for the bird. Another shout got the pilot scrambling to light his turbines. In less than ninety seconds, the Black Hawk was in the air.

BOLAN HEARD the sound of a military chopper approaching hot and low. It could have been just another fly-past to have yet another look-see, but then he heard the distinctive change in sound as the pilot chopped his pitch. Whoever they were, they were going to make a landing and it sounded as though they were coming in on the uppermost deck. He broke off his search and headed up to meet his visitors.

When Bolan heard a voice he recognized bellow a command, he smiled. The Stony Man cavalry had arrived. Somehow Brognola had managed to get Buck Greene and some of his blacksuits into the game. That would make finishing this up a lot easier. If, that was, he could make contact with them without getting shot. With everyone on the boat wearing basic black combat suits, it would be easy for him to be mistaken for one of the Cubans.

Again, a lack of communication was going to make this link-up more difficult than it needed to be, but he knew that Greene would be on the lookout for him and that would slow his trigger finger.

BUCK GREENE was on point as the blacksuits moved through the lounge on the upper deck when he heard a voice he knew well, "Yo! Jarhead!"

Greene looked and spotted Mack Bolan at the far end of the open area. He waved and keyed his throat mike. "I've got him," he transmitted, "and he's on his feet."

"How many people did you bring?" Bolan asked.

"Twenty, counting myself."

"Good, let's get going."

"After I get you properly outfitted." Greene reached into his fanny pack and pulled out a pocket badge bearing Department of Justice insignia and the title Senior Special Agent.

"Here," he said, handing it over. "A little sheep dip. Put it on your left pocket."

"Got a photo ID to go with it?"

Greene went into his left jacket pocket and pulled out a properly battered federal ID card. "Your ticket to the ball, Cinderella."

"It's a little late, but thanks."

"Now," Greene growled, "let's get the rest of this tub cleaned up."

"We'll start from here and work our way down," Bolan said. "And get back to Hal and tell him that it's okay for the medics to come in where you did as long as they're escorted. By the time they get here, we should have most of the rest of this tub under control."

THE WORD of Diego Garcia's death had gone through the remaining Matador fighters like a hurricane.

Some fearing American vengeance decided to fight to the death rather than be executed, but enough of them put their AKs down and their hands up that the odds were evened out considerably.

With Bolan leading, the blacksuits went from one deck down to the next, relentlessly double teaming the remaining Cubans. Those who were smart enough to hang it up when they had a chance got riot cuffs, a swatch of duct tape over the mouth and were left behind. Those who put up a fight were simply taken out of the play—permanently.

After clearing the ship's superstructure, Bolan led the blacksuits onto the open deck at the stern. A quick look revealed that some of the men in the human shield wall had leaped into the water when the firefight had broken out. Others, unwilling to leave their wives and children behind, remained and faced off the Cubans. Several had been killed for their efforts and others lay wounded.

"That's going to be a little tricky," Greene observed.

"Let's sweep both sides at the same time," Bolan said.

"Got it," Greene replied before clicking in his com link to split the blacksuits into two contingents.

While Greene took his group and started up the portside of the ship, Bolan took the remainder and headed for the starboard. They were spotted almost the instant they broke into the open, and the reaction was almost comical.

The first Cuban took one look at what was coming at him and jumped over the railing. The next one made the mistake of trying to fight and was gunned down in an instant. Several of the passengers took this opportunity to vent at their soon to be ex-captors. A few of the ex-hostages were shot for their efforts, but more of them got revenge for their imprisonment, some of it fatal.

Bolan and the blacksuits plunged into this melee, rifle butts and pistols serving very nicely to sort it out. A couple of the enraged passengers got a rifle butt to get them out of the line of fire, but most of them were willing to stand aside to let the pros go to work.

Bolan's group met up with Greene at the bow of the ship after their twin sweeps. Behind them, the decks were littered with more than a dozen bodies, most of them were terrorists. Every time the blacksuits had encountered a wounded passenger, they'd paused to administer combat first aid before moving on.

"There might be a few more still hiding belowdecks," Bolan told the Stony Man security chief, "but we need to secure the upper levels so we can get the medics in here."

"We can handle that." Greene signaled for his squad leaders to assemble.

"And," Bolan said, "while you're taking care of that, I'll hit the lower decks."

"Need a backup?"

"Thanks, but it'll be better if you stay up here and deal with the Feds for me. Tell them that I'm working down there and be on the lookout for me. I would, though, like to borrow a com link from one of your men."

Greene turned to the closest blacksuit. "Wilson, give me your radio."

"You got it, Chief."

Bolan fitted the com link to his harness and ran a com check.

"I'll be in touch."

CHAPTER TWENTY-FOUR

Evacuating the ex-hostages from the *Carib Princess* was going as quickly as could be expected with the ship in midchannel. An aid station had been set up on deck to handle the casualties, and the medics were bringing the wounded out and triaging them before moving them to the rescue boats.

Richard Spellman had been tagged and was awaiting his turn. Though he was strapped to a stretcher with an IV plugged into his arm, he kept twisting to look at the ex-hostages, searching every woman's face as she appeared, trying to catch a glimpse of Mary Hamilton.

"Richard!" he heard a woman scream, and he turned to see Mary Hamilton running toward him. When a medic moved in to hold her back, she brushed past him and threw herself on the wounded man.

"Oh, Richard," she sobbed as she held him in a bear hug that threatened to break the rest of his ribs.

"Careful," he cautioned.

"Oh, God," she said as she pulled back. "Did I hurt you?"

"No, no, I'm okay."

"But where have you been?"

"Well," he said, "there's this man who got on board somehow, some kind of secret-agent commando, and he kept me from being killed. Then we teamed up and he started killing the terrorists. Then, when the ship pulled into the harbor, we both started…"

Hamilton looked in wonderment at the man she had so misjudged. When she'd first met him, she'd thought that he was a nice man, witty and interesting enough to hold her attention, but more or less what she expected from a researcher. In a word, bland and harmless. A medi-nerd in the common vernacular. That he had somehow managed to turn into a commando was a revelation, and it made her smile. Bland and harmless was all fine and good, but there was something exciting about a man who had the courage and fortitude to stand and put his life on the line when the circumstances required it.

She knew that was just her most primitive DNA talking, but she'd take a commando over a researcher anyday.

"You want to get married in the hospital?" she asked. "Or do you want to wait until you're released?"

Spellman smiled. "Whatever floats your boat."

"Don't you ever use that word to me again," she mock snapped.

"Yes, dear."

HAL BROGNOLA was waiting dockside when Mack Bolan stepped off one of the rescue boats. The Executioner looked as if he'd been dragged behind a pickup at high speed down several miles of bad road. Nonetheless, the characteristic demeanor that marked him hadn't been beaten down.

"The next time we think about doing something like this," Brognola said, "we've got to make sure that we've got our com links with us."

Bolan agreed that a lack of communication had been the most serious obstacle they'd had to overcome. But he had a better solution to the problem than keeping a Stony Man com link in his back pocket at all times. Much better.

"I'll tell you what," Bolan said as he put his arm around his old friend's shoulders. "I've got something that will guarantee that you'll never have to go through something like this again."

"What's that?"

"It's real simple, Hal. When I get done making a report to the Man, your ass is never going to be out of eyesight of your bodyguard team unless you're locked in a first-class latrine on a 747 at thirty-eight thousand feet."

"Give me a break, Mack!" Brognola was shocked. "You can't even suggest something like that to him. My life's bad enough as it is without having to tow a Secret Service Personal Protection Team in my wake."

"I can't?" Bolan smiled slowly. "Watch me."

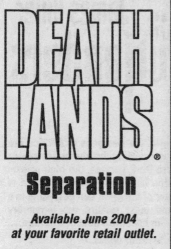

DEATH LANDS®

Separation

*Available June 2004
at your favorite retail outlet.*

The group makes its way to a remote island in hopes of finding brief sanctuary. Instead, they are captured by an isolated tribe of descendants of African slaves from pre–Civil War days. When they declare Mildred Wyeth "free" from her white masters, it is a twist of fate that ultimately leads the battle-hardened medic to question where her true loyalties lie. Will she side with Ryan, J. B. Dix and those with whom she has forged a bond of trust and friendship…or with the people of her own blood?

James Axler
Outlanders®

SUN LORD

In a fabled city of the ancient world, the neo-gods of Mexico are locked in a battle for domination. Harnessing the immutable power of alien technology and Earth's pre-Dark secrets, the high priests and whitecoats have hijacked Kane into the resurrected world of the Aztecs. Invested with the power of the great sun god, Kane is a pawn in the brutal struggle and must restore the legendary Quetzalcoatl to his rightful place—or become a human sacrifice....

Available May 2004 at your favorite retail outlet.

TAKE 'EM FREE

2 action-packed novels plus a mystery bonus

NO RISK

NO OBLIGATION TO BUY